Devotion of a Wolf

Viking Wolves Book 3
CJ Ravenna

Copyright © 2026 by CJ Ravenna

No part of this publication may be reproduced, distributed, or transmitted in any form or by any means, including photocopying, recording, or other electronic or mechanical methods, without the prior written permission of the author, except as permitted by U.S. copyright law.

The story, all names, characters, and incidents portrayed in this production are fictitious. No identification with actual persons (living or deceased), places, buildings, and products is intended or should be inferred.

NO AI TRAINING: Without in any way limiting the author's exclusive rights under copyright, any use of this publication to "train" generative artificial intelligence (AI) technologies to generate text is expressly prohibited. The author reserves all rights to license uses of this work for generative AI training and development of machine learning language models.

No AI was used in the creation of any part of this book. This author supports human creators.

This book contains sexually explicit materials only suitable for mature readers.

First edition 2026

Beta reading by Lark's Literary Nest

Copy edits by Jennifer Smith

Proofreading by Lori Parks

Cover design by Natasha Snow

All rights reserved.

Content Guidelines

Brief mentions of off-page violent deaths including that of a main character's parent and an infant

Chapter 1
Lyall

Iceland, Year 821

The flaming arrow arcs through the sky and lands on the pyre, setting the wood aflame. I can't bring myself to watch as the fire consumes my father's body.

Alpha Erik, son of Thorin and Freda, is dead.

Tears threaten to spill down my cheeks, but I fear weeping will make me look weak. I'm eighteen, my father is dead, and it's time for me to be a man. But how can I when our family is torn to pieces?

Yesterday I wed the man I love. I feasted with my family, not knowing it would be our last meal with Father. Gunnar, next oldest after Anders and me, had cooed over his son, my nephew, sweet baby Bjorn, while his chosen mate Leif had cradled the little lad in his arms. Anders, my twin, had teased Wulfric, our youngest brother, as he always did. Father had chastised him, but always with patience.

I'd danced until my feet hurt, drank mead until my head swam, and laughed myself hoarse. It had truly been the best day of my life. Before I'd left to claim my mate, Father had taken me aside and cupped the nape of my neck.

He said, "I'm proud of you, son. I wish you nothing but happiness."

Blushing, I'd pushed him off before my brothers could see and tease me mercilessly.

If I'd known Father would never touch me again, that only hours later he would be killed on the very beach where my brothers and I had run and played and hunted together... I'd have held on to him and never let him go.

When I was a lad, Father had told me that because we were ulfhednar, there would be those who wouldn't understand the great gift of change bestowed upon us by Fenrir. He'd told me that humans would hate and fear us. He'd been very strict about how far we could stray from the village in our wolf forms and told us to never prey upon livestock from the neighboring villages. We were never to attract attention to ourselves.

As the years passed and trade prospered between us and the human villages, I'd thought we'd succeeded. I had been more wrong than I could have imagined.

Only hours before my wedding, human missionaries had come to our village. The missionaries' leader, a man named Thorald, had brought chests of gold and a strange offer: if we would abandon our pagan gods and accept their Christian god, we would be rewarded with wealth.

Father had politely refused. Although we worshipped many gods, we were most devout to Fenrir. We were loyal to him, and he rewarded us with the gift of the change. Father had feared that by worshipping other gods, we would displease Fenrir and lose his boon. Thorald had smiled as best he could with that scar on his lip and seemed to respect Father's answer. I had wondered at the time how a man of the cloth had gotten such an injury.

Thorald took his missionaries and left... or so we'd thought.

The next time I saw Thorald, he'd donned the armor of a hunter and was holding his blade to my neck. He'd been no man of god, but a hunter in disguise, and we'd unknowingly welcomed him and his men into our village.

Father and Wulfric had beaten the hunters back to the shore, but Father fell in battle. I know Wulfric must blame himself, but I believe he did the best he could. Anders had been tortured until he almost lost himself to his berserker's feral rage. Baby Bjorn and Leif had been cut down right before Gunnar's eyes. What *monsters* could kill a defenseless child? What was my sweet nephew's crime but to be the child of wolves? He'd never harmed anyone.

Wulfric turns to face the crowd. Father's black wolf furs look too big for his narrow shoulders, too heavy. Gods, but I ache for my little brother. He inherited the power of the Alpha from our father's bloodline. We always knew that someday Wulfric would lead our pack as Father and

Mother had. It wasn't supposed to be this soon. He's still just a boy. He deserved the time to be a child while he still could. Now that's been robbed from him too.

"I swear to you all," Wulfric says, hands in fists that tremble at his sides, "I will help lead our pack out of this darkness. We will heal and come back from this terrible loss. I will honor Father's memory and be the Alpha you all deserve." There's a crack in his voice I can't miss. I wonder if he even believes his own words.

Before I can stop myself, I go to him. Gunnar follows and the pair of us put our arms around our little brother. "You won't be alone, Wulfric," I promise him. "I swear, we will be with you every step of the way."

Gunnar doesn't speak, just bumps his forehead against Wulfric's shoulder. The gesture is far too animalistic, and his silence scares me. Gunnar watched his mate and child be killed before his eyes. I fear what such trauma will do to his mind, but most of all to his wolf. Since we found him cradling the bodies of his family, he hasn't spoken a word. It frightens me.

"Thank you," Wulfric says, voice thick.

The only one who hasn't moved is Anders. Hands in fists, he looks at Wulfric with unbridled contempt. An enraged wolf, ready to strike.

My heart is heavy in my chest as I stop outside the basement door. Upstairs my brothers and aunt move through the longhouse. Will I ever stop expecting to see Father moving through our home, to hear his rare but booming laugh and deep voice?

Blinking fast, I unlock the door. I thought my heart had already been broken by the tragedy that struck our family. The sight of Soren, my childhood friend, my *mate*, chained to the wall like a common thief shatters my heart to pieces.

I have never seen Soren so broken, not since that day all those years ago when Father returned from a voyage at sea with him. He'd been orphaned after wolves attacked his village, leaving him the sole survivor. Even so, he overcame his fear and decided to become ulfhednar when he came of age. For me. The furs he fought so hard to earn have been taken away, leaving him as weak and vulnerable as a human.

A broken whine escapes me when his wet, red-rimmed eyes find mine.

"Lyall," he croaks, tears flowing, "oh, Lyall..."

I only take a few steps before I am on my knees and my arms are around Soren. Sobs I've been fighting back all day rattle my chest.

Trembling lips kiss my neck, my wet cheek. He whispers, "I'm here, my love. Right here. I am so sorry. So, so sorry."

Gods, but I am a failure. He should not be comforting me.

Wiping my eyes, I pull away. "Has anyone hurt you?" I frame his face in my hands, looking for any injury.

He shakes his head, dark locks clumped together with dirt, blood, and sweat. "No."

Reaching up, I check the cuffs. They've dug into his wrists and brought blood to the surface. I have seen people lose their hands from how tightly cuffs were fitted to their flesh. Drawing him close, I kiss his dry lips and try to fight back another wave of anguish. "I will get you out of here. I swear it."

My heart sinks when Soren shakes his head. "Wulfric seemed adamant that I was never leaving this basement until the moment of my judgment."

A growl rips from my throat. "You are my mate. He cannot keep you here!"

"Lyall..." Soren's voice is soft, pleading. Even when we were boys, I could never deny him anything when he took that tone with me. "You have lost so much. B-because of me." Tears spill down his cheeks, mixing with blood and sweat. "I will not be the reason you lose the rest of your family."

I press my forehead to his, swallowing back the rush of tears. "This was not your fault."

"But it was," Soren says, face twisted in anguish. "This happened because of me."

Soren and I had met beneath our favorite elm tree and claimed each other as mates at last. He'd still been inside me when a man had come up behind us and touched his blade to my neck. All the blood in my body had turned to ice when I'd recognized the man in hunters' apparel as the leader of the missionaries who'd come to our shores earlier that same day.

Soren had recognized him too, but for very different reasons.

Thorald, the man who'd murdered my father and led the attack on our village, was Soren's father. Soren hadn't been the sole survivor of the attack on his childhood village after all. Unbeknownst to us all, his father had survived and spent years training and gathering an army for this very moment.

"You are not responsible for his actions."

Soren scoffs. "Tell that to your brothers. They have decided my guilt by association with him."

Shock ripples through me, and I shake my head. "No. They can't." It wouldn't be fair to blame Soren for his father's actions. Yet I could envision Wulfric doing exactly that, lost in his grief and rage and guilt, desperate for someone else, anyone else, to blame. "I will speak to him, make him see reason!"

My own brother would not part me from the man I love. He *couldn't*.

"It's too late, Lyall." The finality in Soren's voice turns my blood to ice.

I stare, unblinking, into his defeated eyes. "Why would you say that?"

A broken laugh escapes Soren. "I already confessed."

Bile rises in my throat. "To *what*?"

Soren averts his gaze, lips trembling. "To betraying the pack."

I rock back on my heels, swallowing hard so I won't be sick. "What... why would you..."

"While you were recovering from the battle, mistrust spread through the village. The townsfolk thought I had turned you against your own family, that you were somehow in on my father's plan to attack the village and kill Erik. I couldn't let them think so poorly of you. So I... confessed. Told them I alone knew my father's plan. That I used you all for protection until the day I could be rescued." He swallows hard, and the bond between us sours with despair.

The room spins around me, and I close my eyes and take several deep breaths. Chest tightening, I lurch away from him and pace to the wall, leaning on it for support.

It's all a lie, of course. Soren was as surprised as I was to find hunters in our village. All these years he'd believed his father to be dead and gone, just like his mother and his friends from the village he'd grown up in.

Snarling, I rake my claws down the wall. "Then I will tell them it's not true, any of it! I will make Wulfric listen to reason. I—"

"No!" Soren's broken shout fills the chamber. "I will not be the reason you lose your family, Lyall. I can't!"

"You *are* my family!" My roar tears at my throat. "And I have already lost so much. I will not lose you, too!"

"So... if you had to choose... myself or your family... you would choose me?"

Yes, I want to say, but the word won't come. I swallow hard, trying to speak, but emotion chokes me. I am the eldest brother, and unlike my twin Anders, it's a duty I've always taken to heart. Ever since I held newborn Gunnar in my arms, then Wulfric a couple years later, I knew I would protect them with my life. That is my duty as their big brother. My brothers come first. Always. That is the promise I made to myself. To Father.

How can this world be so cruel, to ask me to choose between my brothers and the man I've loved since I was a boy?

A tender smile breaks on Soren's face. He does not hate me for being too weak to choose. No, he looks as if he loves me all the more for my foolish indecision. "It is all right, Lyall."

A sob chokes me, and the room blurs through my tears as I fall to my knees and pull him into my arms.

No, it is not.

Nothing will ever be all right again.

I hurl open the doors to the longhouse. "Wulfric! I must speak with you, now!"

Sitting in my father's seat at the table makes Wulfric look so very small. A child playing dress-up.

Wulfric sets his mouth into a grim line. "You saw him."

My fists tremble as I curl them. "Release him. Now. Give me the keys." I will rip them from his hand myself if I have to.

"Lyall..." Wulfric begins, as if he's speaking to a wild animal. "I can't do that."

"You can and you will!" I slam my fist down on the table, making it shake. Flinching, Wulfric stumbles out of his seat, not like an Alpha but like the thirteen-year-old boy he is.

Shame burns me up inside. This is my little brother. I shouldn't raise my voice. I should be kinder. I—

No. He is not only my little brother.

He is my Alpha now, and he has to learn that not everyone will agree with his decisions.

Taking in a slow breath, I say, "Why not?"

Balling his hands into fists, Wulfric meets my gaze head-on. "Because he has betrayed us."

I grind my teeth. "You can't believe that. Not after all the years he's spent with us."

"I didn't want to." A sheen dampens Wulfric's silver eyes. "But he told us himself. All these years, he was just using us... using y-you, Lyall."

"That isn't true, Wulfric. You have to know that."

"I..." Wulfric parts his lips, then snaps his mouth shut. "I'm sorry, Lyall. Truly. The pack... *my* pack"—his voice breaks on the word—"want answers. They want justice."

"And this is how you'll get it?" The roar escapes me before I can stop it. "By exiling an innocent man? Why? So you can feel like half the Alpha our father was?"

Wulfric staggers back, looking like I struck him. "Lyall, I know how you feel about him. You care for him. We all did. But he has betrayed us. It's his fault Father is dead! He must be exiled, or I will kill him myself."

Lunging forward, I grab his hands in mine. "Please. Wulfric, please, do not do this. Do not take him from me. Please."

Wulfric's wet eyes widen, his lips working soundlessly.

My knees give out, and I clutch onto his arms to keep myself upright. "Wherever he goes, so will I."

A choked sound escapes Wulfric. "No. Lyall, you can't. I need you here. I can't be an alpha without my pack."

His pleas strike me in the chest. "You'd make me choose?"

How could I decide between my family and my mate? I promised Father after Mother died that I would look after my brothers, but Soren and I are mated, bonded for life.

"How dare you?" My voice breaks, half a sob, half a snarl. "You're no Alpha. You're a coward, looking for someone to blame for your own failures!"

Wulfric's eyes flash with fury. "And where were you?" he bellows. "I was on the beach with Father! We fought for our lives, and you weren't there!"

My claws come out. "You will not blame Soren for your shortcomings! Father died because of you, not Soren!"

As soon as those poisonous words leave my lips, something between us shatters. Perhaps even irrevocably.

Tears blazing in his eyes, Wulfric charges me, and his claw tears across my cheek. I don't try and stop him as he punches, kicks, and claws at me. The wounds on the surface will heal but there's no healing a shattered heart.

"I tried!" Wulfric screams, swinging wildly at me. "I did everything I could! I wish I'd died instead of him! It should be me! I should be dead! Not him!" He sobs freely now, great wrenching gasps that leave him hunched over.

I don't know when it happens, but my arms are around him and we're kneeling on the floor, holding on to each other like we're all that's keeping the other afloat.

"I know," I whisper. "I know, little brother. I know, little Wulf. I'm sorry. I'm so sorry. Please, forgive me."

A tear spills down Wulfric's grimy cheek, his body trembling in my grasp. "Don't make me do this without you, Lyall. Please. I lost Father. Gunnar w-won't even speak to us. Anders blames me for everything. I can't... I c-can't lose you, too. Don't leave me alone. *Please.*"

Gods. He sounds like a little boy. The little boy I'd carried on my shoulders through the woods. The child I soothed as he struggled to shift to his wolf the first time. My little brother, my Alpha, needs me.

I promised my father.

I *promised*.

How can I leave my broken family behind?

How can I part from Soren, half of my heart and soul?

With a gasp, I bury my face in his stomach and break apart.

"It's okay, Lyall." Soren kisses my hair.

I can't bear to look at him. "My family needs me, Soren."

"They do," Soren agrees, and I wonder at how he can be so forgiving, so understanding. "More than ever."

I hold him tight, wondering when I will next get the chance. "I will come for you." When he doesn't speak, I untuck my head from the spot under his chin and look him in the eyes. The anguish sparkling in his gaze nearly breaks me. Framing his face in my hands, I say, "You are my mate, Soren. Half of my very soul."

"And you are mine," he whispers, voice shaking.

I touch my forehead to his, heart aching. "They will exile you at dawn but as soon as I can, I will come for you, whether you are in the past or the future."

"How? I don't want you to get in trouble."

I kiss the tip of his nose. "I will keep a branch of Yggdrasil and hide it away." The branch of our holiest tree will allow me to travel through time to wherever he is. "As soon as I think it is safe, I will find you, and we will be together. I promise."

Soren's lips tremble when he smiles. "I will wait for you. No matter how long it takes."

Leaning in, I capture his lips, sealing the promise that warms the bond between us.

Nothing will keep my mate from me.

Not even time itself.

Chapter 2
Soren

Present Day

"I think we should break up."

Fuck. I knew this was coming the moment Tony asked me to meet him at his place.

"Oh," is all I say.

It's only been four months since we started dating. We met in a gay bar in the West Village, hooked up, and liked each other so much we decided to keep seeing one another outside the bedroom.

It hasn't been that long, I remind myself, but there's no stopping the lump that rises in my throat.

How can this be happening again? Why do none of my relationships ever last longer than a few months?

"Did I do something wrong?" I wait for his answer, heart throbbing. Was I too clingy? Did I rush into things?

"No!" he hurries to assure me. "It's just... you're the first guy I ever dated, and I'm not ready to tie myself down yet. I was closeted for so long and now that I'm out, I want to have fun, you know?"

How can I blame him for that? This isn't on me. "Yeah. Of course. I get it."

It doesn't stop my eyes from stinging.

"I'm sorry. You're a really great guy. Sweet. Sexy. You'll find someone."

I nod and mumble my way through our goodbyes, then make my way to the subway. My body is on autopilot as I board the train. A fog of heartache obscures the world around me, but somehow I manage to get home. All I want is to curl up in bed and lick my wounds, get it all out of my system before I have to go to work tonight.

"From your expression, I take it things didn't go well?" My grandfather Fergus waits for me at the kitchen table. There are two mugs of hot chocolate, one by his spot and another by mine. We have a tradition. Whenever I'm having a bad day, he makes us hot chocolate.

There's nothing chocolate can't fix, he always says.

I huff a bitter laugh. Where do I even start?

"Sit down. Tell me everything."

Wordlessly, I join him at the table. I sip my drink, the warmth and sweetness a soothing distraction. It's not that I don't want to talk to Fergus; I just don't know what to say. I never hide anything from him. As cheesy as it is, my granddad is my best friend. He raised me after my mom decided she couldn't cope with being a parent at eighteen, took off, and never returned. I never met my father. I've got his dark hair and brown eyes, but that's about it.

By the time I hit the bottom of my mug, I've found my voice.

"Tony and I broke up. I swear, there's something wrong with me."

"Oh? Why do you think that?"

I pull at a loose thread in the tablecloth. "I don't think it. I know it. If I weren't so messed up, people wouldn't keep leaving."

A frown tugs at Fergus's mouth. "Did he blame you for the breakup?"

"No, but—"

"Then it wasn't your fault," he says, as if it's as simple as that. "I'm sorry, my boy. I know you cared for him."

I shake my head. "I didn't, not really." Guilt churns in my stomach. "I'm not sad that I'll never see him again. I'm just disappointed he broke up with me." Tony was a nice guy. I had fun with him. But every time we kissed, touched, made love—there was this sense of *wrongness* deep in the pit of my stomach.

"I don't get it!" I scrub my hand down my face, digging my nails into my cheek. "When he texted me this morning, I knew he was going to break up with me. And I was *relieved*. What the hell's wrong with me?"

My grandfather is quiet for a moment, probably wondering why his grandson is so fucked up. He sets down his empty mug and gives me a searching look. His wise stare always reminds me of an owl, like he sees right through me down to my deepest secrets. "Your heart is telling you that Tony isn't the one you're meant to be with, Soren. You listened to it and let the relationship end. That's a good thing. You're young. There's no need to rush into things."

"I just don't get it. None of my relationships have lasted longer than a few months. It doesn't matter how much I like them. It never feels right." Sighing, I slump in my chair. My eyes sting as I wonder if my life will always be like this. How many more times will I sit down with my granddad and spill my heartbreak to him?

"I'm done," I croak. "I can't do this anymore."

"What do you mean?"

"Putting myself out there only to get shit in return! I'm done with dating, done with relationships. All of it."

Before my granddad can reply, a look of pain crosses his face. He coughs so hard, he doubles over. "Gramps?" I run to his side and rub his back, my heart thudding as his coughing fit worsens. Before I can freak out, Fergus takes a few deep breaths. "Are you okay?"

He waves a hand and coughs some more, but it's nowhere near as severe. "I'm fine. Don't trouble yourself."

"You really should see a doctor about that cough." It used to not happen very often, and he usually blamed it on allergies or dust. Lately, though, it's been happening a lot more frequently. Is he sick? What if it's cancer or something else?

Fergus smiles. "I'm fine—"

"Please, Gramps." My heart drops into my stomach. I can't lose him. He's the only family I have left.

He sighs, then pats my hand. "I will, I promise."

"Thanks, Gramps." I squeeze his wrist and wonder if it was always so small and bony or if he's ill. With worry churning in my stomach, I leave him at the table and head into my bedroom. I collapse onto my bed, and the mattress eases the tension from my body. I take my phone out of my back pocket, find Tony's number, and block him.

No more of this shit.

I'm done being heartbroken.

The Closet is always packed on the weekends. Horny guys grind on each other beneath the swirling lights. Scantily clad men move their bodies to the throbbing beat. The air is thicker than a rainforest with body heat and sweat.

I smile and chat with Tom and Franklin, two of my regulars who come in every week. Hopefully, they can't tell I'm dying inside as they cuddle up and whisper together. They have been together for almost three years. What's their secret?

Raising my voice so they can hear me over the music, I ask, "How do you guys do it?"

Tom smirks. "Bit of a personal question."

Franklin throws back his head and laughs. "Fetch us another round and we'll consider it."

Heat warms my cheeks as I let out a laugh. "Ha ha. I meant how have you stayed together this long?"

Tom gives Franklin a squeeze. "We respect each other."

Snorting, Franklin adds, "Oh, we do? I didn't feel so respected when I asked you to fold the laundry this morning." To me, he says, "Do you know what this brat did? He folded the laundry all nice and pretty—and left it inside the dryer."

Tom interjects, "That's what you said! Fold the laundry in the dryer."

The dry look Franklin gives me makes me laugh.

Tom smirks. "The punishment was totally worth it."

Franklin clears his throat. "We want the same things. I think that helps."

My exes and I had similar ideas for the future. A marriage, kids, a life together, but that was never enough. There was always something off. Either they ended things, or I did because that gut feeling of *wrong, wrong, wrong* became too loud to ignore anymore.

Tom adds, "You gotta have four things. Respect. Trust. Communication. Devotion. Those, to me, are key to a happy relationship."

"And it sure helps if he's hot and uh-mazing in bed," Franklin says, bumping his hip against Tom's. Tom never takes his arm from Franklin's wide shoulders, and their bodies press so close Franklin is practically in his lap. They look so comfortable together. I'm not into the kink scene like they are, but I'd give anything to have the kind of love they have.

No, we're not looking for love anymore, remember?

I have to look away from them as bitter jealousy tears through my heart. When my shift finally ends, my stomach is cramping with hunger. I stop at a deli and with a hot foil-wrapped sandwich in my hand, I begin the walk home.

The walk up Ninth Avenue toward West Twentieth is a vibrant one as always. Locals and tourists spill out onto the streets, leaving bars with friends or holding hands with lovers. Loneliness leaves an ache in my throat, but it's a feeling I'm going to have to get used to.

I pull out my keys and approach my front door, exhausted down to my bones. Footsteps approach from behind me, and tension makes my shoulders stiffen.

"H-hello?"

It's a man's voice. Heavily accented, deep, and quivering with emotion.

I swear I've heard it somewhere before...

I turn and my heart leaps into my throat. Behind me stands a man. Tall and muscular, with golden hair tied in a ponytail. Wide glass-green eyes roam over my every feature. For some reason, they're damp with tears. At his sides, his hands shake where they're balled into fists. And then there's the way he's dressed in an antique tunic and cloth trousers despite the freezing weather. As our eyes meet, his lips tremble when he smiles, and shit, it's a beautiful thing, lighting up his face like a sunbeam. No one's ever looked at me like this stranger has.

"Can I help you?" I try to keep my voice steady, though my body betrays me by tensing up like we're about to brawl.

His smile falters to a frown. "It's me. It's Lyall."

Have I heard that name before? When? Where? He says his name as if I should know it. I'm sure I've never met this man before in my life, and yet he's looking at me like I'm his whole world.

"I'm sorry, you must have me mistaken for someone else."

The man, Lyall, takes a step back, blinking like he's coming out of a daze. His voice is barely a whisper. From the look on his face, you'd have thought I'd just slapped him. But it's true. I seriously don't know who he is. Do I?

Damn it, now I'm questioning my own memory.

"I said, you've got me confused with someone else."

Lyall stares at me for so long, it starts to make me uncomfortable.

"I see." He combs a shaking hand through his hair, blinking fast. "I thought you were... someone I cared about." He pauses, swallows hard. Whoever he thought I was, he's clearly shaken up that I'm not them. "Apologies for interrupting your evening." Moisture dampens the corners of his eyes.

Poor guy. I almost wish I were whoever he was looking for.

"No worries, man." I offer him a smile. "Hope you find them. Good night."

He says nothing as he steps backward off the stoop. Guilt's heavy in my chest when I turn away and stick my key in the lock. Should I offer him some help?

"Hey," I say, turning toward him.

He's gone as if I'd imagined him.

A chill that has nothing to do with the crisp night air crawls down my spine.

My legs are shaky as I climb the stairs. It was just a case of mistaken identity. No big deal. Happens to all of us. I didn't know him. I've never met him in my life. Maybe he's a model, and I saw him in an advertisement a time or two. He's sure got a face for modeling.

Once I'm upstairs, I lock the door. I put my sandwich in the fridge, suddenly too unsettled to eat dinner. In my bedroom I toss my clothes onto my desk chair, then fall into bed.

The devastation on his face keeps replaying in my head. *Why was he so familiar?*

It's hours before I finally sleep.

Chapter 3

Lyall

Isle of Ulfheim, year 833

For years, I have searched for Soren.

Using a branch of Yggdrasil, our holy tree whose branches and roots connect all nine realms, I have traveled to the future to find him just as I promised. My search had yielded nothing but heartache, for I had never been able to locate him.

The moment he'd passed through the portal and into exile, I could no longer feel him through the bond. It was as if he'd simply... vanished. In the days following his exile, I'd mourned my mate as if he had died. It had only been when the weeks passed that hope finally found me.

All ulfhednar from an Alpha bloodline need a mate, chosen or fated, or else they risk going berserk. All berserkers are threats that must be put out of their misery. If Soren were dead, surely I would have lost myself to the berserker's rage by now.

My younger brother and Alpha, Wulfric, found his mate, Kieran. Gunnar recently found his mate in Arlo, though he rejected the poor witch. Even Anders, my foul-tempered twin, found his mate in Jamie.

I'd begun to fear that I would live the rest of my days alone.

Until I stepped through the portal to the future once more, and for the first time in so long, I could *feel* the bond connecting us, warm as summer sun bursting through the clouds in my heart.

I thought I'd died the day I'd lost him, that the pain of losing him *and* my father was the lowest I could fall.

I'd been wrong.

When Soren looked at me without a trace of recognition in his eyes, I died a second time.

The days pass. I don't leave my house. I hunger for nothing. Exhaustion weighs on every bone in my body, but I can find no rest. Draugr have more life in them than I do.

The life we built together, the dreams we had, the love we shared… it's gone. All of it. It's not enough to have lost him once before, to have spent years mourning him. No, the gods decreed that I must mourn him a second time. This time will be my last. The heartache will be the end of me.

A sob racks my body, and I curl in on myself, shivering despite the blankets I've tucked myself away in.

Noises beyond my front door make me open my eyes. Familiar grumbling and mumbling tell me it's my brothers. Great. I pull the blankets over my head just as someone kicks the door in. If they broke anything, they had better fix it.

I yelp when the blankets are wrenched off me, forcing me to glower up at my brothers. Wulfric's eyes are full of worry. Gunnar's jaw is set tight with anger. Anders, the bastard, is smirking.

"Get him!" Anders shouts.

Both Gunnar and Wulfric seize me by an arm and haul me out of bed. I kick and thrash, but not eating for days has left me feeling weak, so I settle for cursing them out as they drag me through the village and toward the hot springs. I bellow for help from the villagers, but they only laugh at our antics.

Panic flares within me as the hot springs come into view.

Anders grabs the back of my trousers, lifting my feet off the ground. They start swinging me.

"If you do this, I will kill all of you!" I snarl.

They don't care.

My shout echoes as they hurl me toward the water. Bastards didn't even bother to undress me. I sink like a stone to the bottom of the pool, too stunned to move. My lungs throb, and I kick and claw my way to the surface. They laugh as I come up for air. Sweeping my hair out of my face to glare at them properly, I snap, "May your balls fester and your pricks rot!"

Anders only howls louder, bent over from mirth.

"It was for your own good!" Wulfric insists, arms folded over his chest. "You haven't left your house in a week, brother. We had to do something. Hate us if you like, but you'd have done the same."

Aye, that's true, but fury still burns in my gut. "I would have at least let you undress before throwing you in the spring!"

"We did you a favor. Those clothes need to be burned," Anders says, turning up his nose.

"You lads are horrible!" Aunt Helga huffs as she approaches, carrying a tray laden with food. "Look what you've done to him!"

"It was necessary," Gunnar says. His voice is hoarse, as if he hasn't spoken in a while. The fool's probably been spending more time in that cabin of his up in the mountains. He'll only go berserk faster if he's isolated.

My aunt sets the tray down by the water. "Poor dear." Helga kneels, reaching out to cup my cheek. "I'll bring you some clean clothes and here, use this." She hands me a soap stone. She gives my brothers a look that makes them avert their gazes, then walks back toward the village.

I feel like a fool bathing with my clothes on, so I strip and toss my sodden clothing onto the shore, then lather up the soap stone so I can wash myself. Wulfric and Anders undress and wade out into the spring to join me. Gunnar remains on the shore, leaning against a tree and glowering off into the distance.

Wulfric disappears beneath the water, then surfaces, sweeping his golden hair back from his face with a boyish grin I haven't seen in a while. He's been quicker to smile since he and Kieran mated. Anders motions for the soap, and I fight the urge to throw it at his head.

"Are Jamie and the lad well?" I ask.

Anders nods. "Aye. Jamie tells me there's this special day called Christmas coming up at the end of the month. He wants us to celebrate."

I've never heard of such a thing, so it must be an invention from the future.

"What's happened?" Wulfric asks, turning to me with his arms crossed.

I can't tell him I met Soren. He would view that as a betrayal. Anders is the only one who knows the truth about what really happened on that fateful day. As far as Wulfric and Gunnar are concerned, Soren is still the man who got our father and Gunnar's family killed.

"Nothing."

Anders is quiet, but there's a knowing look in his eyes.

"What a crock of shit," Gunnar says from the shore. "Something's wrong. Tell us."

Sighing, I splash water over my shoulders to rinse off the soap. "It's nothing you can fix."

"Try me." Gunnar cracks his knuckles. His claws are sharp, and there's a feral glow to his eyes. "If someone has harmed you, they won't live to see another day."

I appreciate his protectiveness, but I shake my head. "I... had my heart broken. I fell for someone and they didn't return my feelings."

"I'm sorry to hear that," Wulfric says. "Did they say why?"

My reflection ripples on the surface of the pool. I don't recognize the man looking back at me with bruises under his eyes, his cheeks gaunt. "No."

"There will be others," Wulfric says.

My jaw clenches until my teeth ache.

There was only one, and you took him from me. The words burn the back of my throat like bile. How I want to rage at him, tear into him with words and with claws.

But I can't. Just as Wulfric bears responsibility, so do I. No one forced me to stay. I made my choice. I chose my brothers. I let Soren go.

Anders gives me a knowing look and says through our bond, *"I'm not letting you give up. I didn't watch you pine and mope for years only for you to give up at the slightest inconvenience."*

I take a deep breath to keep my composure, pretending to rinse soap from my shoulders although they're clean already. *"I did not pine. And this is more than an inconvenience. He doesn't remember me. Worse than that, he was frightened of me."*

Anders scoffs, earning him an odd look from Wulfric. He disappears under the water, then surfaces some way off.

I swim out to the center of the pool with him. Quietly, Anders murmurs, "Of course he was frightened. No doubt you went charging in and made a spectacle of yourself."

"Because I thought he knew who I was," I hiss.

"Well, he didn't. Jamie punched me in the face when we first met."

My mouth slips open. Jamie hit him? Sweet slip of a thing, Jamie?

"Wish I'd been there to see that."

He smacks the back of my head, making me chuckle. "Point is, you've got to have some tact. They don't like being told that you're from the past and you've come to knot and mate them."

"But Soren's not a human."

Anders huffs. "He's spent years in their world and for whatever reason, he's lost his memories. He may very well believe he is one of them. So you've got to play by their rules, as Jamie says."

"What's the point? He doesn't remember me."

Anders snaps, "Then you'll just have to make him fall in love with you again, idiot!"

Could he be right? Is it possible for me to find a way to earn Soren's love?

"I did it before..." It had taken years, and my feelings had changed so slowly I hadn't noticed it myself. Surely I can do it again.

"Are you willing to try? Is he worth it?"

My heart skips. "Of course he is!" Within me, hope blossoms like flowers in spring.

Anders grins, eyes lighting up. "Good. Now listen. Here's what we're going to do."

"Where are we going?" I ask as Anders rows us out into the sea.

"To get you registered with the Time Traveler Agency."

My heart skips. "No. Anders, what if they tell Wulfric that I registered? That would give me away!"

Anders rolls his eyes. "Not if you have good reason to visit the future." He thumbs his own chest. "You've got family in the future now. It's hardly suspicious to want to visit your twin, aye?"

I suppose he has a point. I've been very careful not to be seen traveling between realms. All it takes is a human with one of their fancy devices taking a picture or video of me popping out of a portal, and my pack would be in violation of traveler law.

Founded by witches, the TTA helps travelers fit into their new present by providing them with documentation needed to thrive in the modern world. Then there is the

Travelers Council, witches who make the rules of time travel and punish those who violate them.

Anders had landed in trouble with them not long ago when he'd gone berserk and threatened to not only endanger our pack but expose the mundane world to the paranormal one. He could have had his wolf stripped from him by magic. Fortunately, we'd had an unlikely ally in Arlo, an enforcer for the agency. Why he aided us, I cannot say, but I will be forever in his debt for helping my brother find his way back to us.

"You must do this, Lyall. By the grace of the gods, you avoided detection all these years. Sooner or later, you will be caught and punished for breaking the rules. Registering is the safest thing you can do. Besides, it's a simple process. A child could do it."

I hum thoughtfully. "Ah, so that explains how you were able to do it."

He splashes water in my face. Normally I would splash him right back, but I can barely even muster up a smile in response to his teasing.

Anders's scowl deepens. "Odin's beard, brother. You are pathetic. The sooner you get your mate back the better. This sulking about isn't becoming of you."

His words are harsh, but beneath them, his heart skips a beat. My brother is worried about me.

"Why are you helping me?"

Anders's bushy brows furrow.

"You can't tell me you honestly trust Soren after the one conversation we had."

A muscle ticks in Anders's jaw. Years of gnashing his teeth in rage have left his jawline sharp. "You're right. I don't. Not truly. But I've watched you suffer in silence for too long. If I can help you, then I will."

A smile, honest and true, curls my lips. For a time, I wondered if Anders even saw us as family. After losing our father, my twin's kind disposition disappeared. His loss hardened Anders into someone ruled by bitter anger and jealousy of Wulfric's position. Ever since he met Jamie, though, Anders has been a man reborn.

"Thank you."

The branch of Yggdrasil Anders brought with us begins to vibrate, the runes glowing a pale blue. The flash of a portal obscures my vision, and the next thing I know, we're not at sea anymore. The portal carried us into a pool of water within a large chamber where other boats of different sizes and styles are moored.

Beyond the pool, a line of travelers has gathered, all dressed in styles I have never seen before—from big hats adorned with feathers to shiny helmets. Once we're at the head of the line, the woman behind the desk asks for my name, my paranormal identity, and my purpose for being here.

Afterward, I have to wait in yet another line to get my photo taken for this thing called an Eye D. It's a long and dull process, but within the hour I have all the documentation I need and authorization to travel to the present.

"Let's go," Anders says, but I hesitate. There's something I need to ask.

I approach a woman dressed formally like the rest of the staff. "Excuse me. Who is your Alpha?"

She frowns at me. "Alpha? Oh, you mean in charge? Helena Cartwright heads this branch of the TTA."

"I need to see her."

"I'm sorry, sir, but you'll have to schedule an appointment."

An appointment? A schedule? I haven't a clue what any of that means, but it sounds complicated. "No, I must see her now."

She sighs. "Ms. Cartwright does not accept walk-ins, so once again—"

"That's all right, Isabella." A woman with dark hair and fair skin stands behind me. Her scent of ozone tells me she's a witch. "I have time but please be brief." She motions me into her office.

"What're you doing?" Anders asks.

"I want to ask her about Soren." I brush off his hand and follow the witch into her office. Grumbling, Anders follows me in.

She closes the door behind us and motions to the plush armchairs by her desk. "I am Helena Cartwright, head of the Manhattan division of the Time Traveler Agency."

"Lyall Erikson and my brother Anders."

She smiles. "Yes, I recognized you, Anders. It's nice to meet you, Lyall. Please, have a seat."

I sit opposite her desk, drumming my hands on my thighs. I fear I won't like what answers she has for me. "Many years ago, my brother and Alpha, Wulfric, banished Soren Erikson to this time. I... Anders encountered him and Soren had no recollection of ever knowing Anders. I need to know why."

Pursing her lips, she waves her hand and across the room a file cabinet opens. A file flies toward her, pages turning, and settles neatly on the desk. "Just a moment..." She goes through the file, nodding to herself. "He was exiled from your pack after a hunter clan led by his father burned your village and killed your father, the former Alpha Erikson."

"Aye, but he wasn't responsible." My hands curl in my lap. "He had no idea his father was alive. He thought all his kin had been killed in an attack on his village when he was a boy."

She frowns at me. "That's not what I have in his file. It says here he knew about the attack and helped plan it with his father."

"That's a lie!" I snap, fangs sharp as my wolf rears his head to defend our mate.

Anders growls, "Calm yourself."

I take a breath. "Apologies, but that isn't true at all."

"Do you have proof of your version of the story?"

A sigh escapes me. "No. Only my word."

"I see." She closes Soren's file and meets my gaze. "Mr. Erikson, when Soren came to our time, we erased his memories and planted new ones to help him assimilate into his new surroundings as smoothly as possible."

My heart drops into my stomach. They *stole* my mate's memories of our life together. It's their fault Soren doesn't remember me.

"Give them back." My shaking hands curl into fists in my lap.

"I cannot."

"You must!" My fist hits the desk, knocking over some pens. They roll across the desk and quietly thud onto the carpet. "You stole our life together. You took him from me." My voice trembles and cracks.

She speaks gently, as if to a child, when she replies. "Without proof of his innocence, we can't restore his memories. It's simply too great of a risk. I'm sorry."

"You're thieves. Thieves and cowards!" There's a sharp sting in my palms.

"Brother, you're bleeding." Anders lays a hand on my shoulder.

I uncurl my fists, and blood pools in my palms.

"You're welcome to spend time with him. We ask that when you travel to this time, you do so inconspicuously, such as over large bodies of water via boat or, preferably, through one of our own portals in this building. If we find out humans have seen you while traveling to this time or that there have been attempts to remind Soren of his past, then there will be repercussions."

"Such as?" Anders asks, his hand tightening on my shoulder. His worry hits our bond.

"First, we will contact Alpha Erikson and tell him of this violation. He will have a month to come up with a solution. If he cannot, then the Travelers Council will get involved and your pack will lose the ability to travel."

"What?" Anders snarls, outwardly furious. Only I can sense the storm of horror that crashes through the bond.

Dread makes my heart sink. "Why the pack? Why not simply me?"

Anders lives in the future with his family. Kieran still has friends he checks in on in this time as well. If we aren't allowed to travel, I'll never see Anders again, nor he us.

"The Travelers Council takes violations of traveler law seriously. We must maintain the peace and security of travelers in the past, present, and future. Do you have any other questions, Mr. Erikson?"

No, but I want to grab her and shake her. How dare she try to keep us apart! Taking a long breath, I urge my wolf to calm himself. This isn't her fault. She gets her orders from the witch version of an Alpha, the Travelers Council.

"I understand." I don't, but I plaster on a smile. "Thank you. But just to be clear, I am allowed to meet with Soren?"

She returns my false smile. "Of course. As long as no attempts are made to remind him of his past, then you are allowed to see him. Have a good day, Mr. Erikson."

Anders and I are silent as we make our way outside.

My family has suffered so much. Being separated would break our hearts. It isn't fair to put my own happiness before theirs. If Anders is no longer comfortable with my plan to reunite with Soren, then that's it. I will have to stop. If I alone were the one to suffer, I would still risk it all. But I won't be the reason my family is torn apart.

The TTA office is a plain-looking building from the outside. The travelers I'd seen from the past and future spill out into the streets. Not one of them is out of place in their new surroundings. I'd never have guessed they were travelers at all.

With my hands in fists, I force myself to speak. "Being with Soren is risky. I understand if you no longer support my decision. If our family is separated because of me, I'll never forgive myself." My throat thickens, and the streets around me blur. "Say the word, and this will end here and now."

Every second of silence that passes tears at my heart.

Anders huffs, the sound heavy. "Have you always been such a craven?"

Blood heating, I whirl around to strike him. He grabs my fist easily. "How dare you?" I snarl the words through clenched teeth. "It's not craven to sacrifice my happiness for the sake of our family!"

Anders sneers. "All these years, you still haven't learned to put yourself before others."

"Like you do?" Anders may have never taken his role as eldest seriously, but I have. It's my duty to protect my family. Aye, Wulfric is Alpha, but that doesn't mean he must bear the responsibility alone.

His eyes narrow. "Once, Lyall. Just once, allow yourself to come first."

The storm raging within me slows and then settles. "You... you want me to do this? Even if it means being separated."

Anders shrugs. "Just don't be an idiot and get caught. Simple."

I gape at him. Anders would risk losing his connection to our pack, for me, for my happiness?

He grunts when I wrench him into a back-slapping hug. "You've changed, brother. Father would be proud."

The tension leaves Anders's shoulders, and he grips the nape of my neck. "We'll think of something. I promise. Let's ask Jamie. He's got quite the imagination. I'm sure he'll think up a way for you and Soren to reconnect."

We linger a moment, basking in the warm glow of pack and brotherhood. Anders is blinking fast when we separate. My own eyes sting. He coughs. I scuff my boot on the ground.

Although I've been to this timeline often since Soren and I were forced apart, something feels different now. I take a breath and find my chest is lighter, my heart racing with hope rather than fear. For the first time, I've arrived here knowing I will find my mate. Knowing that I will not be leaving brokenhearted.

After all these years, I've been given a second chance with the man I love, and I will be damned before I squander it.

This time, we will never be parted again.

Chapter 4
Soren

New York is a big and sometimes strange place. People have encounters with odd people all the time. So why can't I forget him?

He's in my *dreams* now, dreams where I'm happier than I've ever been. In these dreams, he makes me laugh and smile so hard my cheeks hurt. Wherever we are, it's somewhere cold, full of rugged natural beauty. He looks at me like I'm his entire world, kisses me like he can't get enough. We talk. I don't know what about. Our conversations are muffled, like I'm hearing them from underwater.

Every time, I wake with an ache in my chest and sometimes even tears in my eyes because I know I'll never find anyone who loves me like my dream man does.

My dreams become more and more intense. Tender kisses become heated. Every touch has me aching for more. Beneath me, his eyes dark with lust and adoration, he falls apart as I drive myself deep into the heat and tightness of his body. He feels like home. His gorgeous lips part as he utters moans I can't hear. When he comes, his lips forming the shape of my name over and over again, I realize that all my life, something has been missing.

It's him. It's the love we share in these dreams.

It's so damn pathetic.

"Are you sleeping well? You have bags under your eyes," Fergus points out one night, worriedly rubbing beneath my eyelid.

I move out of his reach to plate up the piping hot veggie lasagna we're having for dinner. "I'm fine. Just having weird dreams."

I hand him his plate and we sit at the table together.

"Nightmare?"

"I guess." No, they're anything but. However, I'm not telling my granddad I've been having wet dreams about a weird stranger.

Fergus's knife scrapes the bottom of his plate. He forks some lasagna into his mouth and sighs contentedly. "This is delicious. Eat, boy. Did anything happen recently that bothered you?"

I shrug. "Something happened last week."

Fergus frowns. "Drunks at the bar causing trouble?"

I take a sip of my coffee, sucking it down like its oxygen. I need the energy since I'm working all night at the bar tonight. I couldn't sleep at all last night. My brain was like a TV that wouldn't shut off, replaying my encounter with that strange man who was both familiar and not.

"I wish. This guy came up to me just as I got home." Where do I even start? Do I mention his antique style of clothing? His archaic way of speaking? How he'd looked at me in a way no one ever had before? The devastation on his face when I'd told him I didn't know who he was?

Fergus frowns. "Are you okay?"

I nod. "Yeah. Yeah, he didn't hurt me. It was just weird, that's all. He acted like he knew me."

"You're sure you'd never met before?"

I nod. "That's the thing. I know I haven't, but there was something familiar about him."

Ceramic clanks hard against the table as Fergus sets his drink down. "What did he look like?"

"Like he'd walked off a film set. Kind of like a character from some Viking movie or something."

Fergus is quiet for so long, I look up and freeze. His face has gotten paler, his knuckles whitening around the handle of his mug.

"Gramps? You okay?"

He jumps, sucking in a breath. "If you see him again, let me know at once. If he comes looking for you again, stay away from him."

My stomach churns. I've never seen him so serious before. "I will."

He exhales slowly. "Good. I'd hate for anything to happen to you." His eyes water, and I chuckle.

"I'm fine, Gramps. Besides, he wasn't dangerous." If I'm sure of anything, it's that. He'd looked at me with such tenderness, I'd known on an instinctual level he'd never hurt me. "He just seemed sad when I didn't know who he was. It's so odd. I could have sworn I'd seen him somewhere before..."

"You haven't, Soren. You're being kind and empathetic, that's all. He was mentally ill. Hopefully, he will get the help he needs but knowing how little this city cares about helping people like him, it's not likely." Fergus gives me a tight smile, his lips whitening. What's with him?

He rises and approaches my chair, then leans down and hugs me tightly.

I chuckle, putting an arm around him. "Hey. What's going on?"

He laughs, low and rusty, and I smile into his shoulder. "Oh, hush and let me hug my grandson." He grips the back of my neck and squeezes. A warm sensation runs through me, making me feel like a boy again, running into his arms for comfort and safety. "Have a good shift, my boy."

I give him a squeeze. "Thanks."

I give the ice-cold shaker a long rattle. It's a good night. The dance floor is packed, and there's only standing room at the bar. I've been busy, bouncing between the bar and the kitchen to bring people food. There's an ache in my feet, and my head's starting to pound with every throb of the music. There's only an hour left, and then I can go home.

I strain the drink into a glass, garnish it with an orange peel twist, and then hand it to my customer. "Here you go."

Jamie takes his drink but doesn't sip right away, taking a moment to admire my work. I do make nice-looking drinks, and I've been told they taste as good as they look. I've come a long way from my days of spilling beer and dropping glasses. Okay, I still drop a glass from time to time.

"This looks amazing! Cheers, puppy dog!" He lifts his glass to the rugged, handsome man beside him.

"Cheers!" Anders returns, and he drinks his beer.

Jamie and Anders are newcomers. They've been showing up at least every other night for the past two weeks. Anders seemed like a broody grump at first, but Jamie, and a few drinks, helped loosen him up.

"So good!" Jamie says. "This may be the best Cosmo I've ever had!"

My face lights up with pride. "Thanks. Glad to hear it."

"How long have you lived in the city?" Anders asks.

"All my life," I answer. "How about you?"

"Just moved here myself. Me and my twin."

Dear God, he has a twin? Is he single?

Nope. Doesn't matter. No more relationships for me.

"Where from?"

"Iceland," Jamie chimes in. "Ever been?"

I had noticed Anders's intriguing accent, but I hadn't been able to place it.

"Wow, that's exciting. Can't say I've thought of visiting."

"Would you be open to showing my twin around the city in your spare time? Jamie and I have busy schedules, or we would offer."

That sounds fun. "Sure," I say. It would be nice to meet someone new and do something outside of work for a change. "Give him my number. My evenings are busy but my weekends are free."

"Thank you," Anders says, smiling gratefully. "He's a good man, my brother. A bit thickheaded."

Jamie laughs. "Not everyone can be as perfect as you."

I give Anders my number so he can pass it along to his brother. My shift gets busier after that, so I'm not able to chat much, and Jamie and Anders leave before my shift is done. Craving a warm bed, I drag myself home and all but collapse.

When I wake up the next day, there's a message on my phone from a new number.

> **Greetings. I am Anders's brother. Thank you for your kind offer.**

> **No problem! This'll be fun. Is there anywhere in particular you'd like to see?**

> **Do you know of any mead halls?**

Mead halls? I guess that's something they have in Iceland.

> **We don't have mead halls, but I bet I can find a place that serves mead.**

Sounds like he's feeling homesick.

After a quick Google Maps search, I find not only a place that serves mead, but it's also Viking themed. It sounds fun.

We make plans to meet at the bar around noon.

I spend the rest of my morning getting ready for the day and brainstorming interesting places we could go. I think I have a pretty good plan by the time I leave the house and ride the train over to Hell's Kitchen, where the bar's supposed to be.

The bar, Valhalla, is nestled amongst a whole block full of bars, mostly catering to the LGBTQ community. It sure stands out with a name like that. The interior is as cool as I'd hoped it would be, full of Viking-esque decor and horned helmets on the walls. It's like I walked into a mead hall from the Viking era.

"Soren?"

That voice... It can't be...

I turn and can barely stop my mouth from falling open. It's Lyall. He's dressed differently from the night we met, in a sweater that hugs his thick chest and a leather jacket. He's tied his golden mane back into a ponytail and shaved his beard to stubble. His eyes. They're identical to Anders's, and now that I've met Anders, there's no mistaking the family resemblance.

Well, shit. What are the chances?

"*You're* Anders's brother?"

"Aye. His twin." He smiles, looking much happier than the night I met him. "Fancy seeing you again."

I chuckle. "I know, right? Only in New York. So. Nice to meet you. Again. I'm Soren."

"I know—my brother told me," he adds quickly. "Lyall. A pleasure to meet you. Again." He gives me a playful smile that I pretend doesn't make my stomach flutter. Shit. He's stunning. That's fine. Nothing wrong with appreciating a handsome guy. We're not dating or anything. There's no harm in looking.

"I hope you like the place. They serve mead."

Lyall looks around with a smile. "Why are there horns on those helmets? Is that not impractical? Suppose you're fighting and someone grabbed onto those horns and pulled. They could easily get a hit on you."

I shrug. "You could gouge an eye out."

Lyall laughs. "I hadn't thought of that! Aye, that could work, but see the way they're curved? You'd leave a bruise for sure but you wouldn't come close to taking an eye out."

"Yeah, but you'll look epic while doing it."

"You'll look *dead*."

"And cool."

He huffs in amusement, but before he can reply, the bartender hands us some menus. Lyall orders right away. "Mead," he says.

"Sure. Which kind?"

He doesn't even look at the menu. "Whichever is your strongest."

"I'll have whatever he's having," I add.

Once she's off preparing our drinks, I rotate my barstool to face Lyall. "How are you liking the city so far?"

"It's loud and smelly but I can see why my brother loves it here. There are interesting things to see around every corner. What about you?"

"It's home," I say. "I grew up here with my granddad."

Lyall frowns at that. "Your grandfather?"

"Yeah. My parents weren't the parenting type, so he raised me."

"He sounds like a good man."

"The best." I don't know where I'd be without him. My life would have turned out so differently, most likely for the worst. I owe him so much.

"Is he the reason you stay?"

"Huh?"

"You said, 'It's home,' and spoke of your grandfather."

He's perceptive as hell. "Oh. Well. I guess I've always wanted to be somewhere else." A twinge of guilt always accompanies these thoughts. Fergus has done so much for me. I can't just leave him, especially now that he's older. He has looked after me all these years. It's only right to be there for him. "The city's great. You can walk everywhere. There's tons to do. But I've always had this feeling that there's something more out there."

"Someone?" Lyall asks softly, almost to himself.

I don't know what to say about that. It's like he read my mind. It's unsettling.

Our bartender brings our drinks over, and Lyall lifts his glass.

"To family," I say.

Lyall smiles. "To charting our own course in life, no matter the consequences."

I drink when he does, his words replaying in my head. "How's it compare to mead in Iceland?"

He smacks his lips, then takes another gulp. "Delicious. Thank you for bringing me here. I wonder if there are any similar places we could visit."

"You mean, more themed bars?"

"Something like that, aye."

"Maybe there's some other medieval-themed activity we can do."

I didn't mean for today to turn into a Viking-era adventure in NYC, but I'm here for it. Especially if I can make Lyall smile like that again.

Damn it. No, this is just a fun outing. Not a date. Get it together, me.

By the time we've drained our glasses, I've found something else that sounds interesting. "How about a sword fighting class?"

Lyall slams a fist on the bar. "I will conquer this class!"

I bark out a laugh. "Sounds like a yes to me." I close out our tab and motion for Lyall to follow me. "Come on. The class starts in thirty minutes. We'll get there faster if we take the train."

Lyall frowns. "A train?"

"No, the F train. It'll take us right there."

We zip up our coats and I lead the way to the nearest station. "Have you ever taken a sword fighting class before?"

Lyall grips my arm as cars rush past, and I realize I was so busy looking at him that I almost walked into oncoming traffic. Whoops. "I've mastered all manner of blades and blunt weaponry. My father trained us lads as soon as we were old enough to swing a blade."

Whoa, that's pretty hardcore. It sounds like he had an unusual upbringing. Once we're down in the subway, I tap my phone to pass through the turnstiles. Lyall simply hoists himself over and looks confused when other people don't do the same.

"Show off," I say.

Lyall grins. "It seemed the faster way."

"Excuse me, sir," a police officer calls, marching toward us. "You've got to pay the fare!"

"Shit!" I grab Lyall's hand. "Let's go!" I take off, leading him down onto the platform just as our train roars into the station. Lyall freezes, wide-eyed as the train screeches to a stop.

"Excuse me, pardon me!" I call out, dragging Lyall onto the cramped train before the passengers can get off. They grumble and some curse us out, but enough people exit the train that the flow of foot traffic cuts the cop off from us. Collapsing into a seat, I laugh as the cop's scowling face becomes a blur out the window.

"Next time, pay the fare. Or make sure the cops don't see you if you decide to jump it."

Lyall doesn't respond. He's standing and gripping a pole with both hands. His knuckles are white from how hard he's holding on. Wide green eyes dart around the train car, and his shoulders heave less from exertion and more from panic.

Shit. That chase with the cop must have freaked him out.

"Hey. You good?" I stand and quickly grab onto the pole so I don't fall as the train rocks on the tracks.

"I... I don't think so." Lyall gulps, wincing as the train's wheels screech over the tracks.

"It's okay," I tell him, not sure what else to say. "Worst-case scenario, the cop would have made us pay a fine. He probably wouldn't have arrested us."

"That's not—"

The train stops in the middle of the tunnel. I don't even blink when the announcement that we're being held momentarily by a train ahead of us crackles over our heads, but Lyall gasps, one hand rubbing his ear like the noise hurt him.

Shit. I don't want him to have a panic attack. What do I do?

"Lyall, everything's okay. We're safe." I reach out to touch his arm. Instead, he grabs my hand and holds on tight. His hand is unsteady in mine, skin clammy. Damn. He's really unsettled. He's been through a lot of changes. Anyone would be overwhelmed. Heat warms my neck, but I don't pull away. I squeeze his fingers, rubbing my thumb over his knuckles. Lyall inhales softly, his gaze capturing mine.

"I... I won't let anything happen to you." Even though his voice shakes, he grips my hand and never breaks my gaze. The promise in every word makes my heart skip.

A soft laugh escapes me. "Okay."

I don't know why, but I believe every word.

"Welcome, everyone!" our instructor says, a muscular woman with box braids and a bright smile. "Y'all here for the sword fighting class?"

"Yup," I say, setting my bag down by the door.

"Good, because I've had a few folks askin' for Pilates and this *definitely* isn't Pilates." She coaxes a laugh out of the crowd and then introduces herself as Briana. After encouraging us to introduce ourselves, she goes over a brief history of medieval sword fighting. Briana calls up another instructor for a demonstration of a few beginner moves we can try. There are quite a few oohs and aahs, and I'm impressed by the skillful parrying and counter-attacks the instructors show off.

Then finally we're allowed to get our hands on some swords. The swords themselves are metal but blunt and fitted with rubber at the tip for extra safety measures. Lyall inspects his blade, a longsword. "Blunt. Good. No children will get hurt. Decent weight too. It beats the wooden sword I trained with..."

"How often did you train?" I ask, intrigued. Lyall's an interesting guy.

"My father made sure I practiced every day."

"Sounds like a cool guy." A smile tilts my mouth. "Was he a professional fighter?" It sounds like he wanted his sons to follow in his footsteps.

"All right, everyone, let's pair up and do some sword fighting!" Briana says before Lyall can reply.

He tugs on my arm, bringing me close to him. Heat flushes my cheeks. "We're together," he declares.

She laughs. "You two can go stand on the mat over there, okay?"

We face each other, longswords at the ready. "Do you remember how they did the parry and the counterattack?" I ask, trying not to think about how warm and sturdy he'd felt against my side.

"Let's try it," he says. "But first..." Setting down his sword, he walks into my space. My breath catches when he touches my wrists. "Hold the sword like this." He adjusts my grip, his hands warm and his fingertips rough with calluses.

Something about the weight of the sword in my hand feels familiar. Right.

"Spread your legs," he murmurs low in my ear. "Like this."

He kneels before me. All my blood rushes past my hips when he touches my ankle, guiding my foot to where it should be. He'd look good on his knees in other scenarios, too…

No, think unsexy thoughts. Cockroaches. Rats. Bags of garbage.

"There we go, perfect!" Lyall says cheerfully, patting my shoulder. He picks up his sword and faces me. "I'll swing at you. You push my blade away, then counter."

"Just like that?" A nervous laugh escapes me.

"I'll take it easy on you, don't worry. Ready?" When I nod, though I feel far from ready, he swings.

As the blade comes toward me, something inside me… wakes up. I had braced myself to dodge or jump back. Instead, I throw myself into my swing, deflect his attack, and knock his sword right out of his hand.

Lyall's mouth falls open. Heads turn and the chatter in the room falls quiet as the sword clangs loudly to the floor.

What the hell just happened? Somehow that came as naturally as breathing to me.

"I'm so sorry! Are you okay?" I hope I didn't hurt him.

Wide, unreadable green eyes find mine. Then Lyall spins on his heel and picks up the sword. "Again," he says.

"Wh-what?" I ask Lyall.

He grins and beckons to me. "I said *again*. Give me all you've got." He shifts into a battle-ready stance, and I mirror him without even having to think about it. I don't know what's going on with me, but I don't care. My blood's heating up, heart racing.

I swing and I don't hold back. Lyall deflects, and as soon as he smacks the blade aside, he lunges in for a counter-attack. I sweep his attack aside without a second thought, and a thrill makes my hair stand on end. Lyall curses under his breath, then goes charging back in. The room blurs around us as we move, parrying, swinging, dodging.

It's like a fierce dance, one we've practiced together many times. Lyall is big but graceful and fluid as water. Sometimes he hits my shoulder while I manage to catch him a few times, but he just laughs and keeps going. My own face hurts from smiling, chest heaving with exertion.

Our swords cross, and he leans into my space. He's panting, breath hot against my face, eyes wild and dancing with exhilaration. Locks of blond hair cling to his sweaty forehead. I push back against his sword, bringing us closer. Those emerald eyes darken, lids lowering as he glances down at my mouth.

I toss him a smirk, drawing my tongue over my bottom lip to tease him. "What's wrong? Need to take a break?"

He laughs, low and gravelly, then leans in. "Oh, no. I was just going to tell you that you should watch your footwork."

"Huh—"

He sweeps my feet out from under me in a move that's somehow familiar. I grab hold of his shirt and haul him down with me and roll. Our bodies slam together as I pin him beneath me, my knee on his wrist, my other leg sprawled across his hip. With a grunt, he drops his sword and glares defiantly up at me. We pant together, foreheads almost touching, sharing the same breath.

I've never felt such a rush before. Something about what we just did feels so familiar, so intimate, in a way nothing else ever has.

"You win," he says breathlessly and shifts his hips against me. "Now what?"

I buck against him, keeping him pinned in place, and bite my lip so I don't groan as our groins come into contact. He's getting hard, and me? I could pound nails.

"Think I deserve a prize…"

A shiver goes through him. "Whatever you want."

"Wow, that was amazing!" The class erupts into applause, making us both jump.

Mortified, I roll off him, making sure I stay on my stomach so nobody sees just how worked up I really am.

Briana claps for us. "You guys should be the ones teaching the class! Bravo!"

As the adrenaline fades, all I'm left with is confusion.

What the hell just came over me? I've never held a sword before in my life. All that action got me thirsty, so I escape into the hall and find a water fountain by the restroom. I take a long drink, then lean on the fountain for support.

"Are you well?" Lyall regards me with a concerned tilt of his head.

"Fine, just... I feel like I've done that before," I say, pushing my sweaty hair out of my face.

Something odd brightens Lyall's face. "What makes you say that?" For some reason, his whole body has tensed, and he's looking at me with such intensity, it unsettles me.

"I don't know. I've really never done this before. So I don't understand why that came so naturally."

Lyall's eyes widen. "Tell me what you remember." There's an odd urgency in his voice.

"What do you mean? I don't remember anything."

Lyall's shoulders slump. "Nothing?" He sounds almost disappointed.

I don't understand. "No. Why should I?"

But Lyall just shakes his head. "It's nothing. Never mind." He turns away before I can ask more questions. "We should get back to class."

And as he walks away, it's only then that I understand what that desperate look in his eyes was. It was hope that had brightened his eyes, and something about what I said took that hope and crushed it beneath my boot.

Chapter 5
Lyall

Today has been a day like no other.

This afternoon I was overjoyed to see Soren. Only in my wildest fantasies could I have imagined we would sit down and have mead together like we used to. Everything about him is so familiar. It's easy to slip up and share information about life from my timeline. I have to remind myself to be careful, but it's hard. I have never kept secrets from Soren. We knew each other so well, as if we were extensions of each other's souls.

Then I made the mistake of jumping over that obstacle in the subway. It was only later that I remembered Anders had given me this thing called an OMNY card, some magical scroll that would help open those barriers so I could enter the underworld. He'd said that the guards might get angry if I didn't use the scroll, but I had forgotten—and I'd wanted to impress Soren.

As we'd rushed deeper into the underworld and a giant metal dragon had come charging in from the tunnel toward us, I'd begun to panic. The humans had willingly walked right into the beast's belly! Why? It was then I realized... they were human souls, already passed on from this life. This metal beast had been spiriting them away to the Hel's realm.

It was nothing like the stories Father had told us lads about Helheim.

Soren hadn't been afraid. No, he was the one who'd comforted *me*. Human as he is now, unaware of his past, he'd shown such bravery in the face of an uncertain journey we might never have returned from.

I'd uttered a prayer to the gods when we left the underworld behind and returned to Midgard. Hel would not have our souls this day. Not yet.

My spirits had lifted considerably when Soren and I had sparred. For a glorious moment, the man I knew and loved had shone through. He'd fought with the same skill and ferocity as the warrior I'd proudly called my mate.

But it hadn't been enough for him to remember me. The disappointment had nearly brought me to my knees, and so I'd escaped outside for some fresh air. I'd taken the portal back down the tower to the city streets below and used the magic box—the phone, I think it's called—to contact Anders and tell him everything.

"This is a good thing, though!" Jamie's voice says.

I fail to see the positive in this. "Is it?"

"Pet, are you thinking what I am?"

"You bet your sexy ass I am."

Anders adds, "Think about it, brother. His memories may be gone, but his body still remembers. The person he used to be still resides within him. Mayhap with more encouragement—"

My heart leaps as understanding hits me. "He'll remember our history! Yes! That's brilliant!"

Jamie says, "Keep doing stuff that's similar to what you used to do together. Maybe it will help."

"Such as? This timeline is too different."

"Hang on, let me look something up," Jamie says. After a short pause, he says, "How about axe throwing? There's a place on Lafayette that does it. I'll send you the link."

We hang up and, true to his word, Jamie sends me directions to the place.

"Hey." Soren's voice makes me jump. "You okay?"

"Aye. It was hot up there, that's all. Do you know how to get here?" I hold up the phone. Soren leans in to read the message, then nods.

"Yeah. It's not too far. Why, what's there?"

I shrug. "A surprise."

Soren lifts his brows, lips curling playfully. "I like surprises."

To my relief, we don't go back into the underworld this time. Soren waves, and a yellow car pulls up to the curb. Driving is much more pleasant, especially when I roll down the window and the crisp, cold breeze blows my hair back.

"You're crazy," Soren says, laughing. "You're gonna get frostbite!"

"It will be worth it. This breeze is wonderful!"

Soren mutters something about a golden retriever, whatever that is.

Once we arrive at our destination, we take another one of those portals up. I can't fight back my nerves as the doors close, confining us in the narrow space. Soren doesn't even blink, just pushes a button for our floor.

"You sure you're okay?" Soren asks me.

I nod, forcing myself to laugh. "F-fine."

"Not a fan of enclosed spaces, are you?"

Not sure what that means.

Soren leans back against the wall, his shoulder brushing mine. "We'll be fine," he says, and the confidence in his words makes the knot in my chest unwind. I exhale and lean into his side, my heart slowing to a steady thump. I trust Soren with my life. If he says we're safe, then we are.

A flurry of delicious smells hits me as we step out of the portal and into a large dining hall. There's a crowded bar, and many of the tables are full of people enjoying delectable meals. The music is loud, making me wince. I know human hearing is weaker than an ulfhednar's superior senses, but do they really need the music *that* loud?

"A restaurant?" Soren guesses.

A woman smiles and waves at us. "Welcome, guys! Would you like a table or are you here for the axe throwing?"

Soren gapes at me. "Axe throwing? We're throwing axes?" His face splits into a grin that I haven't seen in years, one bright with the promise of adventure.

"The axes, please," I say.

She leads the way through the crowded hall and up a set of stairs. There are several loud *thwacks* followed by cheering.

"Whoa!" Soren says, rushing ahead to watch as a woman in a cage throws an axe at a target and misses. Her friends laugh at her. Soren shakes his head, laughing too. "Drunk people throwing weapons. That can't possibly backfire."

There are several cages, all occupied by men and women throwing axes. Some hit their targets while others miss, but everyone appears to be having a good time. My fingers are already twitching to get my hands on an axe.

While we wait, an instructor gives us advice on stances and grips so that by the time Soren and I enter cages next to each other, we're prepared. Soren appears a little uneasy as he glances back at the instructor for advice on his posture. I heft the axe with ease, unable to hold back my grin. "What's wrong, Soren? Afraid I'll best you?"

"I mean, you probably will."

"Come on! Show me what you've got!" I fling the axe at the target, barking a laugh when it lands dead center just as I knew it would.

"We get it, you're awesome," Soren says, voice devoid of emotion. He steps up toward the target, shoulders tense. He's in his head; I can see it in the way he keeps readjusting his grip.

"You can always walk away, Soren. No one will blame you for being a craven."

Soren's eyes light up at my teasing. "Fuck you," he says, grinning, and hurls the axe across the room. It lands on target, and Soren throws his arms in the air and shouts in excitement.

I can't help but laugh at his joy. I knew he could do it. He was always a natural. "A wager!" I say challengingly. "Whoever hits the most targets gets a free round of drinks!"

"You're on!"

And so it begins. I work up a sweat as I throw and throw and throw. My arms start to ache, and when I miss one of my shots, Soren howls with laughter. Seeing him so happy and in his element suddenly becomes much more important than winning. When the timer goes off, Soren has bested me. I may have deliberately missed a few of my targets, but that will be my little secret.

Soren does a little dance, holding the axe over his head. "How do you like my dance? I'm calling it the free drinks dance!"

I lift my hands and show him my middle fingers, a gesture I learned from Kieran.

Soren laughs until he's doubled over.

"Aye, you'll have your drinks. Hope you choke on them," I say, but without any venom. I'll buy Soren whatever he wishes so long as it makes him happy. Swinging my arm around his shoulders, I guide him back to the bar and happily hand over my—well, Anders's—card to pay for the first round.

Beyond the windows, the city lights come on as the sky darkens. By our second round of beers, Soren has regaled me with countless stories from his job as a tender of bars, each one more humorous than the last. I've laughed until my stomach aches and I fear I'll throw up my beer.

"You jest!" I wheeze for air and thumb away a tear from the corner of my eye.

Soren shakes his head, cheeks red from drink and mirth. "Swear on my life! Five thousand dollars if I'd blow a line of coke up his ass!"

I am not sure what this coke is, but the visuals are enough for me to understand. "Tell me you refused!"

"Of course I did. Kept the money, though. He was so drunk, he didn't even ask for it back!"

I slap the bar with a guffaw of laughter. "What did you spend it on?"

Soren's humor sobers. "My granddad needed knee surgery, and his insurance wouldn't cover it, so I chipped in."

His grandfather? Soren never had a grandfather. All his family except for his father were killed in the attack on his village. Whoever this man is, he isn't his relative. So who is he?

"That was kind of you. You must care for him deeply."

Soren smiles, soft and loving. I missed that sight. "He's the best. My mom had me really young, and she took off and left me with him. I can't imagine raising kids was something he wanted to do after he retired, but he gave it his all."

What? His mother? Realization slams into me, making my hand curl into a fist. These must be the memories the Council planted in Soren's mind to help him adjust to this new timeline. It's not real, any of it, but he believes it is with his whole heart.

I push my drink aside, the taste like ash in my mouth. If Soren were to learn the truth, that his entire life has been a lie... it would devastate him. Who is his grandfather? Is he somehow in on this whole thing?

Gods, I wish I could tell Soren the truth. He deserves to know. But I can't. It would bring ruin to my family. I can't risk it.

"You okay?" Soren nudges my foot, his gaze soft and concerned. He rubs my shoulder, and I lean into the warmth and sturdiness of his touch.

"Aye. Just... happy you had him." A lump rises in my throat, but I smile around it.

It should have been me. I should have been there with him. If I had gone, mayhap the Council would have taken both our memories of the past, but let us be together.

What have I done?

"Hey, there's a rage room!" Soren says, pointing toward a door with a big flashing sign above it. "Wanna go smash shit up?"

That sounds like a good way to let loose all my despair and frustration. "Sounds good." I rise when he does.

We're handed safety gear and shown the way to the dressing room. Once we're alone, Soren clears his throat. "Guess we better... strip." While I can't catch Soren's natural scent, I can still smell his emotions and hear the skip in his heart. He's nervous and... aroused. Turning away to hide my smirk, I make a show of slowly peeling up my sweater and tossing it onto the bench. I rotate my shoulders, my muscles popping. In the quiet, the sharp hitch in Soren's breathing is quite loud.

He's watching me.

I toss my hair over my shoulder and turn to glance at him. Soren looks away and focuses on removing his own clothing. His coat comes off, then his sweater, revealing fair skin and a hairy chest I want to nuzzle into. His body looks different, soft in places where he used to be toned and hard. In my time, he had the body of a warrior, honed for battle. This Soren lives a different life now, a softer, easier life.

Even if we did get back together, would he still feel at home in the past?

Our lives have gone in such different directions.

"See something you like?" Soren asks.

I look away, my neck warming. "Oh, aye. Very much."

Soren sweeps his gaze up and down my bare chest. "Okay." He snorts, not sounding as if he believes me at all.

"I do," I insist. Why doesn't he believe me? He looks different now, but that hardly matters. I still want to put my hands and mouth anywhere he'll let me. "Shall I prove it to you?"

Soren swallows loudly. "Prove... what?"

A smile lifts the edge of my mouth. Soren leans back against the lockers as I close in until the space between us diminishes. The heat from his body warms me from head to toe, and his breath ghosts over my lips. Reaching out, my hand oddly shaky, I trace his jaw with the back of my knuckles. My stomach swoops.

I'm touching him. Soren's *letting* me touch him.

His eyelids lower and he angles his head, leaning into my touch. His lips look so soft, and they're so close that the warm gust of his breath tickles my mouth. Gods, I've dreamed every night about kissing him again, of having him in my arms. My chest aches with the need to lean in and kiss him.

"Soren." His name cracks in my throat. "I've thought of nothing but this all day."

Years. I've wanted you for years.

"Tell me you feel the same, and I'll spend all night proving how desperately I want you."

"Why?" Soren's voice is barely above a whisper. "I don't get it. You don't know me."

Gods, but I *do*. I know him better than I know the depths of my heart. If only he knew that.

"I know enough," I say, lowering my face so our foreheads touch. "I know that you're loyal to your family. That you're brave and adventurous. Kind. For now, that's good enough."

Soren's breath quickens, but not from desire. No, he's *scared*. Horrified, I step back. My heart drops into my stomach. Shit. What have I done?

"Look, I, uh..." Soren shoves past me and grabs his sweater. "I had fun today, but it's late. I've gotta get home."

No, no, *no*. "Why?"

Soren tugs on his sweater. "Early shift at the bar, so—" He disappears into his clothing, arms flailing.

Going to him, I grab his sleeves and help tug them down over his arms. His hair is tousled, his cheeks flushed. "What did I say?" I ask him, giving his wrists a gentle squeeze.

He shakes his head. "Nothing, just… Okay. Lyall, I just got out of a relationship. I had a good feeling about him, but he didn't feel the same."

"Then he's a fool," I growl.

Soren tugs out of my grip and grabs his coat. "You're great, okay? But I'm not looking for a relationship right now. Or ever."

His words make my heart sink. He… doesn't want me. My mate doesn't want me.

"I wouldn't hurt you," I say.

Soren looks down at the tiled floor, the muscles in his jaw jumping. "I wish I could believe you. But I can't. I've been burned too many times. It's not your fault. I'm not in a good place right now, and you deserve better."

Someone has hurt my mate, made him afraid to trust me. I want to hunt them down and rip them limb from limb.

Soren turns away, and I catch the glimmer of unshed tears in his eyes. I can't stop myself from taking hold of his wrist again. I can't let him leave when he's hurting. "Please don't leave."

Soren exhales shakily. "Let go."

I unwind my fingers from his skin, the disappointment heavy enough to crush me. Swallowing hard, I step back. My wolf howls in my soul, asking me why I'm letting him go, why I'm not taking him in my arms. I can't. I've yearned for him all these years, but to him, we're only strangers. I'd only frighten him if I showed how desperate I am to have him.

I can only watch as the man I love walks out on me, taking all the broken pieces of my heart with him.

"He rejected you?" Jamie's pitiful gaze makes me want to hide behind the kitchen counter.

I stick another spoonful of raw cookie dough into my mouth. This dessert from the future is irresistible. I wonder if I can make it back home. "Must I repeat myself?"

Jamie shakes his head. "No, no, I was just surprised."

Anders scoffs. "You were too blunt, as always."

I point my spoon at him. "You're hardly one to talk about being blunt!"

Jamie elbows Anders. "He's got a point. I don't think this has anything to do with you, Lyall. Soren said it himself. He just got out of a relationship. He's scared of being hurt again. It's not easy to open yourself to someone after being burned so many times."

My heart aches as I recall the sadness in Soren's eyes. The man I knew and loved was a risk-taker. This man is the very opposite. If only I could make him understand I would never hurt him. I would treasure his heart until the end of my days, should I be worthy enough to earn his love.

"While you were together, did you get the sense that he was attracted to you?" Jamie asks.

"Aye. Very. We would have kissed if he hadn't run from me."

"So there's still hope!"

I wish I could see things the way he does. From where I stand, everything feels hopeless. "How can I help him understand? None of his relationships lasted because those men weren't who he was meant to be with!" I toss my spoon into the container with a sigh. "I can't tell him we're fated mates. He'd never believe me. If I could learn more about him, mayhap I could understand him better. But how?"

Jamie and Anders are quiet, seemingly as stumped as I am.

"Oh my god." Jamie suddenly springs to his feet. "I just had the craziest idea!"

Anders smiles. "Crazy may be just what we need right now, pet."

Jamie paces up and down, murmuring to himself. "Wait. Wait, this is actually brilliant. Go me!"

"What?" I ask, struggling to stay patient.

"He rejected Lyall the man. But what if he met Lyall the wolf?"

My brain tries and fails to make the connection. "How would that help? I wouldn't be able to talk to him in that form."

"Let me cook!" Jamie snaps.

"Now is not the time for cooking!"

Anders chuckles. "It's a saying. He's thinking."

Sighing, I slump against the counter. "Fine. Go and cook. Or however you say it."

"So, he's afraid of relationships but we've established that he likes you. He's not going to let you close. But! What if you found another way to get to know him?"

Understanding dawns bright like the sunrise. "As a wolf! I could learn more about him. His fears. What he wants."

"Exactly! So if you see him again in human form, you'll know how to reassure him."

"Your mate is brilliant," I tell Anders.

Smirking, Anders puffs out his chest. "Obviously."

Jamie's plan is a good one, but my spirits quickly sour when I realize it has a flaw. "How do we get him to meet with me in my shifted form?"

Jamie waves away my concerns. "Leave that to me."

I hope I don't regret this...

Chapter 6
Soren

"How do you feel about dogs?"

I'm not sure I understand the question or why Jamie is asking. I hand a customer their Guinness and say, "I mean, they're pretty cool. I've never had one, but I never pass up the opportunity to say hi to a friendly pup. I saw the cutest golden retriever on my way to work. He had this big goofy smile and…"

And it had reminded me so much of Lyall, I'd had to walk away. I hadn't been able to outrun the sucker punch of guilt and the awful feeling I'd made a huge mistake. Usually after I break up with someone or they dump me, there's the initial hurt, but it's mixed with relief. As sad as it was to end things, I knew it was the right thing to do. They hadn't been my person.

Could Lyall have been my person? Did I fuck things up for good?

"You good, Soren?"

I rearrange my face into a smile I hope is more sincere than I feel. "Yeah. Fine. Why'd you ask about dogs?"

"My friend is going out of town and he needs someone to pet sit his dog."

"What kind of dog?"

"A Tamaskan."

I've never heard of those before. Jamie pulls out his phone and shows me a picture. My jaw drops. "That's a wolf."

Jamie laughs. "Nope! Tamaskans are bred to look like wolves."

Could have fooled me. The dog is beautiful. Huge, with pure white fur and beautiful eyes. I'd still probably piss myself if I saw it watching me from a shadowed corner of my bedroom, though. "Gorgeous dog. What's their name?"

"I know, right? If Anders and I weren't so busy, we'd love to have him over. His name's Buddy."

Imagine having a dog that looks like they walked off the set of *Game of Thrones* and giving it the most average name imaginable. What a missed opportunity.

"Is he friendly? House trained?"

"Yes and yes!"

That's a relief. "I'll need to check with my grandfather first, but I'll let you know." Having a dog around could be just the thing to lift my spirits.

Fergus seemed apprehensive, but when I told him the dog was trained and friendly, he was on board. So early the next morning, I go downstairs to meet Jamie. His car pulls up to the curb, and Jamie gets out to open the back door.

If I thought the dog was big in the picture, he's even larger in person. The white wolf-like dog jumps out of the car and shakes his thick pelt of fur. His coat is so bright when the sun shines on it, it almost hurts to look at. Stunning green eyes find mine, and his big, bushy tail starts to wag so hard his entire backside wiggles with it.

I kneel and beckon him over. "Here, Buddy. What a gorgeous boy you are!"

With a big gaping grin, the dog lopes over and covers my face in sloppy licks. Sputtering, I tilt my head back so he licks my neck instead. "Whoa! Friendly, aren't you?" I sink my fingers into his dense coat and give him a good rubdown.

"He's the best, isn't he?" Jamie asks. "And between you and me, he's a great free therapist!"

"Who could be depressed with you around?" I ask Buddy, stroking his soft ears.

"We'll come and pick him up around the same time on Friday," Jamie says. "Oh! And here." He pops open the trunk and hauls out a huge bag of dog food I'm not excited to carry upstairs. He's also got a big bag of other pet supplies, like toys, food dishes, and some treats.

"Does he need anything else?" I ask. *Please say no...*

"He should be all set! Call us if you run into any problems."

I shoulder the large, very heavy bag of stuff. I'll have to make two trips. No way am I carrying the food and—

To my amazement, Buddy grabs the food bag and carries it toward the front door. He paws at it and looks back at me expectantly.

"That solves that problem then."

Once we're upstairs, Fergus greets us at the door. The second he lays eyes on Buddy, he takes a step back, color draining from his face.

"Gramps? It's okay. He's very friendly."

"Y-you're sure that's a dog?" Fergus asks.

"He is!"

Buddy whines, dropping the food bag. He backs away from the threshold, ears flat and eyes fixed on my grandfather.

What the hell is going on? I can't tell which of them looks more unsettled. Crap. Maybe this won't work out after all.

"I could rent a place and take Buddy with me," I offer.

"No," Fergus says, so sharply I jump. "I don't want you alone with that thing." I've never heard his voice so harsh before. "Fine, just see that it behaves."

My shoulders loosen a little, but I can't shake the feeling that something is wrong. "Go on," I say, motioning Buddy inside.

The dog lifts a paw and places it over the threshold, almost as if he's testing thin ice. He hesitates, then darts inside, giving his pelt a shake. Maybe this wasn't such a good idea. Hopefully, once Fergus sees how friendly Buddy is, he'll relax. I make myself busy, setting up the food and water bowls in the kitchen and scattering some toys around the living room for Buddy to choose from.

I'm grateful I have the day off so I can supervise Buddy. Fergus keeps darting looks at the dog from where he's sitting at the kitchen counter. He even flinches when Buddy goes past him. Buddy jumps at the sudden movement and scurries across the room.

Man, they're so fucking weird around each other. "Hey, Buddy, wanna watch some TV?" I pat the sofa. Buddy doesn't hesitate to jump up and join me, laying his big head in my lap with a contented huff. "What a sweet fella," I say, glancing at Fergus and hoping he'll notice Buddy's cuddly nature.

Fergus wrinkles his nose in distaste. "If he sheds on the sofa, you're cleaning it up."

I raise both hands in surrender. "Fine." As I continue season three of *You,* I keep sensing Fergus's eyes on us. Seriously, would he relax? It's a dog, not an alligator. Unable to focus, I pause the show and look over the back of the sofa at Fergus. "Is this going to be a problem? You told me you were fine with boarding a dog."

Fergus's shoulders stiffen. "That was before I knew how big he was."

"I showed you a picture of him."

"Yes, well... I forgot."

Damn it, what am I going to do? I'm technically doing this for Jamie's friend, but I don't want to disappoint Jamie by going back on my word and dumping the dog on him. Jamie's a nice guy, tips really well too, and I want to stay on friendly terms with him. "Look, Gramps, the dog's staying. I'm helping out a friend of my new regular. Just give him a chance. He's sweet." Buddy nudges my hand with his big, cold nose, reminding me that I'd stopped petting him. "Sorry, fella," I say, resuming the strokes between his ears.

"I'll try," Fergus says. He places his empty mug in the dishwasher and heads to the bathroom. When the shower starts running, I relax back onto the sofa. Crisis averted. Maybe.

After finishing the remaining minute of the episode, I decide it's time for something a bit more lighthearted. A comedy or a romance. I don't usually watch or read romance, but there's a sexy actor I like who is starring in a new rom-com. Maybe some eye candy will cheer me up.

I put on the movie, but instead of distracting myself, my mood worsens the more madly in love the couple becomes. Did I make a mistake when I rejected Lyall? If I called him right now and apologized, would he forgive me? For what feels like the tenth time that day, I check my phone and find no new messages. No surprise there. I rejected him. Of course he's going to be a decent guy and respect my decision.

No, enough of this. I made my choice, and it was the right one. All my relationships have ended in disaster. This one wouldn't have been any different.

But being with him felt so right...

Yeah, for now, I remind myself with a sigh. Relationships always feel great in the beginning until the rose-tinted glasses come off and leave me disappointed in them, or the other way around.

"Ugh, stop it," I mutter, smacking my forehead. "You made the right choice. End of story."

Buddy lifts his head from my lap and whines at me. I'm still petting him, so I don't know what the problem is. "What?" I ask, looking down into his big green eyes. Buddy watches me with a tilt of his head. Maybe he can smell my bad mood.

"I'm fine," I tell him, then snort at myself. Am I seriously going to talk to a dog right now? Better than venting to my granddad or my friends. Lately my problems all boil down to the same thing, and I don't want to annoy them. Just because they're supportive doesn't mean I should take advantage of that. "Okay, I'm not. I feel like shit, Bud."

I should feel stupid, but it feels good to get things off my chest. Animals are great listeners, and they don't judge.

"Is there a girl dog you like? Or a boy dog. That's fine too. Can dogs be gay? Ugh. Never mind." I scratch between his ears. Buddy stares up at me, tongue lolling as he pants. He's probably waiting for me to say a word he knows like *food* or *treat* or *ball*. But it looks like he's listening. "Well, there's this guy. He's really sweet. Super sexy. We had tons of fun together and I felt great around him. But I've been burned by so many guys before. Every time I think I've found my person, it never works out."

Buddy stops panting and tilts his head, whining low in his chest.

I run my fingers through his fur, sighing. "I had a really good feeling about him, but I've been wrong before. So many times. I don't know how to trust my instincts anymore. I want to call him, tell him I'm sorry. I'm too much of a damn coward. Lyall's never going to want to see me again anyway. I blew it for good."

Buddy paws at me suddenly, making me jump.

"What?"

He whines and nudges my hand with his nose.

I rub his head and his tail swishes side to side.

"You're a real sweetheart, you know that?"

Jamie was right. Buddy really is a great therapist.

By the end of the weekend, things are still off with Fergus and Buddy. Fergus keeps watching us whenever we're sitting together, and Buddy avoids Fergus like he's a bag of garbage. Don't dogs like garbage? A bag of cats, maybe. I feel a little uneasy when I leave them alone to go to work at the bar later that evening. Buddy was snoozing on the sofa when I left, and Fergus was in his room reading. Hopefully, they'll stay away from each other.

About two hours into my shift, a pleasant Anders-and-Jamie-shaped distraction walks in through the doors and waves at me. I was bummed when Franklin texted to tell me he and Tom weren't coming in this week since they were in California visiting family.

"Hey, guys. The usual?"

"Aww, you remember our orders?" Jamie asks, smiling as he takes a seat in Anders's lap. Anders wraps an arm around his waist to steady the smaller man. Their casual intimacy makes jealousy twist in my gut.

"Of course. I'd be a pretty bad bartender if I didn't." I pour Anders his beer and gather the ingredients to make Jamie's cocktail.

"Hey, how's Buddy doing?"

I pour the ingredients into my shaker. "He's great. Super sweet." I leave out the fact that he and my granddad are engaged in a cold-war standoff.

"Isn't he?" Jamie beams. "And a great listener, right?"

"He really is. I swear, it's like he understands me." I shake the drink until the shaker is ice cold, then pour it neatly into a glass. "Did your friend like the pics I took of—"

I almost choke on my tongue as Lyall comes up behind Jamie and Anders, putting a hand on each of their shoulders. Oh shit.

Those beautiful green eyes that haunted me all weekend find mine. "Hello, Soren." Lyall's voice is soft and uncertain.

"I, uh—" In my shock, the glass slips from my hand and bounces on the rubber mats. It doesn't break, but the drink spatters all over my shoes. "I'm so sorry, Jamie! I'll make you another!" I reach for my Cointreau and curse when I realize the bottle only has a tiny amount left. "Fuck! Be right back!"

Wow, me. So chill, very professional. Could I have been more obviously freaked out? Face burning, I dart downstairs and find the liquor cabinet. My shaky hands drop the keys before I can stick them in the lock. I punch the cabinet, snarling as an ache throbs in the side of my fist.

Sucking in a harsh breath, I close my eyes and lean my forehead against the cool metal.

How can this man reduce me to a wreck with nothing but my name on his lips?

I've got to get it together.

Chapter 7
Lyall

Spending three whole days pretending to be a dog was harder than I thought it would be, but it gave me the chance to be close to Soren at last.

It's not without its challenges, of course. The pitiful burned pellets Soren calls "kibble" taste foul, for one thing. How do domesticated dogs tolerate eating it every day? Nothing will ever compare to meat fresh from the bone.

For another, I can't speak a word to Soren. All I can do is listen as he pours his heart out to me. It aches deep inside that he can bare his soul to me in this form but shuts me out in my human form.

But now I understand why.

My mate has been hurt so many times before. It's left him terrified to trust because none of the other men he was with appreciated his tender heart and fierce loyalty. I've got to prove to him that I'm not going anywhere and that I'd never hurt him.

I just need to know how. The Soren I knew wore his heart on his sleeve. He wasn't afraid to make his feelings known. This Soren is far more wary. Mayhap Anders and Jamie can help me come up with ideas.

And then there's the biggest obstacle to my plan.

Fergus, Soren's so-called grandfather.

He's a witch. The scent of his magic was a dead giveaway. With one look, he knew exactly what I was. I've done my best to keep my distance. Soren seems to have placated him so far since he hasn't made a move against me.

That will change the moment we're alone. I know it.

After Soren leaves for work, I perk up my ears and listen for any movement in the bedroom. Just as I anticipated, the mattress creaks. Footsteps thud on the floorboards. The door opens.

My fur peels back from my body, crawling back up my shoulders into the shape of a fur cloak. I'm never naked after a shift as the fur grows over whatever I am wearing, but I can't help feeling vulnerable as a newborn babe in nothing but my human skin and delicate clothes when Fergus enters the living room. The wrinkles on his brow deepen as he glares at me. "Wolf," he says with all the pleasure of a man who's just stepped in horse shit.

"Witch." The word comes out as a growl. My jaw aches from how hard I'm clenching it. What has this man done to Soren?

"What do you want with my grandson, wolf?" Fergus's eyes are as cold as glaciers as he looks me over from head to toe as if I'm a rotten scrap of meat.

My lip curls. "To remind him of everything you took from him."

Fergus folds his arms. "You'll do no such thing. Soren has built a life here. He has friends. A family. A job he loves. He belongs to this world now."

"Only because he thinks he has no other choice!" My snarl fills the room. "You aren't his real family!"

"And you are?" he counters, voice thick with fury. "Your pack cast him aside like trash."

"You've *lied* to him! You used your magic to hide him from me for all these years!"

"To protect him!" he snaps. "When he came to this time, he was *broken*, wolf."

My throat thickens. I know. I was there the day he was banished. I'd held him as he wept in my arms. That day he'd lost his family all over again.

"I took him in and helped him grow into the man he is now. Whatever happened to him, it devastated him. If he were to remember, it would break him all over again. He's happy now, wolf. Let him have that."

I blink hard down at the floor. The last thing I want to do is hurt Soren. Would remembering our history cause him pain? Would he feel torn between worlds? I have no way of knowing how he'll react.

"Mayhap you're correct, witch. But he deserves to have a choice."

The witch is quiet for a moment, knuckles bone-white. My words ruffled him. Good.

"Even if I wanted to restore his memories, I can't. They're gone. He can never get them back."

Even though I knew this to be true, his words are like an axe straight to my chest, knocking the wind from my lungs.

Fergus looks into my eyes when he asks, "If he never remembers you, can you still love him as he is now?"

My tongue is a deadweight in my mouth. I should say yes, but the word won't come, because it wouldn't be the truth. Soren and I come from different worlds now. He's built a life here, Fergus is right, and it would be selfish to try to take him away from it.

Blinking hard, I force my head up to face the witch head-on. "Time has changed us, it's true, but nothing will ever change the love I have for him. I know he feels the same."

I *hope* he does. More than anything.

"He will remember, and he will love me again!"

"If you so much as try to make him remember, I will report you to the TTA!" Fergus shouts. The photos on the wall rattle. The lights flicker.

I fold my arms, smirking. "And if he remembers of his own accord?"

Fergus's jaw tightens. "Then he will decide for himself what to do with that information. I would hope that he remembers who raised him and who *abandoned* him."

My fingers curl, a snarl building in my throat. "We'll see about that." Turning on my heels, my fur cloak swishing against my back, I march from the apartment.

Fergus isn't keeping me from my mate any longer.

We will be together, whether he likes it or not!

I headed to Jamie and Anders's home, and all three of us came up with a plan. They'll go to Soren's bar like they normally do, and I'll come with them. We leave the apartment together, and Jamie drives us to the bar. I hesitate outside the doors. "What will I say?"

Jamie huffs. "Look, let us go in first. We'll chat with him while you decide what to do."

I exhale, my heart pounding so hard I fear it will fly up my throat and out with my breath. "Aye."

They head inside while I linger. What if Soren isn't happy to see me? How will I convince him to give me another chance? I've got to. I can't be without him again. The pressure to get this right feels heavy enough to crush me. What did Kieran call this feeling? Anxiety? I take deep breaths in, exhaling out through my mouth. It's something he taught me to do. My heart slows with each exhale, and I open my eyes.

Nothing has to happen tonight. If I push too hard, he'll run. I've just got to encourage him to give me another chance.

I lift my head, push my shoulders back, and march into the bar and toward my mate. I place a hand on Jamie's and Anders's shoulders, squeezing lightly. Soren turns toward us, drink in hand, and freezes. His expression of shock is almost amusing enough to make me smile. As our eyes meet, my heart leaps up into my throat.

"Hello, Soren," I say, but before I can say anything more, the glass slips from his hand.

Soren jumps as if he's been bitten in the ass by a goat, babbles something about making Jamie another drink, and races through a door.

Anders smirks. "That went well."

Jamie smacks his shoulder. "Hey. Don't be bitchy."

With a groan, I drop into the empty seat beside them. "He hates me."

"He does not! He's scared, remember? He likes you, Lyall, so you're already halfway there. Just convince him to give you another chance."

"How?"

"Tell him what he needs to hear!"

The door behind the bar opens and Soren reappears, cradling a bottle under his arm. I try to make eye contact, but he's got his head down.

Jamie clears his throat. "So. Lyall told us you two had a great day." He elbows my ribs, making me grimace.

Soren laughs, but it's forced and insincere as he pours various liquids into a metal cup. "That's great. Always glad to help newcomers to the city."

"It was an evening like no other," I say to his back.

Soren makes a pleased sound through his teeth as he shakes the drink up and down.

"I'd love to do it again."

"Here you go," Soren says, setting the glass down in front of Jamie a little too hard, liquid sloshing onto the counter. "Sorry!" He dabs the counter around Jamie's glass with a rag. "I'm off to take my dinner break but if you need anything, talk to my barback." Soren practically runs from the bar and out the door.

"Wow. He's really skittish. You've got your work cut out for you," Jamie says.

"Thanks," I grumble as I leave my seat.

Outside, Soren sits on a bench, shoulders up to his ears. Everything he confided to me when I was a wolf echoes in my mind. Mayhap what he needs isn't a lover, not yet at least, but a friend. We were always friends first.

"I'm sorry if I pushed you too hard. It wasn't my intention to cause you any distress."

Soren sighs, his shoulders drooping with the motion. "You were fine. I'm the one who should apologize for ditching you after how much fun we had. That was really shitty of me."

"Apology accepted. May I sit?"

When Soren nods, I fill the empty space on the bench beside him, mindful enough to keep some space between our bodies. Soren opens his bag and pulls out two wrapped items, each roughly the same size.

"Are you hungry? I made sandwiches. You can have one if you want. It's peanut butter and jelly." His face flushes. "Kiddie food, I know, but it's always been a comfort food of mine."

"Aye, I'm famished."

He laughs for some reason. "You and your words..."

The metal-stuff crinkles as I take the sandwich. Hmm. Do I just take a bite? Maybe this metal-stuff is for flavor? I open my mouth and—

"Uh, Lyall?" Soren gives me a strange look. "Aren't you going to unwrap it first?"

Heat rushes to my cheeks. "O-oh! Right. Of course." I carefully remove the wrapper, glancing at Soren to watch what he does so I don't make any mistakes. How interesting. It's two pieces of bread with something brown and red slathered between the slices. Humans are so creative.

I inhale long and deep, mouth watering as the sweet and salty aroma of the sandwich fills my nose. Beside me,

Soren's watching me like I've grown two heads. I must look strange. I take a small bite and—

"By the gods!"

Soren jumps at my exclamation.

"It's *sweet* and"—I take another, bigger bite and moan—"salty and sticky and—"

So good! is what I'd say if I weren't devouring another huge bite of sandwich. The peanut butter, or is it the jelly, gets stuck to the roof of my mouth as I chew, but I don't mind at all.

"What the..." Soren mutters.

"You made this yourself?" I lick a glob of the salty stuff off my thumb.

"Yes..." Soren is giving me a wide-eyed, amused look. "Wow. You love your PB and J, huh?"

"This," I declare, "is the food of the gods themselves!"

Soren bursts out laughing beside me, cackling so hard he doubles over. "Oh man. I should have made more! You're killing me here."

What? No! I don't want to kill him. "What's wrong?" I grip his shoulder. "Are you suffocating? Can you breathe?"

Soren wipes his eyes and waves me off. "I'm fine. I'm fine!"

The sight of his smile leaves me speechless. I did that. I made him happy. I'd eat more of these sandwiches until I burst if it would make him laugh again.

"I'm glad you liked the sandwich."

"I *love it*."

Snorting, Soren offers me some napkins. "You're the messiest eater I've ever seen."

I scrub at my face. "Better?"

"Give it here." Shaking his head like I'm the most foolish man in the world, Soren takes the napkin from me and rubs the corner of my mouth. A thrill ripples through my stomach as he leans in. The cloth keeps his fingertips from my skin, but I still shiver at his touch. Soren glances up, and I lose myself in the earthen-brown of his eyes. When was the last time we were so close?

We were such different people then.

Wetting his lips, Soren looks away. "There. All better." He pats my thigh, cheeks flushed.

Having his hand so close to my cock makes heat stir in the pit of my stomach.

I long then to touch him, to reach out and turn his face to mine and let him taste the sweetness of the strawberries that still lingers on my tongue.

Clearing my throat, I say, "Thank you for the food."

He grins. "It was so worth it."

We share a chuckle before Soren looks away and watches the traffic go by.

"I understand if you don't want a lover," I say, watching him closely. Soren's jaw tenses. "But how about a friend?"

He sighs with such uncertainty in his eyes that I have to fight back the urge to reach out and comfort him. "Lyall... are you sure?"

"If all you ever feel for me is friendship, then that's fine."

It isn't a lie, not really, because we've been here before.

When my feelings for Soren had started to shift from friendship to love, I'd thought for sure I was the only one who felt that way. I'd feared that if I confessed what was in my heart, he'd run from me.

So I'd stayed silent and fought the way my wolf howled for him to be mine alone. If I had to choose between having some of Soren or none at all, then the decision was easy. I would always choose him, again and again. His friendship was the greatest gift of all.

To have his whole heart in one timeline and only parts of it in another will always hurt. But I will be grateful for what I have and, most of all, I will have patience. We're fated for each other, and Soren's heart will find its way back to me. It's just a matter of time, but I will always wait for him.

"I would be honored to be your friend, Soren."

He looks at me with what I can only describe as awe. Smiling, he shakes his head. "Well, then... I'd be honored to be your friend, too."

I can't fight the grin that springs across my face. Before I can say a word, Soren's phone rings. He frowns at the screen and answers. "Hey, Fergus. Everything okay?"

I focus, homing in on the distant sound of Fergus's voice.

"Something's wrong..." The witch sounds weak and feeble. If this is a ploy to keep me away from Soren—

Soren's heart skips a beat. "What is it?"

"I don't feel well. The whole room is spinning, I—" There's a crashing sound that makes me wince.

"Fergus?" Panic tightens Soren's voice. "Hello? Answer me, Gramps! Oh shit. I'm calling an ambulance." Soren taps hard on the screen and paces away from the bench.

"Nine-one-one, what's your emergency?" a faint female voice asks.

"My granddad just called and said he was feeling sick and—and then it sounded like he fell over. I think he passed out. He's not responding!" Soren fumbles out some more information about Fergus and gives them his address before hanging up. He whirls around, eyes wide and face pale. "I've got to go, Lyall. Sorry!" He races past me and back into the bar.

Shit. If he's going home, then that means I'll need to shift into Buddy again. He'll only be more upset if he thinks Buddy has run off on him. I run to Soren's apartment, which is nearby. Fortunately, a group of friends is leaving the building, and they hold the door for me on my way in.

I climb the stairs two at a time until I'm outside the door. It's locked, but all it takes is a hard twist of the knob, and I'm in. Fergus lies in the middle of the living room. The scent of magic that permeated the air around him is gone, but his heart rate is strong.

Thank the gods, he's not dead then. I know what's wrong. He expended too much magic trying to keep Soren hidden from me all these years, and it's taken a toll on his body. The same happened to our village healer after the attack on our village. She was well after rest and prayers to Freya. Fergus should be the same.

Distant footsteps make me tense. Someone is coming fast. I shift to my wolf form just as Soren bursts into the apartment. He doesn't stop to question why the door is open. "No, please, no!" The devastation in his voice tears my heart to shreds.

"Granddad. Please, don't do this. Not yet. I need you!" Soren clasps the older man's hand. Sobs shake his shoulders, tears bright in his eyes. "Come on, everyone else left me alone. Don't you leave me, too!"

Oh gods. He doesn't remember that my family abandoned him. I know this, but it still feels like an accusation. Tears had still been wet on his cheeks as he'd sat in the boat and faced the horizon. He'd cried alone in that boat as he rowed toward the portal that had taken him away from me.

I won't let him suffer alone again.

"Soren. I'm here. It's okay."

He looks up, and his mouth falls open. "W-what? Lyall? When did you get here? How? And where's Buddy?"

Shit. I'd shifted without even realizing in my haste to comfort him.

I don't know how I'm going to talk my way out of this.

If the TTA finds out I've exposed Soren to the paranormal world against their orders, then we'll be over before we've even had a chance to start.

Chapter 8
Soren

When we arrive at the hospital, only a short ride away in the West Village, Lyall and I follow the paramedics as they wheel Fergus into the emergency room. My granddad doesn't always look his age, but seeing him sprawled out on a stretcher with an oxygen mask over his nose and mouth reminds me that he won't always be here. I just never thought that day would be today. I thought we had more time together. I—

"He'll be all right," Lyall says. His hand is big and warm on my shoulder.

I blow out a shuddery breath, blinking fast. "God. I hope so."

I can't lose him. He's all the family I have left.

The nurses wheel Fergus down the hall, and he disappears from my sight. "Come. Let's find somewhere to rest." If it weren't for Lyall's hand on my shoulder keeping me grounded, I probably would have walked into walls as he steers me back in the direction we came from.

I'm in such a daze, I don't realize where we are until Lyall says, "Soren. Have a seat."

I all but collapse into the chair. Lyall showed up to the bar wearing this big fluffy fur cloak, and the fur is warm and soft against my shoulder. It kind of reminds me of—

"Shit. Buddy. We left him!" Who is taking care of him?

I try to stand, but Lyall forces me back down.

"Soren, listen to me. There's something I need to tell you." Lyall heaves a sigh, shoulders slumping. In a low voice, he says, "I... I am Buddy."

That makes no sense. "Sorry, what?" A few other patients look at me, and I realize I practically shouted the question at him.

Lyall hisses, "I am Buddy, and he is me. I'm ulfhednar. But you call our kind wolf shifters."

Wolf shifters. Is he for real? I can't believe he'd joke around at a time like this. "You know, now really isn't the time to be making jokes!" I hiss, trying to escape his grip.

Lyall pulls me back into the chair before I can get far. "I would never lie to you, Soren! Even as a jest." Lyall's eyes are pleading with me, and maybe I'm crazy too because I almost believe him. How can I not when he looks at me like that?

As crazy as that whole statement sounds, it almost makes sense. Lyall was nowhere to be seen until Buddy just disappeared in the split second I was distracted with Fergus.

A laugh escapes me. "You're insane."

"I can show you."

I bark a laugh at the thought. Exhausted, I slump over with my face in my hands. "Just... later, I guess."

For a long while, we're quiet. Lyall rubs my shoulders in soothing circular motions. As strange as he can be, I'm still so grateful he's here. I'd hate to be alone right now with my thoughts.

"Mr. Smith?"

I jump to my feet. "Here!"

A doctor approaches and shakes my hand, introducing himself, but I barely listen. All that matters is when he says, "Your grandfather is stable. He's going to be just fine, but he'll need to stay the night for monitoring."

"Can I see him?"

The doctor leads us to my grandfather's room. He's propped up against the pillows, eyes closed. The doctor leaves us alone before I start bawling like a scared little kid.

Lyall locks the door behind us. "Soren, I—"

"No. Enough of this 'I'm a wolf' crap. Just... just go away, Lyall."

I regret my harsh words when Lyall flinches. "Please, just hear me out!"

I can't. This is all too much.

"Soren?" My throat thickens when I lay eyes on Fergus, and he gives me a tired smile.

I rush to his bedside and put my arm around him, squeezing gently. "You scared the hell out of me!" Tears sting my eyes when he laughs that rusty, warm laugh.

"I'll be fine, my boy."

"Soren—" Lyall begins, but I hush him and focus on my grandfather.

"What happened? You were passed out when I came in." I can't keep the fear out of my voice.

Fergus's lips twist in pity. "I'm sorry I worried you. I just felt so tired all of a sudden—" He goes quiet, glaring over my shoulder at Lyall.

"Oh, this is my friend Lyall." I motion to the man. Except he's not a man at all. There's a motherfucking wolf right in front of me. A second ago he was Lyall, and now he's a wolf. A wolf that looks a lot like Buddy the wolf-dog. Because he is. It's just like Lyall said. They're one and the same. But... but *how*?

"Can you see that?" I ask hoarsely, pointing at the wolf.

Fergus sighs, his head dropping back against his pillow. "Yes."

Somehow that's worse. If we can both see it, then this is real. I just saw a man turn into a wolf. A wolf who is scratching himself in the middle of the room like he has every right to be here.

"W-why aren't you more surprised?" I ask with mounting suspicion.

Fergus looks tired. "Because I'm a witch."

A bark of laughter escapes me, but my grandfather doesn't return my humor.

Lifting a hand, he curls his finger as if he's beckoning to me. I jump out of my skin when the faucet turns on all by itself. Before my eyes, a paper cup levitates right out of the stack, fills itself, then flies right into my grandfather's waiting hand.

"Do you believe me now?"

I can't speak. There has to be a logical explanation for this. Maybe there's something in the water, or—

The wolf whines, making me jump. The huge beast lowers himself down to his belly. His green eyes are identical to Lyall's, the only thing human in his beastly body. They're mournful. Is he feeling sad? Why?

A shudder racks the wolf, and his fur pulls back from his body, revealing Lyall on his knees before me, still dressed in his streetwear as if he didn't shift into a wolf at all. "I didn't mean to frighten you."

I can't hold back my burst of hysterical laughter. "I'm sorry, you just turned into a fucking wolf! What else was I supposed to feel? Happy?"

Closing my eyes tightly, I suck in quick breaths. Magic is a thing. Werewolves are real. My grandfather is a fucking witch. Oh my god. Fergus knew. He knew all this time, and he kept this from me!

"Soren, it's all right," Fergus says, but his voice is far away, like I'm underwater, like I'm drowning.

"It's not!" My voice fills the room, cracking under the strain. "You're a witch! You can do magic! He just turned into a wolf! Nothing about this is all right!" I stumble, gripping onto the doorknob for support.

"No, I suppose it isn't..."

Lyall clears his throat. "I didn't show you what I am to upset you. I showed you because you deserve to know the truth."

"Which is?" I snap, wiping sweat from my forehead. "What? That I'm crazy? That nothing I know is real? That you've kept this from me all my life?" I turn to my grandfather, who averts his gaze down to his hands, where they're clenching the blanket. "What else did you lie about?"

Fergus flinches.

Oh fuck.

Is there more he hasn't told me? I try to swallow, but my mouth has gone bone dry.

"Tell him," Lyall says, making me look at him now. Somehow the two of them are in on this. It makes my stomach cramp with dread.

Fergus closes his eyes tight. When he opens them, they're glassy with tears. "No matter what, Soren, I want you to know that the love I have for you has always been real."

Silence descends upon the room, and I hold my breath, terrified of what I'll learn when it finally breaks.

The paper cup of water shakes in Fergus's grip. He takes a gulp, then lowers the cup into his lap. "It's true. I am a witch. So was everyone in my family before me. Since the Viking age, witches have worshipped Freya. It's through her blessing that we receive our magical gifts. Much like how Lyall's people worship Fenrir and are rewarded with the ability to shift."

I want to call bullshit, but I just saw this guy turn into a wolf and a cup fly into my granddad's hand on command like a bird.

"Long ago my ancestors performed a magic ritual that allowed them to travel between the past, present, and future. There was chaos at first as the timelines clashed. My ancestors sealed the portals and created magical artifacts that would allow travel between realms without disturbing the balance of all three."

"Wait. Stop. Why are we talking about time travel? That's a thing too?" The doorknob isn't doing a good job of keeping me on my feet anymore. I stumble to the nearest chair and collapse onto it.

"Aye," Lyall answers, and something clicks into place in my brain. "We're in your present world, but the time I'm from is long past."

When I look at him, it's like I'm seeing him for the first time. The antique clothes he wore the night we met... his archaic way of speaking...

"You're a…" The words get trapped behind my teeth. Even after everything I've seen tonight, saying this out loud still feels wrong. Like saying the Earth is flat, or that the moon landing was fake. There are undeniable truths in this world. Time travel, magic, werewolves, witches… these are all things I believed could never exist.

"I'm a time traveler," Lyall says. His gaze never wavers from mine as he speaks with such conviction, I have no choice but to believe him.

"Fuck…" I lower my face into my hands.

"Shall we continue?" Fergus asks.

Speechless, I can only nod.

He clears his throat. "Lyall isn't the only traveler I know, Soren." He hesitates for a long moment. I look up and wish I hadn't. Fergus looks more devastated than I've ever seen him. "You are too."

I shake my head. "What are you talking about?"

No, this is some kind of joke. I can almost get behind the whole time travel thing, but me being a time traveler? That's not possible. I would have remembered that.

"When you were eighteen, you arrived in this timeline from the past. You were alone and in need of help. My employers at the Travelers Council assigned me to care for you and help you adjust to this new time."

"No." I push myself up. "This isn't funny." I pace from one side of the room to the other. This room is so fucking small, and it's only getting smaller. Everything narrows down to me and my grandfather.

Who is he? Are we even related?

"This isn't true. My mom ran off when I was a baby. You raised me. You're my family."

Fergus's lips tremble, and my heart cracks.

"Aren't you?" I whisper.

"That was the story my employers decided on. Those memories you have of your past, they were planted there."

I gasp as my chest tightens. When I try to suck in air, it won't come. "No. No, that's not true. You're lying."

"Think, Soren," Lyall says softly. "Really think. What's your earliest memory of Fergus?"

"That's easy. It was... it was..."

I can't. I'm trying, but there's *nothing* there. There's a fucking hole in my head where something should be. A part of me is missing, and I don't know how to get it back. A gaping void opens up in my head the deeper I probe, searching for memories of childhood friends I would have met in school, a first boyfriend, high school, college... But there's nothing.

It's a lie. My entire life has been one big lie.

The room tilts, there's a whooshing in my ears, and the tiled floor gets closer. Big arms wrap around me, holding me tight.

"I've got you. Breathe, Soren. I have you."

I'm safe, a voice inside whispers. *Lyall's here, and I'm safe.*

It makes no sense. I don't know this man at all—do I?

Gasping, I clutch onto him. His clothes are soft. The scent of coconut blankets me. A shampoo or body wash, I don't know. Warmth spreads through every part of me when he strokes my back. At some point, my frantic gasps shift to deep, slow breaths. I've never felt so safe. Not with Fergus. Not with any of the guys I've dated.

For all my life, I've always felt like something was missing.

Here in Lyall's arms, I realize that it was never something I was searching for, but some*one*. Lyall is who I was missing. The piece of my heart that I thought I'd lost has finally come home.

"Why are you so familiar?" I whisper into his chest.

His fingers sweep through my hair. "Because deep down inside, your soul recognizes mine."

My breath catches. I look up into his eyes. "You're saying we... knew each other?"

Lyall dips his head, never looking away as he runs his knuckles along my jaw. "We may be from different times now, but that matters not. In every life, in every time, we would find each other. I'm sorry it took me so long to find you but I am here now. I'll do whatever it takes to help you remember."

I swallow with some difficulty. "Remember what?"

Lyall takes my hand and brushes a kiss over my skin. "You are mine. From the beginning you were my first love, and you will be my last until the day I take my final breath."

We knew each other. Loved each other. Lost each other.

I can't remember any of it, but God, I wish I could remember being loved by this man. I'd take it all, the good parts, the painful parts. I found the kind of love I've searched for all my life, and it was stolen from me, from *us*.

Tears sting my eyes, and I wriggle out of his arms before he can see them. On the cool tile, I take in a breath, then another. The lump in my throat slowly fades, and I wipe my eyes.

"Give them back." I don't recognize my own voice, hoarse like I've been screaming in agony for hours.

Lyall doesn't speak. Fergus does, though, like somehow he knew I was talking to him.

"I can't."

A fresh wave of tears floods my eyes. "Please, Fergus. I won't be mad. I'll forgive everything else, just—"

"Your memories are gone, my boy." Fergus's voice shakes.

I choke on a sob, wrapping my arms around myself so I don't fall apart.

"I'm so sorry. If I'd known we would grow so close, that this would hurt you so deeply—"

My anguish grows claws, morphing into a beast full of wrath. "How could you do this to me?" My roar fills the room.

Fergus flinches, his face wet with tears. "It was for the best, Soren."

"You don't get to decide that!"

I barely recognize him. This man who cared for me, who loved me, who lied to me, who *stole* something so precious from me. Just looking at him fills me with so much anger and hurt and still, beneath it all, I want to wrap him in my arms and tell him I love him, that I forgive him. It's too much.

There's a knock at the door. I unlock it and duck my head just as the doctor walks in, hoping he won't notice what a mess we are. "Visiting hours are over. I'll need you to stay the night so we can monitor you, Fergus, but depending on how you're feeling, I think you'll be able to go home tomorrow."

Wiping my nose on my sleeve, I squeeze past him. "Lyall, can you come with me?"

"Oh. Certainly!" His enthusiasm makes my lips twitch in an attempted smile.

"Soren—"

I can't even look at Fergus. I let the door slam shut on the man who raised me and follow Lyall into a new, uncertain reality.

Werewolves. Time travel. Witches. Lyall.

Those are the four things that cycle through my mind, keeping me so entrenched in thought that I don't even notice when our taxi driver stops outside my apartment.

"Soren? We're here."

I jump even though Lyall's voice is low and soft.

"Right. Thanks," I say to the driver, swiping my card to pay for the ride.

Once we're upstairs, I open the door. Lyall hesitates outside, shoulders hunched and chin to his chest. I flash back to the big white wolf with green eyes. Seeing him shift had shocked me, but never for a second had I worried he'd bite or attack me.

Some part of me had known I could trust him. Maybe the part of me that Fergus said was taken from me. I need to know everything about this history he claims we have together.

"Coming in?" I ask.

He perks up like a freshly watered flower. "Aye. Thank you." He follows me inside.

"Sorry about the mess. Fergus and I aren't the neatest guys." Wait, what am I talking about? He's been in my apartment before as Buddy and then again in human form.

I have a time-traveling Viking werewolf in my apartment.

What the fuck do I even do with that? With him?

"Want something to drink? Tea, coffee?" Booze, I want to suggest. I feel like I need it after all the craziness of tonight.

"Coffee," he says immediately.

A curious smile tugs at my mouth. "Do you even have coffee where you're from?"

"Not before my twin's mate Jamie started coming to visit us. He brings us coffee from his cafe. It's delicious."

I trip over my own feet. "Jamie? As in your brother's boyfriend?"

Holy shit. Of course! Anders and Jamie planned all of this. They were setting me up with Lyall from the moment I met him!

Lyall has the look of a dog who crapped on the carpet. "Me and my mouth." He sighs. "Yes, Anders is from the past. He moved to the present when he met Jamie."

So, people can travel to and from different timelines as easily as getting on a bus, apparently. "I'm going to have a word with those two... Why did they set us up? Why make me believe you were a wolf-dog of all things?"

"Anders and Jamie have graciously helped me adjust to this timeline. They've driven me places and Anders loaned me his phone, just to name a few things they've done. Anders knows how long I've been searching for you. He only wanted to help introduce us properly."

"But we'd already met."

He nods. "Aye, but it didn't go at all to plan. The night we met, I realized you had no recollection of me. I knew then if I wanted to be with you, I would have to do things differently."

"So Anders and Jamie asked me to show you around the city." I have to say, it's not a bad plan. "But that still doesn't explain why Jamie asked me to pet sit you." I choke back a laugh at the ridiculousness of it all.

Lyall's cheeks redden. "That was Jamie's idea, not mine!" He hangs his head sheepishly. "After you... rejected me, I lost hope that we could reconnect. I knew you felt the same pull, but you were holding back. I hoped if I knew why, I'd be able to prove that all your fears and doubts were misplaced. That I'd never hurt you the way those other men had."

My cheeks warm, and I want to hide under the counter. I can't believe I told him all that. "But wait a second. Even after I told you, you still stuck around as Buddy. Why?"

Lyall looks confused. "To be with you. Why else?"

My mouth slips open. "But... you had to eat kibble, you couldn't talk, I made you go on walks! And you never even went to the bathroom on those walks!"

Lyall laughs. "I held it in and went to my brother's place to take care of business. Didn't want you cleaning up after me."

I can't stop myself from laughing with him. "Well, thanks for that. That would have been a bit too intimate for me. Still, how can any of that have been enjoyable for you?"

"It had its difficulties compared to being in my human form." He smiles. "But it was worth it."

My heart does a flip in my chest. This guy's tenderness and sincerity keep catching me off guard. Despite everything, I trust Lyall, I'm attracted to him, and it's dangerous. Just when I've decided I'm giving up on love and relationships, this man from the past—my past?—bursts into my life and throws everything on its head.

The kettle beeps, telling me it's done heating the water. Once the coffee has been filtered, I hand him a mug. "Milk, sugar?"

Lyall shakes his head and takes a sip, humming his approval. "You wished to talk?"

I squeeze the mug in my hands, fingers shaking as I take a cautious sip from the steaming cup. One thing at a time.

There's so much I want to know about him, about us. "Why are you here?"

He frowns. "Because you invited me."

Somehow I manage a huff of laughter. Lyall grins, dimples popping in his cheeks. It's the cutest thing. "I guess I did, didn't I? I meant why are you *here*, in the present day."

"I thought that was obvious. To find you."

My grandfather had said that I arrived in this time alone. Lyall claims I was from the past with him, and we knew each other. "If I'm from the past, then why am I here?"

The grin falls off Lyall's face and without it, his face darkens. "When we were young men, hunters attacked our village."

"Hunters? Why?"

"Because of what my people are. Ulfhednar. What your people call werewolves or wolf shifters, mine call ulfhednar."

"But why?"

Lyall's lips twist into a scowl. "They came to our village to rescue you. Their leader believed we had taken you as a captive. They attacked us."

The coffee in my stomach churns unpleasantly. I can't believe I have no recollection of this. He might as well be talking about someone else's life, not mine.

Lyall's knuckles whiten around the mug's handle. "They killed my father. Tortured my twin. Slaughtered my brother's son and his mate." Lyall's voice is low and calm, but every word shakes with an undercurrent of rage and pain.

"Oh God..." I may not be able to remember this, but it doesn't matter. Lyall has never forgotten, and there's no questioning the effect this tragedy still has on him. "What happened then?"

Lyall shakes his head, lip curling to reveal the tip of a fang. A shiver runs down my spine. "The man who led the attack on our village... was your father, Soren."

His words don't hit like they should. I shake my head. "No, that's not—I never knew my father. He ran off on my mother when I was a baby."

Lyall says softly, "That's what you were made to believe."

I don't know what to think anymore. Everything Lyall's telling me goes against what I was told by Fergus. Shaking my head, I exhale slowly. "Right. Sorry. I keep forgetting."

"It's fine. I know this is a lot to take in. After the fight, the survivors believed that you had been conspiring with your father to attack the village."

My heart drops into my stomach. Even if I don't remember the past, if Lyall and I really were in love, I never would have betrayed him. "I wouldn't have done that," I say, interrupting him.

Lyall's eyes widen. "What makes you so sure?"

"Because that's not who I am. If what we have meant so much to you that you've been searching for me all these years—since I was *eighteen*—I would never have taken that for granted. I'd never have hurt you that way."

Smiling, Lyall slides his hand across the counter. His fingers bump against mine. There's a spark there, like an electric current, that makes my heart jolt. "I know," he whispers. "No one else believed you, but I did, Soren. Never once did I doubt you." When I don't pull away, he slowly drapes his hand over mine. My breath catches, my chest tightening with too many feelings to name.

There's something about Lyall's touch that makes me think of northern lights dancing in a moonlit sky. Meadows full of small blue flowers. Of laughter in my chest and love in my heart, burning bright and fierce.

God. Whatever we shared, it was powerful. I know it because after all these years, all that's left is a void nothing and no one could ever fill because there was no getting over Lyall. Once, I knew this man like I knew myself, loved him like I loved no one before him and no one after.

He was it for me, and if there's a chance for me to remember why I felt that way... I've got to take it, or I will never know true happiness again.

Chapter 9
Lyall

At first, I'd feared that turning into a wolf in front of Soren was not the best idea.

Sure, it made sense in my head in that moment, but history has shown I don't usually have the best ideas. Rather like that time I thought I could chug a whole barrel of mead in under ten seconds. Aye, I could and I did. Was it a good idea? I spent all night vomiting, so likely not.

If Anders were here, he could have talked me out of such a rash decision. Of the two of us, I have the strength of Thor while my brother has the smarts of Odin—or mayhap Loki is a more apt comparison.

"Lyall? What happened next?"

"The pack blamed you for the attack." Closing my eyes, I run my thumb over Soren's knuckles just like I used to do. "You were exiled. I tried to change the hearts and minds of my family. No one would believe that you weren't responsible." Tears sting the back of my eyelids. It was my fault as well. I should have gone with Soren. If I had, I could have protected him from the Council. He might still have his memories. We wouldn't have lost so much time.

Soren's hand grips mine, and the storm of guilt and grief in my heart quiets. "I'm sure you did. I can understand why people would think I was responsible."

A snarl crawls up my throat, and my canines lengthen, pricking my lower lip. "They wanted someone to blame and they chose you. It wasn't right."

"Maybe it wasn't." His low, even tone soothes my wolf's fury. "What's done is done. We can't change it." His fingers tense around my hand. "Unless, can we? If we can go back in time or to the present—"

I shake my head before he's finished speaking. "Believe me, love. I have revisited that day so many times. I could not speak or even touch the ghosts from the past. You cannot change what has already come to pass. If I could..." A lump sticks in my throat and I close my eyes against a sharp, sudden sting.

"It's okay. I get it." He squeezes my hand. "I guess there's nothing we can do about it." Disappointment lines Soren's brow. "I wish I could remember even a little bit."

Soren's words plant a seed of an idea, and my heart races as that seed grows into a tree, branches reaching toward countless possibilities.

"What if I were to show you?"

Soren's quiet for a moment. "What do you mean?"

Launching to my feet, I pace the length of the counter and back. "I don't always have the best ideas," I preface, hands up so he'll hear me out uninterrupted. "My twin, Anders, will tell you as much. Once I tried to blend in with a family of walruses. I got these sticks and put them right here." I point to where my canines are. "I thought if I could convince them I was one of them, they would teach me how to swim like they do so I could catch all the fish I could eat. Oh, and once I burned my tongue eating my aunt Helga's boar stew, so I found a chunk of ice and stuck my tongue to it and—"

"Lyall."

"—I was stuck there for two days!"

"Lyall." Soren has a smile on his face, amusement crinkling the corners of his eyes. "What do you mean, 'show me'?"

"Oh, right." I give my head a shake. "I don't have the best ideas. Not always. But if I were to take you back in time with me to see these events for yourself, mayhap that would stir your memories."

Soren's eyes widen. "Could we do that?"

I nod fervently. "Aye. If that's what you wish."

"If we did... would we be able to come back?"

"Of course. My twin and his mate travel back and forth often to visit our family."

Soren runs his tongue over his bottom lip, like he's tasting the idea, letting it linger on his palate like a fine mead. If ideas had a taste, what would it be? No, focus, Lyall.

"In movies and books there are all these consequences to time travel. Would we get in trouble?"

I'm about to shake my head, but as much as I wish to, I can't deny the truth. I'm breaking every rule the TTA explicitly warned me not to break. In one night I've revealed the paranormal world and told him of our shared history. There is still time to back away before I get myself and my pack in trouble we may not be able to get ourselves out of. To put my family first.

But I look at Soren, and not even Thor himself could lend me the strength to leave him again.

Soren *is* my family, and I promised myself that this time I would choose him above everything and everyone else.

"Lyall?" Soren watches me with wide eyes full of uncertainty.

I make myself smile, wishing only to reassure him. "There are risks, but you are worth all of them."

Soren's jaw tightens. "Could you get in trouble because of me?"

I nod. "Aye."

"And you're just... okay with that?" The bewildered expression on his face reminds me of just how far I have yet to go to remind him of what he means to me.

Good thing I've always loved a challenge.

Except for the time I shoved my snout in a beehive to get at the honey before the bears could. My nose was swollen for weeks.

Looking Soren in the eyes, I hold on tight to his hand, reaffirming my commitment to him. "I've never been surer about anything."

Soren looks at me the way I imagine I must look at the northern lights when they dance above the mountains. "You're either brave or crazy as hell. Not sure which."

I grin. "I've been called both. Once, you were quite the risk-taker yourself."

"Really?" he asks as if he can't believe it.

"Oh, aye. The pair of us were always getting into trouble, but we were always there to get each other out of it."

Soren tilts his head. "Hang on. Just how long did we know each other?"

I give his knee a squeeze. "You'll find out soon enough."

Chapter 10
Soren

I'm exhausted when I arrive at the hospital the next morning. All night long, all I did was replay the day's events. I second-guessed everything, from whether any of this was even real to how I'd reacted to Fergus. Had I been too hard on him? How else was I supposed to react? There isn't exactly a self-help book for this stuff. *So You Just Discovered You're A Time Traveler: A Guide to Werewolves, Witches, and All Matter of Fuckery.*

Maybe I should write one.

I've still got no idea what to say when I pick up Fergus from the hospital. He smiles, and I return the gesture, though it doesn't feel genuine. All this time I thought we were related, that I was just an average guy who couldn't hold down a relationship. Fergus kept so much from me, and I don't think he had any intention of telling me.

It's hard not to hold that against him, but the least I can do is hear his side of the story.

"Hey." I wince at how awkward I sound. "Feeling better?"

Fergus nods. "Much. I am hungry, though. How about some lunch? My treat."

I'll accept the olive branch he's offering. At the end of the day, he's my family, even if we aren't related.

A few streets down, we find a cafe to sit and chat in. Fergus buys us both a coffee and a couple of breakfast sandwiches. I unwrap mine and take a bite, melted cheese, bacon, and eggs exploding in a flavor bomb on my tongue.

Fergus doesn't touch his coffee, eyes full of guilt when he looks at me. "Soren—"

"I'm sorry I got mad, Gramps." It hurts to look at him and remember the pained look on his face.

"I shouldn't have kept things from you," he says. "I was selfish. I feared that if you knew the truth, you'd want to return to the past and stay there."

I snort. "Why would I? I want to know, yeah, but my life is here. My job. My friends. My family." I tap his foot with mine beneath the table.

Fergus smiles and gives my shoulder a squeeze. "I should have trusted you. Maybe if I had, I wouldn't have fallen ill."

"What does all this time travel stuff have to do with you being sick?"

Fergus's shoulders slump. Great. More secrets, I'm guessing. "I've used my magic to mask your presence from other supernatural creatures, but specifically the Erikson pack. I couldn't be sure they wouldn't come looking for you."

"Because I betrayed them."

Fergus nods glumly. "After all these years, using so much of my magic reserves took its toll on me."

Shit. Could he have died? "No more," I tell him, looking him in the eyes. "You can't do that to yourself. Okay?"

I can't lose him.

Fergus smiles and pats my cheek. "No more," he agrees. "But Soren, you need to be careful around that wolf. Is he still here?"

My defenses go back up. "He's not dangerous." The part of me that once knew and loved Lyall prickles with anger at my grandfather's assumptions.

"You can't know that."

"I do, Gramps," I say, voice sharp. Taking a breath, I try to calm down. Fergus furrows his brows, like I've grown a second head or something. "He and I... we were close. He loved me."

Fergus purses his lips the way he does when he wants to say something I probably won't like.

"What?"

"If he loved you so much, then why did he let you go?"

Because everyone does.

Faces flash before my eyes. Men I knew for a night, a few weeks, a handful of months. Men who left me, men I rejected because I knew deep down they weren't *it* for me.

But Lyall is—was. I have no idea if we can be what we once were. It's too overwhelming. Maybe nothing will happen between us. Maybe my heart will just end up broken all over again.

"I don't know, Gramps. Okay? But I'm going to find out. Lyall's offered to help me remember."

"You can't!" he hisses, gripping onto my arm hard. "Soren, he could be trying to trick you. And what's more, you do not have the TTA's permission to travel. There are rules that must be obeyed!"

"Lyall's willing to break the rules for me. He's been looking for me all these years. I trust him, and I need to know why."

Fergus heaves a sigh, and I hate that I'm worrying him like this.

"I'll come back," I say, needing him to know. "I promise, Gramps. You're my family. You know that, right?"

A watery sheen mists Fergus's eyes, making a lump rise in my own throat. "Be careful, my boy. Please."

Leaning over, I pull him into a hug. "I will."

No matter what I learn in the past, I'll aways have a home here in the present with Fergus.

"So, how does this time travel stuff work exactly?"

Lyall doesn't answer my question right away, too busy chewing a big mouthful of the blueberry muffin I brought back from the cafe. His eyes roll back, and he moans low in his throat. I wonder what else could make him moan like that?

No. Bad. We're not doing relationships, remember?

But that doesn't mean I have to be celibate, does it? Maybe we could just have one night together, or—

No, Lyall feels... something for me. I can't lead him on like that. I guess I have no other option but to pine after him then. To imagine what his hair might feel like between my fingers, his body drawn taut with pleasure beneath mine like in my dreams...

"—and we're there. Simple. Soren?"

I blink away the images of Lyall and clear my throat. "Sorry?" Shit. My voice sounds as if I just gargled with gravel.

An indulgent smile spreads over Lyall's face. His nostrils flare as he leans forward, the table between us the only thing stopping him from being within kissing distance. "I said..." His voice is low and husky, like a caress right over my dick. "I must take you... to a body of water." Shit. He's teasing me. Has to be. "There I will open a portal that will take us wherever I will it."

Keep your eyes on his face. Don't look at his lips. His eyes are up here.

My throat convulses around a swallow. "Oh. Okay. Sounds good." His knees brush mine beneath the table.

"You aren't nervous?"

His question drains my arousal, making me more aware of the nerves churning in my stomach. "A little."

"Fear not." His hand slides across the table and squeezes mine. "I'll protect you."

My face flushes. "I can protect myself."

"I know." Melancholy clouds his eyes. "You were always strong and capable. It never stopped me from worrying after you." The tenderness in his voice makes my breath catch. Nobody's spoken about me in this way. I haven't done anything to deserve it. The man Lyall knew and the man I am now aren't the same person. Once Lyall realizes that, will he be disappointed?

Probably. Another reason I can't let myself get attached to him. I'll never be the same person he speaks about with such reverence.

I pull my hand away and try not to notice the hurt that flashes across Lyall's face.

I know Lyall's hoping that this journey into the past will help me remember, but what if it doesn't? He'll just be disappointed. He'll leave, the same as everyone else. These feelings I have for him... they can't lead anywhere good.

What if he just disappoints me like all the others have? I need to remember that's a possibility.

Lyall swallows the last bite of food. "Ready?" he asks.

There are crumbs in his beard. My fingers twitch, but I ball my hand into a fist so I don't brush them away. "Yeah. Let's do this."

He grins like I've made his day. "Then let's go. You take the lead. You know the city better than I do."

My heart's in my throat as I lead the way to Chelsea Piers. It's not far, and Lyall makes the walk pass even more quickly with all his chatter. "Wait until you see the ocean! You used to love going for swims with me. We'd race each other out as far as we could go."

Racing? Ugh, no thanks. I get enough exercise climbing the five flights up to my apartment. Still, I smile as Lyall's face lights up while describing our antics. I like the version of Soren he talks about. He's adventurous, daring, and passionate.

Nothing like the man I am now. My life is simple. I wake up, eat a quick breakfast, go to work, come home and experiment with new drink recipes, then go to sleep. Lather, rinse, repeat. A guy like Lyall must live an adventurous life. Which is fine. I'm not dating him. He's just helping me remember my past. That's all this is.

Once we're at the piers, I rent a kayak and we settle into it. The day is crisp and cold. There's a thin layer of broken ice that floats over the river's surface. Gray clouds let in pale sunlight. In seconds, the cold air has numbed my cheeks. "What now?" I ask, teeth chattering.

Lyall reaches into his bag and withdraws what looks like a tree branch covered in odd symbols. "It's a branch of Yggdrasil," he explains, "the world tree that connects all the realms of this world. Using it, we can travel wherever we wish." Before my eyes, the symbols begin to glow pale blue.

The branch shakes in Lyall's hand the farther out into the water we get. The wind picks up, rocking the kayak. I grab onto the sides, terrified it will tip us into the icy water. There's a flash that briefly obscures my vision, and my mouth falls open as a tear appears ahead of us. A portal. It's a fucking portal!

I close my eyes tight, heart racing.

Shit, shit, shit. This is happening. This is real. I'm going back in time.

There's no time to regret this choice.

The tip of the kayak passes into the portal, swallowing Lyall, coming for me.

My stomach lurches like I've missed a step going downstairs, like I'm falling and there's nothing to catch me, only an endless abyss.

I slam back into my body with a gasp as the world spins around me, tipping—

"Soren!"

Frigid water crashes over my head. My limbs stiffen, my lungs seizing. I've never known such cold in my whole life. I can't think around it, can't fucking *breathe*.

A hand clasps mine, pulling me toward the surface. I collide with Lyall's firm body, and he holds me tight as the surface gets closer. I suck in air, gasping and shaking.

"I've got you, Soren. I'm here." Lyall hooks his arms beneath mine and kicks toward the shore. My ankles drag over stones, and then there's solid land beneath my body. My muscles have locked up. I can't move, just shudder and gasp for air. I'm as vulnerable as a baby, and it's fucking terrifying. "Don't be afraid. I'm going to look after you."

I'm hoisted into strong arms, held to a powerful chest. Lyall runs, jostling me from side to side. "Let me think... there was a cave around here. Gods, I must remember! Where was it... There!"

The howling wind around us becomes muffled as Lyall squeezes us through a narrow opening and into a dark, quiet space. I huddle into him, desperate for any warmth I can get even though he's as soaked as I am. He lays me down on the hard ground. "I need to get you out of these wet cloths. Will you let me?"

Yes, I want to scream, but my teeth are chattering too hard. I nod, and Lyall gets to work. My limbs are stiff, and it takes several minutes of pulling on Lyall's part, but finally my wet clothes are thrown off. My eyes grow heavy.

"Easy, Soren. You'll feel better soon."

Lyall throws on his furs, and the white pelt crawls over his body. In seconds, a white wolf stands before me, his fur dry. The wolf—Lyall—lies down atop me like a big blanket. His fur itches my bare skin at first, but the warmth radiating from him nearly makes me cry in relief. I wrap my arms around his neck and hold him close. There's a slight breeze as his tail whips back and forth, a happy little squeak escaping him.

Lyall rests his big head on my chest, sighing in a way I could almost call content. I close my eyes and lose myself in his warmth. The numbness fades slowly from my fingers as I run them through his thick, coarse fur. A huff of laughter escapes me. I have a huge wolf lying on top of me, but what I feel isn't fear. Far from it.

No.

I've never felt safer.

"Thanks, Lyall."

He whines, tail wagging.

"Guess that's a 'you're welcome.'" I stroke the tip of his big ear. "You know, for such a fearsome predator, you're just the goodest of boys, aren't you?" He growls at my teasing tone, but I just laugh. I take his furry cheeks in my hands and squish them. "So cute. I've always wanted a dog. Who's da good boy? You is! You is da goodest boi."

Lyall's tail only wags faster. He's loving this.

I scratch his side. "Ready for the good stuff? Want some belly rubs?"

Lyall sighs happily and flops off me. I'm nice and warm now, so I don't mind. I give his chest some scratches, then ruffle the floof on his belly, grinning when his huge paw starts to kick in response. His eyes close, tongue lolling in bliss. "Yeah. That's the good stuff, huh?"

Am I nuts for thinking this wolf is the cutest creature I've ever laid eyes on? It doesn't help that he's more golden retriever than vicious predator. At least, around me he is. Sighing, I flop down beside him, carding my fingers through his fur. His long snout is inches from my face, his big cold nose almost touching mine. His teeth are freaking huge, but I don't feel an ounce of fear.

Reaching out, I put my finger between his teeth. He closes his jaws, applying the barest hint of pressure against the digit. My chest tightens. The trust I have in him must be left over from the bond we shared. If our bond was so strong I trust him even in his most dangerous of forms, then...

"I wouldn't have forgotten you without one hell of a fight," I whisper into what little space there is between us. "What we had... it must have been something special."

The wolf's emerald eyes open, with such a human look of awe in them that it takes my breath away. His body ripples and then Lyall the human lies inches from me, my finger to his lips. His throat clicks loudly in the quiet, a glossy sheen to his eyes.

"It was." He clears his throat, voice thick with emotion.

"I wish I could remember."

He takes my hand, and I let him. The walls I've built around my heart don't stand a chance, not when he looks at me like I'm his whole world. "You will."

I wet my lips, my heart skipping. "And if I don't?"

Lyall's intake of breath is loud, and my heart sinks. "You will."

Shit. It's exactly what I feared. "Lyall—"

"No," he says sharply, holding my hand to his chest. "You will remember."

And if I don't... then he'll leave.

And I'll be left to pick up the pieces again.

Chapter 11
Lyall

What if Soren never remembers?

The question haunts me as I get a fire going. I lay Soren's soaked clothes as close to the flames as I safely can. Nearby, Soren rests beneath my furs, sleeping away the stress of the day. Having him beneath me, flesh to flesh, had felt like a dream. The urge to kiss him had nearly consumed me, but I'd sooner cut off my arm than take advantage of him in such a vulnerable state.

I must have patience and trust that this is all part of fate's plans for us. Surely if we were so incompatible after so much time and change, we wouldn't still be meant for each other? I have to believe that.

When I wake later, Soren still slumbers. His clothes have dried so I drape his coat over him and take back my fur cloak. He'll no doubt want to wake up to a meal, and my wolf and I are more than happy to provide for him. I leave the cave and pull up my fur hood. The shift takes hold, and I gallop on four paws along the shore.

One day Soren will join me on hunts, and we will run on all fours side by side. My heart will finally be complete when he returns my love. Cold water laps at my paws as I venture out into the frothing waves. I catch us each a fish, and when I return to the cave, Soren's dressed and ready for the day.

"Morning," I say. "I caught your favorite. Salmon."

Soren stiffens, and when he smiles, it's forced.

Oh no. Have I done something wrong already?

"Thanks," he says.

"Something's wrong. Tell me."

"No, no. I just—"

"Soren."

His shoulders slump. "Thank you so much, Lyall. I'm not the biggest fan of seafood."

I work hard to keep my expression neutral. We used to sit on the shore together, light a fire, and cook our catch together. He'd smile as I hand-fed him pieces of salmon. He'd lay his head on my shoulder and sigh as the waves crashed on the shore.

This is perfect, Lyall. There's nowhere else I'd rather be.

I try to smile, though I'm unsure how convincing it is. "That's all right. No need to force yourself."

So what if he doesn't like fish? Tastes can change. It doesn't mean anything.

Soren sighs heavily. "I'm sorry. I shouldn't have said anything. That was rude of me. I'm sure it will taste great if you cook it."

"Sit tight. It'll be ready soon." I grab my tools from my pack.

"Do you know where we are?" Soren asks.

I sharpen my hunting knife. "I've brought us to the island of your birth. Your village is only a few miles from this cave. After we break our fast, I will lead you there."

"What's there that's so important?"

I look over my shoulder at him, needing to see his reaction to make certain he is comfortable with this. "Your childhood. Your parents. The fate of your village."

"Fate of my village..." Soren wets his lips. "Guessing it wasn't a happy ending."

I set down my knife and reach out to take his hand. "Was I wrong to bring you here?"

Soren shakes his head, and his eyes burn with resolve. "No. I need to see them. My parents. Fergus lied and told me that my mother had abandoned me. I want to know who they were. That's all that matters."

Then I will support him in this. I lift the knife and bring it down hard, preparing the fish for roasting.

"Oh. That's a lot of blood..." Soren's faint voice alarms me. When I look back at him, he's astonishingly pale. I look down at my hands, red and wet, then back at him.

"So?"

Soren swallows thickly. "Nothing. Just... Excuse me." He lurches to his feet and stumbles outside.

Before I can ask what's wrong, the sound of puking makes me wince. The sight of a dead fish did *that* to him? The man I knew didn't bat an eye at the sight of blood. This version of Soren is soft and sheltered. Nothing like the man I fell in love with.

Are we too different now to share a life together?

I lead the way to the village of Soren's birth. I've visited here many times over the years in my search for anything that reminded me of my mate. I made sure to send us back only a day before the attack on the village so we could witness it together, but now I'm second-guessing myself.

Soren said he wanted to know, and I must respect that, but I fear seeing such a painful memory will do more harm than good. I'd only wanted him to see our story from the beginning.

"Mayhap we should visit another memory."

Soren shakes his head. "No. I want to see my parents." He moves past me, quickening his pace. "Can anyone in this time see us?"

I shake my head. "No. We cannot change events that have already come to pass. It goes against the laws of time travel. There are exceptions, of course."

"What kind of exceptions?"

"Meeting those we are destined for. The witches could never find a way to prevent those fated for each other from altering the timelines. Some things are simply meant to be."

Soren looks back at me, frowning. "Fated? Like soulmates?"

I nod slowly, worrying that he will ask if that's what we are to each other. I want to explain, but at my own pace. He's already been through quite a shock.

The wind carries the sounds of civilization toward us. Before I know it, we're walking the dirt road into Soren's village. The market is packed. Farmers sell their goods. Children chase each other through the crowd, passing right through us as if we aren't there at all. I reach for Soren and take his hand before I can stop myself. He tenses, cheeks flushing as he looks my way.

I clear my throat. "Best to stick together, aye?"

"Y-yeah." He smiles sweetly and doesn't pull away as we venture farther into town. "Everything looks normal," he remarks.

If only he knew how quickly things can turn for the worst in this time. "It will happen soon."

Soren worries his lip. "What will?"

"The attack. Come, let's find your family."

"My family?" Soren grips my hand tighter.

I lead the way from the market, walking the familiar path to Soren's family home. It's a large home. Thanks to their thriving farm and his mother's skills as a seamstress, they're able to afford a comfortable life. In the pasture, cattle graze and chickens roam freely from the yard and into the home.

Soren's mouth quirks. "We let our animals inside the house?"

"Many do." It's strange to him, no doubt.

Soren gasps softly as a boy follows one of the chickens out into the yard. He's got the same dark hair and eyes as the man beside me. "Is that... that's me, isn't it?" Soren hurries closer, leaning on the fence to get a better look at his younger self.

Past Soren scatters feed around the pasture for the chickens, smiling when a cow wanders over to sniff curiously at his hand. "Holy shit. That's me." Soren covers his mouth, eyes wide.

I chuckle. "Aye, it is. You were a cute pup."

Soren shakes his head, mouth agape. "I thought I believed you but seeing it for myself... it's something else."

A woman walks from the house, her dress swishing around her ankles in the breeze. She has the same dark hair as Soren, the same eyes, and even the same nose. Beside me, Soren's eyes water and his hand falls away from his mouth.

Soren's mother rushes forward, scooping up her son. Past Soren laughs, squirming to get free. "Mother, you scared me!"

She kisses his hair. "Come inside and eat. I made your favorite." She takes his hand and leads him into the house.

"She didn't leave me," Soren whispers beside me. He wipes away a tear that spilled down his cheek. "She loved me."

I give his shoulder a squeeze. "Want to go inside?"

"Can we?"

Smiling, I take his hand, and we pass right through the door and into the home. Fire burns in the hearth as Soren and his mother sit at the table, eating together. The door swings open, and my grip on Soren's hand tightens as a man enters the room. He has the same dark hair as Soren, but that's where the resemblance ends, and I'm glad for it.

"How did the hunt fare?" Soren's mother asks, smiling brightly.

Soren's father leans down to kiss her cheek. "Our larders are full. We will have full bellies this winter." He turns to Soren. "Did you take care of the farm and mind your mother in my absence, boy?"

Soren nods seriously. "Yes, sir."

His father's face softens, and he ruffles Soren's hair. My hands twitch, longing to smack his hand away from Soren.

"Are you okay?" Soren asks.

I exhale. "It's... difficult to see your father, knowing the things he will do. But here, he was a different man. Grief and loss changed him."

Soren frowns beside me. "Why? What happened?"

Screams fill the air beyond the hut.

"What's happened?" Soren's mother rushes to the window, and Present Soren hurries to look past her. "Oh gods! Wolves!"

Soren looks at me with wide eyes. "What's going on?"

Before I can answer, Soren's father is on his feet and grabbing a pitchfork by the door. "Stay inside!" he orders, then rushes outside to fend off the attack.

"Pa!" Past Soren cries, running after him. His mother grabs his shoulders and hauls him back. She kicks the door shut and turns to her son.

"Your father will be fine. It's just wolves."

"But they aren't, are they?" Present Soren asks beside me, his face pale.

I shake my head. "No wolves would be so cruel as to attack a village. They are a pack of ulfhednar. They came from across the sea to raid and kill." Soren's hand quivers in mine. "We don't have to stay for this."

Soren's mother screams as dozens of paws slam into the front door. Furious snarls and barks come from beyond, and the door rattles under the pressure of countless claws tearing into the wood.

Soren's mother scoops up her son and races for the back door just as a storm of wolves bursts into the cabin. She runs outside and slams the back door on them, and Present Soren races through the walls and outside, bringing me with him.

Soren's mother runs toward the woods, carrying Soren in her arms. Wolves pursue her. A voice cries out, "To me, foul beasts!" Soren's father hoists his pitchfork and points it at the pack. A few wolves rush him, but a couple others chase after Soren and his mother. The wolves hurl themselves at Soren's father, and though he manages to stab a few, he's tackled to the ground. Present Soren looks away, eyes shut tight as his father screams.

"We need to follow my mother!" Soren races off toward the woods.

I know that despite his injuries, Soren's father will live, the only survivor of the attack aside from his son. He'll get stronger, driven by fury and lust for revenge, and years from now he will come to our shores with a small army disguised as missionaries.

If I could kill him now and prevent the suffering to come, I would do so in a heartbeat.

But I can't. Nothing can change what has already come to pass. All that matters now is that I have Soren, and he needs me. Grabbing hold of my resolve, I race after Soren and into the woods. His mother has managed to shake the wolves for now. They sniff among the leaves, growling in agitation.

"Where is she?" Present Soren asks, looking around.

I grab his hand and lead the way deeper into the trees. Ahead of us, Soren's mother's run has slowed to a limp. Blood weeps from her ankle.

"M-Ma?" Past Soren whimpers in her arms. "Hurry. You have to hurry!"

With a gasp of pain, his mother stumbles, Soren toppling from her arms. He scrambles up and grabs her hand.

"I... I can't go any faster, my love," his mother says through pained gasps.

"Yes, you can!" Soren urges, pulling on her hand. Tears and dirt streak his cheeks. "Please, Ma!"

The pain clouding his mother's eyes disperses. I follow her stare to the hollowed base of a tree. Grabbing her son's arm, she drags him toward the trunk. "Inside, boy, hurry!"

Soren's lip quivers as he looks up at his mother. "You hide too."

"Listen to me." She grips both his shoulders. "We're going to play a game. You be as quiet as you can and don't move from this spot. No matter what happens. I'm going to lead the beasts away but I will come back. When I do, we'll find your father and we'll go far away. We'll start anew somewhere else."

Tears spill down Soren's cheeks. "Promise."

She takes his small hand and kisses his palm. "I promise." She wipes his tears away with her thumbs. "Now, you be strong for me. Quiet as a mouse and still as a tree."

Sniffling, Soren squeezes into the large hole in the trunk.

"Good lad," his mother says, eyes damp but voice full of pride. She backs away from the trunk, eyes never straying from her son's.

Leaves crunch under paws. Snarls get louder, closer.

Soren's mother rips off the hem of her dress and binds it tight around her bloodied ankle. "Beasts! Here I am!" She takes off running. Several wolves tear past the trunk where Past Soren is hidden. True to his word, he remains still.

It will be three days before my father and a few of his men find him and take him away.

He will never see his mother again.

"She left me," Soren whispers. It hurts to look at the tears glinting on his cheeks. "She comes back. Doesn't she?"

I don't know what to say, so I say nothing.

Soren exhales shakily. "Does anyone come for me?"

"Aye," I say quickly. Slipping my arm around his shoulders, I turn him away from the tree his younger self hides in. "Not right away, but my father finds you and brings you to our village."

"Can we, I don't know, skip ahead to that?"

"Of course."

Soren wipes away his tears and gifts me with a wobbly smile. "Thank you, Lyall."

Chapter 12
Soren

"We're leaving?"

"For the day, aye," Lyall says as he leads the way back to the boat. "Tomorrow we will return and you can see the rest of the memories. It's best we pace ourselves."

Secretly, I'm relieved. Seeing my family for the first time only to lose them took a lot out of me. I need time to think, and I want to speak to Fergus as soon as possible.

As we settle into the boat, Lyall lifts the oars. A frown twists his face. "My apologies, Soren. It was inconsiderate to allow that to be your first memory."

"No, I'm glad I know the truth," I insist. As painful as today was, I'd rather know the truth than continue believing the lies Fergus told me.

My parents hadn't abandoned me. My mother had given her life to save mine, and so had my father. Because they'd loved me. Tears sting my eyes, and I focus on the churning waves around us. I hope Lyall will think it's just the sea spray making me misty-eyed.

There's a flash and my stomach flips over, and then the skyscrapers of the city materialize ahead of us. The world spins around me, and I close my eyes. "Don't think I'll get used to that."

"You will." Lyall sounds confident and calm. He's clearly used to traveling from one time to another.

He moors the boat and we leave the piers together. "You're not going back?" I ask.

He shakes his head. "I'll stay at Anders's home. What time would you like to meet again in the morn?"

"Same as today?"

"Will do."

I look back at him, feeling like I should say something. "Thank you for showing me what really happened. It was rough but... I appreciate it. A lot."

Lyall smiles. "You're sure you're well?"

I shrug. "I will be. See you, Lyall."

Once I'm home, I shower and dress for bed. When I leave the bathroom, my heart skips at the sight of Fergus sitting at the table. He must have heard me come in. "Does your magic stuff tell you when I'm home?"

"I have wards around the home that alert me when the threshold's been breached."

I don't know what any of that means. "You know, a Ring cam would work, too."

He doesn't react to my attempt at humor. "What did the wolf show you?"

I want to go and sit with him like we've always done but I'm not the same person I was. The man I loved and trusted like a father lied to me, and I don't know how to forgive that. I settle for gripping the back of my chair instead. Not sitting, but close enough to have a conversation with him. "Why did you tell me my parents had abandoned me?"

Fergus lowers his gaze. "It was not my choice."

"Then whose was it?" I'd like to find them and wring their damn necks.

"The Council decided upon your backstory. My job was to enforce it."

"And the Council is?"

"The Travelers Council is a group of witches. They govern the laws of time travel and protect the secrets of the paranormal world."

Even after everything I've seen today, it still feels weird as fuck to be talking about witches and time travel so casually. "Do they, what, have an office somewhere?"

"They do, actually. Several."

There's so much more I want to ask, but I need to stay focused. "So they made you lie to me about my past." My hands curl around the back of my empty chair.

"Yes, and about your reason for being here in this time, that being your exile and life with the Erikson Pack. But the details of your childhood, your life before you were adopted into the pack, were unknown to us. It's something I had wondered about myself from time to time."

"Really?"

When he nods, the fist in my stomach unclenches. "Yes. So if you'd like to share what you learned, I would be interested in hearing it."

I settle into my seat at the table. Where do I even start? "I had two parents. My mom and dad. We lived in a little village by the sea. We owned a farm. Wolves attacked the village." A lump rises in my throat, and I pause to clear it. "Pa held them off long enough for Ma and me to escape. Ma hid me inside a tree trunk and led the wolves away from me."

My parents are gone. I can't remember them, but I wish I could. I wish I could talk to them, wish I'd been able to feel the love they had for me.

At least when I'd believed they'd abandoned me, I'd known it was possible to find them again.

But my parents are dead.

I'll never get to meet them.

"Oh, Soren."

As I gulp in a breath, tears wet my cheeks, and Fergus comes to me and cups the back of my neck.

I hide my face in his stomach and sob. I don't know how long it lasts. He holds me through it, and though he doesn't say a word, he rubs my back until there are no more tears left to cry.

"Sorry about that," I croak, wiping my face dry. He leaves and returns with some tissues. I blow my nose and try to get myself back in semi-functional shape.

"Soren..." His voice is hesitant. "If you want me to, I can make the pain go away."

"No." I recoil from him, shaking my head emphatically. "I don't want to forget. Not again."

Fergus holds up his hands. "All right. I won't. I promise."

I lean back in my chair, eyes closing from exhaustion. "It hurts. A lot. But I'd rather know the truth than some lie the Council made you tell me."

"I understand." He squeezes my shoulder.

"He's going to show me how we met tomorrow. Hopefully, that'll be more cheerful."

"Soren, you know he's expecting you to remember."

My jaw tightens. "And?"

"If you can't, do you think he'll still want anything from you?"

I don't know how to answer. "I'm tired. Need to get some sleep."

Once I'm alone in my room, I flop into bed and sigh as all the tension slowly leaves my body. On my dresser, my phone pings. Who would be texting this late? I sure hope it's not my boss. I'm supposed to have off tomorrow.

It's of a pigeon perched on the air conditioner outside his window.

My phone rings.

"Hey," I answer, unable to wipe my grin off my face.

"What type of bird is this?" Lyall asks, sounding so confused it's hard not to burst into laughter.

"It's a pigeon. They're, like, the bird of New York."

"Ah. I liked that picture you sent."

Heat crawls up my cheeks. "Yours was better." It was funny and authentic.

"Are you all right?"

I sigh. "I'm... okay. Today was just a lot. Do things get better for us in the past?"

"Aye. They do."

"I sense a 'but.'"

"Our story... it doesn't have a happy ending. But I am working on it, Soren. I'm going to give us both the happy ending we deserve."

I sure hope traveling into the past gets easier. The boat didn't overturn this time, but man, my stomach feels like it got flipped upside down.

Lyall grins at me. "Looking rather green there."

I rub my roiling stomach. "Hey, cut me some slack. It's only my second time."

Laughing, Lyall guides me from the shore toward the woods. "You'll be a natural soon."

"Where are we?"

We're on an island now, but it looks different from the one I grew up on. The trees are denser; the beach is longer.

"The island where I grew up." Lyall motions toward a port farther down the beach. "Look there. That's my father Erik's ship. You'll be stepping off with him in a moment."

Interest piqued, I hurry after him toward the longship. Rugged men disembark, bringing cattle, boxes of goods, and even some people in chains, I note with unease. A big man who shares Lyall's golden hair leaves the boat and at his side is my younger self.

With a hand on my shoulder, Lyall's father says, "Here we are, boy. This will be your new home."

Past Soren bites his bottom lip. "Are you going to make me a thrall, sir?"

Lyall's father snorts. "You're far too scrawny for labor. No, you will live in my house with me and my boys. They're around your age."

Past Soren's eyes widen. "Are... are they wolves, too?" Fear creeps into his voice.

"Aye, I told you, my whole village are ulfhednar. But we are nothing like the cravens who attacked your village, I assure you. We never target humans or those weaker than ourselves. In fact, we do trade with many human settlements, and quite a few of them are aware of our gift. You are safe here. I promise."

Past Soren frowns down at his feet, not looking convinced. I don't blame the poor kid. I'd be scared too if I were going to go live in a village full of wolves, especially after they killed my family and destroyed my home. I hope things will work out for him.

I hurry after the ghosts of the past. From the beach, it's a short walk to the village. We pass several farms before we arrive at the gates. Lyall sighs beside me, a wistful sound that aches. "It's been too long since I've seen our old home."

The streets bustle with villagers shopping at the market stalls, herding cattle, and going about their day. I jump when two wolves race right through me, bounding through the streets like overgrown puppies. My younger self gasps and hides behind Lyall's father as they run past.

Erik chuckles. "Be brave, boy. They will not harm you."

Past Soren's eyes are wide as he darts anxious looks around the village, but when we arrive at the longhouse, his shoulders loosen. As Erik enters, a woman rushes up and hugs him. "You're home!"

"Oof, Helga, easy!" Erik chuckles. "Soren, this is my sister, Helga."

Helga's smile falters, her eyes turning soft and sad. "Poor dear. Whatever happened to you?"

Past Soren hangs his head and doesn't reply.

Erik takes Helga aside, and I move closer to catch what he says.

"The Blackbriar pack attacked his village. He is an orphan. Not a soul from the village survived."

Helga clasps a hand to her mouth. "Oh, by the gods. Poor dear. Those wretched beasts..."

Erik nods grimly. "Where are the boys?"

"Anders and Gunnar are training in the yard. Wulfric and Lyall went to the market together but they should be back any moment."

"Good. The boy needs some space before those rascals descend upon him."

Helga smiles. "I know just the thing!" She approaches Past Soren with a big warm smile. "How would you like a bath and a spot of food?"

Past Soren twists his fingers together and nods. "Yes, ma'am."

She laughs. "Call me Helga, dear." She calls out to the thralls, "Take him to the springs. The poor dear needs a relaxing warm soak."

The thralls lead Past Soren back outdoors. The air warms as we walk until we arrive at a large hot spring. The thralls leave my younger self with a soap stone and a towel, and the silence of the wilderness descends on us.

Past Soren undresses, then sinks into the bath. Out in the wilderness, he looks so small. He hangs his head, and his narrow shoulders start to shake. Great wrenching sobs tear from his body.

Tears prickle my eyes. I wish I could go to him and hug him and tell him everything will be okay, even if I'm not sure it will.

"Don't be sad." Lyall puts a hand on my shoulder.

"Is he... Am I going to be okay?"

Lyall smiles. "Just watch."

Twigs snap. A white wolf prowls from the trees. He's not very big, not an adult or a pup, but I recognize him instantly. The tension in my chest unwinds. My child self has nothing to fear, not from this wolf. Terror bleaches Past Soren's face as the wolf nears the edge of the water. He freezes, screwing his eyes shut tight.

"D-don't. Please. Stay back!" Past Soren whimpers.

The wolf halts, ears flattening. His tail droops as he whines. I don't know how, but I know he's apologizing. His body ripples as the shift pulls back.

"Are you scared of me?"

The wolf is gone. In his place is a boy as wild looking as the wolf. He's got long messy blond hair, and his emerald eyes are a perfect match to Lyall's.

"Where did it go?" Past Soren looks every which way, but there's no trace of the wolf. Well, except for the white wolf furs around the boy's shoulders.

"What?" Lyall looks around.

"The wolf!" Past Soren is clearly wondering how he could've missed it.

Understanding widens the boy's eyes. He grins, sunny and bright. "That was me! Oh, Father didn't tell you? Hang on..." The boy throws the furs over his head. I give a start as his body ripples, shifting before my eyes into the white wolf. Fear stiffens Past Soren's spine as the wolf regards him. Then a smile curls the wolf's mouth, tongue lolling out. With a pounce, he leaps into the hot spring, and my younger self's cry of alarm becomes a laugh as water sprays all over his face.

A chuckle escapes me. It's nice to hear my child self laugh after everything.

After splashing around together for a time, Past Soren gets dressed and collapses on the warm tundra. The wolf shakes off, making Past Soren sputter as drops of water fly at him. Lyall shifts back to his human form.

"How did you do that?" Past Soren asks.

Lyall tugs at his furs. "It's a blessing from Fenrir. He grants us the gift of the change if we worship him and hunt in his name." He leans in and sniffs curiously. "You're human."

"You're not," he states.

Lyall shakes his head with pride. "No. I'm ulfhednar. Sorry I scared you. Are you still afraid?"

"At first," Past Soren admits. "But you're not all that frightening."

Lyall puffs out his chest. "I am so! Where'd you come from anyway?" he asks, circling around the boy and sniffing curiously. "Why do you smell like... like..."

When Lyall burrows his nose into the hair behind Past Soren's ear and inhales long and deep, he squawks and shoves Lyall away. He growls, but it sounds more playful than scary. "Stop that."

"Where's your pack?"

"I don't have a pack." Tears glimmer in his eyes. "My mother and father... they're..." Face reddening, he scrubs his eyes. "Wolves a-attacked my village. I don't know where my father is. My mother left me and never came back."

"Oh. I'm sorry." For a moment, he's quiet. Then he says, "My mother too. When I was little."

"Sorry."

Past Lyall sits beside my younger self, their shoulders touching. "Sometimes ulfhednar hurt humans. Humans hurt us too. I wish we'd stop hurting each other and learn to all be friends." He grabs my past self's shoulders suddenly. A smile blooms on his face. It's like staring into the sun itself. "I'll be your pack."

"Why?" Past Soren asks.

He shrugs. "Because. You're nice. You smell good. My wolf likes you."

I don't know what any of that means. I don't think my younger self does either.

"Don't want a pack. But... maybe just a friend? If you want," Past Soren adds, lowering his head.

My chest aches because I know what he's thinking.

Maybe we'll be friends at first. Then he'll get tired of me and leave.

Suddenly, Lyall grabs Past Soren's hands. He's grinning so big and bright, like I just offered him the moon. "Yes! I'd love to be your friend!"

"Really?"

"Yes! Everyone wants to be friends with my baby brother, Wulfric, because he's going to be Alpha someday. Now I'll have my own friend! But you have to promise to be *my* friend. No one else's. My wolf doesn't like sharing." He scuffs his toe and averts his gaze, like he knows that's not a good thing, but there's a stubborn set to his jaw.

Past Soren smiles. "Okay. I'll be your friend. I don't need a lot of friends. Just one really good one."

Lyall's eyes light up, and he hauls Past Soren to his feet and tousles his hair. "Yes! I'll be the best friend you could ever ask for. You'll never be alone, not ever."

Beside me, adult Lyall huffs a laugh.

"What's your name?" Past Soren asks.

"Lyall. What about you?"

My younger self holds out his hand. "Soren."

Lyall snatches his hand up and sniffs it, then licks his palm.

"Eww!" Past Soren snatches his hand back.

Lyall's eyes widen, his cheeks flushing. "Sorry! It's a wolf greeting. How do humans greet each other?"

"Oh. Just like this." Past Soren holds out his hand and Lyall takes it.

"You'll never be alone again, Soren. I promise."

And somehow, I believe every word.

I think Past Soren does, too.

Chapter 13
Lyall

I could stay in the past forever and relive those precious childhood years, but the future calls. My future in my time, and Soren has responsibilities in his time as well. The longer I stay away, the more suspicious my brothers will be.

Once we return to Soren's present, I accompany him home. Soren's quiet beside me, eyes staring miles ahead. I bump his shoulder with mine. "Don't think too hard. You'll get a headache."

A smile brightens his face. "Speaking from experience?"

"Thinking only hurts after one too many cups of mead."

When he laughs, I feel the way Thor must have felt when he felled the great World Serpent itself. Of the two of us, Soren was always a touch moodier. He gets in his head, analyzes all possible outcomes. He's amazing in that way, but he needs someone to ground him.

"Are you well?"

Soren hums, the sound light and easy. "Just thinking."

"About?"

He shrugs, averting his gaze with a small smile. "How glad I am that we were friends. I have friends in this time. They're great. But you and me, we go way back. It makes sense why you're so easy to talk to. Why you know what I'm thinking or how I'm feeling just by looking at me."

I feel a burst of pride at his words. "I do know you! Better than anyone, I'd wager."

He snorts. "That so?"

"Aye. I can prove it."

"Okay then. Let's do this." Soren suddenly takes a detour. Usually, we leave from Chelsea Piers and walk straight to his home along the Hudson River. Instead, he leads me down a stretch of pier until we've found a bench to sit on.

Soren plops down with a big sigh, eyes closing. I settle in beside him. At this late hour, the world is quiet. It's just us, the seagulls, and the water. "What's my favorite color?"

"Easy. Green, like my eyes. You told me so long ago."

"My favorite food?"

"My Aunt Helga's beef stew."

Soren frowns thoughtfully. "Huh. I did ask Fergus for beef stew for dinner a lot. Okay. Favorite hobby?"

"A hobby?"

"That's something you like to do."

"Oh. I see. You always enjoyed fishing."

He gawks at me. "Fishing?"

"Aye. You loved being out on the water. You didn't often keep what you caught but that wasn't what it was about. You enjoyed the experience. And I enjoyed seeing you happy. So I often went with you."

"Fishing..." Soren looks out over the water with newfound intrigue. "It's something I thought about, but I never committed to actually doing it."

"Why not?"

"Just didn't sound like a ton of fun being out on the water by myself. Hey, we should do that sometime. You and me."

I smile so hard it hurts. "I'd love that."

Soren returns my smile, kicking my foot. "It's not fair, you know. You know all this stuff about me, but I'm drawing blanks over here. Come on. Spill."

"Spill what?"

He huffs in amusement. "Tell me something about you! Otherwise I'm just gonna sit here guessing that you, I don't know, wrestle bears in your spare time."

A bark of laughter bucks my chest. "Is that something people do in this time?"

Soren snorts. "Honestly? Probably."

He wants to know more about me, but I'm not sure what else there is to know. "Well... I enjoy a good hunt. A mug or two of mead—after, not before. I learned that the hard way. I once tried to ride a reindeer in my wolf form rather than hunt it. Not my smartest decision." Soren laughs beside me, making me smile. "And... well. Mayhap this is unmanly but I enjoy the smell of flowers."

Soren bites his lip. "That's cute as hell."

I rub the back of my neck, feeling it warm under my palm. "My mother... she loved flowers." A lump sticks in my throat. I clear it, blinking back the sting in my eyes. After all these years, her loss is a wound that has never quite healed.

"Yeah?" Soren's voice is soft as he scoots closer. Our thighs touch, and his shoulder brushes mine.

I cough. "Aye. So, anytime we lads were out training or doing our chores, I'd slip away and bring her back some. She'd sniff them and smile like they were the best thing she ever smelled." I swallow with some difficulty. "I haven't picked any in years since we lost her."

"I'm sorry. Didn't mean to upset you."

I thumb away the dampness in my eyes. "You did not. I chose to tell you, Soren. Of all the souls in this world, you knew mine like I was simply an extension of yours. Losing you was like losing a part of myself but finding you again after all this time... it's as if my heart has finally come home."

Soren blinks rapidly and looks out over the water. "That's, uh... Wow. It's weird but I know what you mean." He rubs his chest. "For the longest time, I felt like something was missing. There was this absence nothing could ever fill, no matter how happy I was."

It hurts my heart to imagine the loneliness he's experienced for so long. I lean in closer, needing to know the answer when I ask, "Have you found what your soul was seeking?"

Soren looks over, eyes widening when he realizes how close we are. His breath gusts over my mouth, so warm against my skin it makes me feel dizzy. Soren drags his tongue along his bottom lip, and I ache with how badly I need to kiss him, to take him in my arms after all these years.

"I think so," Soren says, his voice low and barely audible over the chilly winter wind and the cry of the gulls. "God. I hope so." His voice shakes, the scent of his fear and longing palpable.

Lifting my hand, I settle my palm against his cheek. Stubble rasps against my skin; the sensation is so familiar it takes my breath away. I can't believe he's really here. So close to me. "You have. I promise you, Soren. You are not alone anymore, nor will you ever be from here on out."

I don't know when he closes the space between us. All I know is that when his lips find mine, the world around me disappears.

He's kissing me.

Soren's kissing me.

Closing my eyes, I fall into the kiss. The softness of his lips, the scratch of his stubble. He pulls back, and I realize

I've closed my eyes when I open them and find him flushed and looking at me with both awe and fear.

"Was that okay?" Soren asks.

I gently bump my nose against his. "I don't know. Kiss me again, and mayhap I'll make up my mind."

He laughs, breath warm on my damp lips, then leans back in.

This time he grabs my shirt and hauls me in. Our lips crash together the way a wave breaks upon the shore. Closing my eyes tight, I drink in every little detail.

The hitch in his breath when I lean into him, pleading for more. His hair between my fingers, shorter than I remember. Soren cups the nape of my neck, pulling me closer, kissing me deeper. A sob kicks in my chest.

I can't believe it. Oh gods, I hoped and prayed and wished so desperately for this moment, but a part of me, one that had grown larger over the years the way a bear cub grows into a fearsome predator, had feared this moment would never happen.

Soren's in my arms, kissing me the way I've yearned to kiss him.

I've dreamed of this moment almost every night for years, but nothing compares to the reality of having my mate's lips on mine.

Finally, we part for air, breath mingling.

"That was... very, very good," I say, making him chuckle.

"I can tell." At some point, his leg ended up straddling my hips. There's no hiding just how good that kiss was, how good it felt to have him so close after so long. It pleases me to no end that I've affected him, too.

"Do you, uh..." Soren rocks his hips, making us both gasp.

I push him back against the bench, kissing his warm, swollen lips. "There is nothing I want more, but I will not rush this. The longer the hunt, the sweeter the reward."

Soren smirks up at me, arching a brow. "You saying I'm your prey?"

"As much as I am yours." With one final kiss, I take his hands and pull him to his feet. "Are you willing to wait for me?" I can't stop the hint of fear, that mayhap I have disappointed him.

Soren squeezes my hands. "Yeah. Of course. Whatever you want. I'll be here."

I smile, relieved.

"But, uh, just so we're clear... we've done that before, right? Sex?"

"Oh, aye. We were very good at it."

Soren laughs, cheeks reddening. "Were you with anyone else since?"

I shake my head. "I was not. It would have felt like a betrayal to you."

Soren's fingers grip mine tighter, eyes widening. "Oh. Uh..."

The scent of his worry makes me slip my arm over his shoulders, pulling him near to kiss his temple. "Tell me."

"I've been with other guys, Lyall."

That makes sense. He had no clue about our past. "It does not bother me. You were unaware of our history." But are there any now? He smells like lots of people, but the only scent that lingers is that of his grandfather's magic. "Are you with someone now?" I find myself holding my breath while I await his answer.

"No. But I was with someone for a while," he admits.

"Did you care for them?"

"Yeah, but also... not really? No one I've been with has ever stuck around." Soren lowers his gaze, shoulders slumping. "My relationships never last. They either leave me, or I leave them because there's something they were always missing."

My poor Soren. While my heart was breaking, his was being broken time and again. His soul was seeking mine, but he didn't know it.

I stop and make him turn toward me. Leaning in, I touch my forehead to his. "I am sorry."

"For what?"

My eyes sting, so I close them tight. "If I'd only known how to find you, I would have. I could have spared you so much heartache."

"You think so?"

I open my eyes, rubbing my thumb along his jawline. "I know so. Your heart knew those people weren't who you were meant to be with. Your soul was crying out for mine."

Soren blinks fast. "You think that's why none of my relationships have worked? Because they weren't you? But how does that even work?"

How do I explain what we are to each other? He's already learned so much so quickly. I fear this will overwhelm him. "You were made for me, Soren, and I for you. I will explain more. I promise. For now, let's get you home, get you rested. Aye?"

Soren lets himself smile. "Sounds good."

With his hand in mine, we leave the piers behind and head for his home.

We shared several more kisses, each sweeter than the last, before we parted ways for the night. I try to wipe the smile from my face several times as I return to my time and row to shore. I fear it's become permanent. My brothers will surely be suspicious.

The village slumbers as I walk the road to my home, but the candles are lit inside the longhouse where Wulfric lives.

Odd that he would be up so late. The front door opens, and my brother calls out, "Lyall."

I freeze, heart dropping into my stomach. "Aye, brother?" I force a smile onto my face as I turn around.

Wulfric has his arms crossed, his brow furrowed.

Shit.

"Come inside. I need to speak with you."

Thank the gods I had the good sense to shift to my wolf and roll around in leaves and dirt before returning to the village. Soren's scent shouldn't still cling to me. I hope.

Wulfric isn't the only one up. Kieran smiles and waves from where he sits by the roaring hearth, nursing a cup of tea. "Hey, Lyall."

"Alpha-Mate." I dip my head.

Kieran rolls his eyes. "Quit it with the titles. It makes me feel all weird and important."

I chuckle. "Because you are."

A low growl makes me jump. Gunnar glowers at me from where he reclines against the wall, arms folded over his big chest. It's the first time I've seen him in several days, and something has shifted. There's a wide, feral look in his eyes, and when he speaks, it's through a mouthful of fangs.

"Where have you been?"

I glance at Wulfric and find his expression just as grim as mine must be.

Our brother is slipping further into his wolf, and it's happening faster than before. Ever since he found and rejected his fated mate, his wolf has been riding him hard. I can only imagine the conflict raging in his heart. His animal instincts would be howling to find Arlo, but Gunnar's human half is determined to push him away.

It's a dangerous game he's playing.

"Answer me," Gunnar snarls.

I flinch at the harshness in his voice. "I was visiting Anders and Jamie." It's not a lie. I do see them every time I visit.

"All day?"

My temper sparks. I fold my arms and stare my brother down. "Aye. I can go where I please, with whoever I please."

"You spend too much time there. Have you forgotten they live among humans? What if they find out who you are?"

"Anders *lives* there. I never hear you pestering him about safety," I snap. I know bloody well why he worries for me and not Anders. I was the one who fell for a human, a human he believes betrayed us. He thinks Soren's a traitor, that I'm a gullible fool, and it makes my blood boil. "If I were you, I'd worry about yourself, brother. Have you looked in a mirror as of late?"

Gunnar curls his lip, revealing a pointed fang. "It isn't safe for you to be there. If anything were to happen to you—"

"Worry about yourself!" I snap. Gunnar has no business lecturing me about safety. None. He can't even take care of himself—he won't even try. It's infuriating and terrifying to watch him lose himself to his wolf.

Wulfric clears his throat before I can argue. "Lyall, we only want to make sure that you're safe. That's all. Besides, Helga misses you at dinner, and we need you during hunts."

Guilt sags my shoulders. Damn it all. Have I truly been that absent? "Apologies."

"It's all right," Wulfric assures me. "You're welcome to visit Anders, but remember your responsibilities here. Aye?"

Gunnar growls low in his chest. "Don't be a fool, Wulfric. It's not Anders he's seeing. It's someone else."

Shit… Does he know? No. If he knew it was Soren I was meeting with, we wouldn't be talking. Gunnar would lose himself in his fury and hunt Soren down. He still mistakenly believes that Soren betrayed our pack and caused the deaths of his chosen mate and son.

He would hurt Soren. Mayhap even worse. The thought makes me sick to my stomach.

"It's none of your business, Gunnar. Mind yourself, not me."

Gunnar snaps his teeth, the gesture so wolfish that Kieran jumps. Wulfric grips his mate's shoulder, shifting his body so he's between our brother and Kieran.

"Who is it? Who are you seeing? Are they safe?" Gunnar advances on me. His fur comes to life, crawling down his arms, his nails sharpening to claws. I back up, the doorknob jamming into my hip. My hands fist at my sides. My own wolf stirs under muscle and bone, ready to defend ourselves and our mate from the feral wolf before us.

"I am safe, Gunnar."

"Are you? Because the last time you thought that, our father was killed, Leif and—and Bjorn. They were—" He blinks fast, shoulders heaving.

Sorrow threatens to choke me, but I fight it back. Anger nips at my patience. "You blame me."

"No. Never you. I blame *him*." Gunnar's eyes flare wolf-bright. "Is it him? Are you seeing him?" His hand shoots out, grabbing my shirt and shaking it.

"Gunnar, that's enough!" Wulfric snaps.

It's too late. Just the suspicion that I am seeing Soren has Gunnar shifting. His head snaps from side to side as his face starts to reshape itself. His claws bite into my chest.

Shit, shit, shit!

I shove him back and blurt out, "You want to know who I'm seeing? It's—it's—"

What do I say? What do I do?

Gods help me.

"It's Arlo."

Gunnar goes completely still.

I want to reach down my throat and shove the words back down, but it's too late. The damage is done.

"I just... I assumed that since you did not want him, that it was all right if I did," I blabber, desperately looking at anything but my brother. In our culture, courting another wolf's fated mate is considered a serious offense. Wolves have come to blows over it, killing each other. But Gunnar rejected Arlo. We all witnessed it.

I should be safe.

Should.

"I see." Gunnar's voice is so startlingly human, I almost don't recognize it as his. When I find the guts to face him, I notice he's reverted back to his normal appearance. There are dark circles under his eyes, like his beast has been restless at night, but they have ceased to glow. His nails are no longer sharp, bitten down until they're blunted.

Somehow he looks worse as a man than he does when his wolf rides him.

"Have I offended you?" I ask.

Gunnar blinks several times, eyes unfocused. "The witch is not mine. Do as you like with him."

He can't possibly mean that. "Gunnar, he's your—"

"He's nothing to me!" Gunnar's roar rattles the windows. "My mate, the one I chose... he's gone." Gunnar's jaw works furiously, his eyes glistening and full of anguish.

My heart breaks for him. "Brother—" I reach for him, but he storms past me and out into the night.

A shuddering sigh heaves from my chest.

Gods, what have I done?

"Hope you're happy, Lyall," Wulfric says, voice heavy with disapproval. He might as well have stabbed me.

"Wulfric, enough. Let's go to bed." Kieran gives me a searching look, like he knows more than I'm letting on. He knows I've been visiting the present long before we met Arlo. I just shake my head.

"Don't," I plead through our bond. *"This is my burden to bear."*

Kieran sighs. *"Be careful. Please."*

My brother and Kieran leave me alone to stare into the fire, hating everything I've just done.

Mayhap Loki has taken possession of my fate.

What other god would be so cruel as to give me everything I've ever wanted at such a terrible cost?

Chapter 14
Soren

"What's got you smiling?" Tom gives me a teasing smile as I slide his and Franklin's drinks across the bar.

Shit. Was I doing it again? I rub my mouth, trying to physically scrub away the evidence. "I was not."

Franklin elbows Tom's side. "You either got that promotion to manager or you got laid."

"Warmer."

Franklin whistles while Tom laughs. "Wait, wait, I got it. You're doing your manager."

"Tom!" Franklin smacks his shoulder.

I snort. "Stone cold. No, I've been seeing this guy." I flush when they both cheer. "He's super sweet, sexy as hell, and I really like him. Great kisser too."

"That's so great! When do we meet him?"

I hesitate, my cheer fading. A customer orders a drink, so I focus on preparing it. I don't usually tell Franklin and Tom about the guys I'm seeing. I've been burned enough times that I've decided to wait about a month into the relationship before even mentioning them.

I can't explain it, but after last night I have a good feeling about Lyall. The kiss we shared was so sweet, and it gave me a thrill I haven't felt in a long time. I'm talking butterflies in my stomach all day and a goofy grin I haven't been able to shake. Kissing him felt so right, like I'd found something I hadn't even known was missing for so long.

But talking to Tom and Franklin makes me feel like I'm jinxing something, and an old familiar fear gnaws at the edges of my happiness. I know how quickly things can change. As right as things feel now, what if it doesn't last?

Scowling, I give the drink I'm making a good, aggressive shake and imagine I'm shaking all the negative crap out of my head. I want to hold on to this giddy infatuation for as long as I can.

Lyall seems to think my past relationships didn't work because they weren't him. He makes it sound like some unconscious part of me has been waiting for him, like he's waited for me. Like destiny or something. I'm too cynical to believe in that sort of thing, so I don't know what to feel.

I want to trust him, even if I can't trust myself.

Once I'm done with the drink, I hand it off to the customer, then stop by Franklin's and Tom's seats. "His name's Lyall. Things are still really new and we're taking it slow, but I've got a good feeling about him."

"That's great, Ren." Franklin smiles brightly. "I hope we get to meet him."

So do I...

After work, I head over to the Hudson River to meet with Lyall. I try to squash as many of the butterflies in my stomach as I can. *Just be cool. Be calm.* Will he want to kiss me again? Fuck, I hope so. Will things be awkward? What do I say? What do I do?

My phone chimes. Lyall sent me a text. Well, a picture.

It's of a seagull perched proudly on a railing, the setting sun casting an orange glow over his feathers.

I stop in my tracks, smiling like an idiot at my screen. Why's this guy so wholesome and cute?

> **Don't be fooled. He may look innocent, but he's got murder in his eyes.**

Lyall replies with a voice message. "Are they dangerous?"

I bark a laugh at the very real concern in his voice, causing some people to stare at me, but I don't care.

> **Very. Five out of ten people are killed by seagulls every year.**

Lyall replies, "By this little bird? If they're so dangerous, why are they allowed free?"

I cover my mouth but can't hold back my laughter.

> **Who knows? This city's gone to the dogs.**

"Dogs are responsible for this?" Lyall sounds both baffled and horrified.

Oh right. He's not familiar with the sayings and slang of this time. I probably shouldn't say those things all the time then, just out of respect—but his reactions are really fucking funny, so I'm gonna do it anyway.

I quicken my pace until I spot him sitting on one of the stone benches and glaring at the seagull still perched on the railing. "You know," I say as I approach, "there are some places where dogs and cats are mayors of towns."

"You jest," he says, huffing. He stands, and my heart trips as he comes closer. We stand toe to toe. We're roughly the same height, so his lips are tantalizingly within reach. His hand drifts along my hip, just touching, not demanding. "You look good today."

My face flushes. "Thanks. So do you."

His throat bobs, and his eyes catch on my mouth. Heat flares low in my stomach.

"I couldn't sleep," I admit. "Kept thinking about you."

The corner of Lyall's mouth tips up. "Good thoughts?"

I grin and lean in until his breath warms my lips. His lips smell of mint, cool and fresh. "Very, very good."

A low laugh rumbles in his chest. "My memories of last night are a bit... blurry. Kiss me again, love. It may just spark my memory."

I don't need telling twice. The low, pleased sound Lyall makes when I take his lips in a deep, lingering kiss makes my heart flip. It's chaste and sweet, and when we pull apart, I want to dive back in for another taste. Lyall leans his forehead against mine, eyes still closed, a smile on his flushed lips.

"Gods. I could kiss you until the end of the world and it would never be enough."

My heart races with joy. "Is there an afterlife in Norse myths?"

"Aye. Warriors go to Valhalla to join Odin's army and prepare for Ragnarok. Those who do not die in battle go to Hel's realm."

"Hell? That sounds scary."

Lyall chuckles. "No. Not the Christian idea of Hell. Helheim. Hel cares for the souls who die of sickness or old age. She is supposedly quite fearsome to gaze upon but tender-hearted."

"Oh. Okay. Well, maybe when we die, we can go there. That way, we'll still be able to kiss, even in death."

Lyall smiles, making the sunlight feel dimmer by comparison, and I realize I've essentially said I want to be with him for the rest of our lives and on into the afterlife.

Oops. So much for taking things slow.

Swinging an arm over my shoulders, he leads me toward the boats. "That's a good idea. To tell the truth, Helheim was always more appealing to me than Valhalla. I want to die in my bed, surrounded by my family. I'd rather spend my life farming than fighting."

"Honestly? Sounds good to me."

Lyall squeezes me close. "Anders used to tease me for it, but he has a family and a nice, cozy life with his mate. Dying in battle seems a worthy death until you've found someone you want to live for. Now, enough talk of death, we have memories to explore."

"What will we see today?"

"I thought we could skip ahead until we're both older." Lyall drops his arm from my shoulders and takes my hand as we walk the stretch of pier toward the rental shack. Once we're in our boat and far enough from shore that nobody should notice, Lyall opens a portal with the branch of Yggdrasil.

This time when we pass through, the sensation is less unpleasant. It still feels like tripping on my way down the stairs, but at least I don't feel nauseous this time. It's night here in the past. The full moon hangs overhead, and stars blanket the sky. We drag the boat ashore and walk the path to the village. Lyall leads the way, my hand in his, walking with confidence while I trip and stumble in the dark.

"Stop laughing," I grumble after almost falling on my face.

"Stop amusing me then," he counters, "unless you'd like for me to carry you?"

"Don't you dare!"

Distant howls drown out his answering laugh. A chill runs down my spine. "Fuck!" I look every which way, but I can't see for shit in the darkness.

"It's all right," Lyall assures me, leading me *toward* the howling rather than away. "It's my pack. We're celebrating."

"What?"

"You."

Curious but still unsettled, I grip his hand tight and let him guide me through the dark. Soon enough, torches light the village road, although the village itself appears empty.

"Where is everyone?"

"This way." Lyall guides me along a dirt road east from the village. Torches flicker ahead like fireflies. Drums thunder through the woods, vibrating the ground. There's a crowd gathered in a clearing in the middle of the woods. Many are humanoid, but others have shifted fully to wolves and watch whatever is in the center of the circle with an awareness that's all too human.

We pass through the crowd like ghosts and stop when we've made it to the front.

A man with long dark hair kneels before an altar. Bones and wolf fur decorate the stony surface. A wolf skull has been mounted to the structure, empty eyes gazing down at the man prostrate before it. The man who, when he lifts his head, looks startlingly similar to me. I barely recognize him. His hair is long and braided; his beard is full but neat. Blood smears his lips and clots in his beard.

A shiver runs through me. This man is nothing like the scared little boy Erik brought to the village. He's a man now, wild and fierce. The crowd parts, allowing Erik to make his way toward us. In his arms, he carries a mound of wolf fur. He stops before Past Soren, who gazes up at Erik not with fear, but with something close to reverence.

The drums fall silent, and the wolves stop howling.

In the quiet, it's as if the wilderness itself holds its breath.

Erik says, "You are one of us now. Blood of our blood, flesh of our flesh. We are your pack. I am your Alpha. You will never hunt or howl alone in this life."

Past Soren's face softens into a smile. "Thank you, Alpha. All of you." He looks past us at someone. I turn, heart tripping when I spot a younger version of the man beside me. Past Lyall has shaken off the gangliness of youth. He's grown out a golden beard and a mane of hair, and his body is hard and trained for battle. When he smiles, it's full of pride and warmth and... love. There's no other way to interpret how he's looking at my past self.

Past Soren throws the furs over his shoulders, and a spasm runs through his body. His shift is nothing like

Lyall's, which is fluid as water. His limbs jerk. His bones creak. He throws back his head and screams through a mouthful of bloody fangs. The fur comes alive, wrapping around him only to recede.

"Soren!" Past Lyall breaks from the crowd and crashes into the dirt beside him. "I know it hurts. Don't fight it. I'm here. Right here."

Past Soren's eyes are wide and wild as he snarls, "L-Lyall..."

Past Lyall takes his face in his hands. "You can do this. This is who you were meant to be. You're part of our pack and always will be."

The furs settle over Past Soren's skin, consuming him until the man has disappeared and only a wolf remains.

Beside me, Lyall smiles. "You did so well."

"I did? That looked agonizing."

"You were scared. Most are before they accept the change. Before the ceremony, you told me you were worried you wouldn't make a good wolf, that you'd be thrown out of the pack and lose your family all over again."

My wolf self bounds among the crowd, most of whom have shifted or are in the process of shifting. Lyall's gorgeous white wolf tackles him and they chase each other into the woods. It's easy to distinguish Lyall and his brothers as well as their dad. They're all huge, making the other wolves, even the full-grown ones, look like puppies.

A lump rises in my throat. "But that didn't happen." I had found a family in the past. One who loved me and accepted me as one of their own. "We looked close."

Lyall nods. "Aye."

"How old were we here?"

"We'd just seen our seventeenth winter."

After a while, the wolves return to human form and make their way back to the village. I could have watched them all run and play for the rest of the night. It was a sweet sight. We follow Lyall and Soren as they peel off from the crowd and head inside a cabin, which turns out to be a sauna. Steam clouds the air, though I can't feel the heat or the cold our past selves escaped from.

"What a hunt!" Past Lyall says, undressing.

"Wish I could have caught that rabbit. Your father would have been proud," Past Soren says, looking put out.

Past Lyall ruffles his hair. "He was. I could tell."

"Really?"

"Aye. If he were not, you would have known. Trust me."

My past self removes his clothes, then sits on a bench. Past Lyall joins him, breathing out a contented sigh. Swallowing nervously, Past Soren bumps his shoulder against his friend's. "Thank you. I could not have done it without your help."

Past Lyall scoffs. "Of course you could. You are stronger than you realize."

"I mean it, Lyall." Past Soren takes in a breath, then reaches out to twine his fingers with Lyall's. Past Lyall stiffens, his lips parting. "You're always saving me. From the moment we met. Thank you for... for everything."

Past Lyall's gaze falls to Soren's lips, his chest rising and falling faster. "I... of course. We're—we're friends, after all."

"Lyall." Past Soren hesitates, looking away.

"What's wrong? Your heart is racing." Past Lyall's face creases in concern.

"It's been a long time since I... since I saw you as only a friend."

There's a long beat of silence. Past Lyall laughs nervously. "I... I'm not sure what you—"

Past Soren takes Lyall's face in his hands and lunges in, closing the distance as he seals their lips in an urgent kiss. Past Lyall's eyes widen, but he doesn't return the kiss, still as a statue. My past self lurches away and stumbles across the room, a hand over his mouth.

"Gods, I—I am so sorry. I don't know what I was thinking."

Past Lyall's expression is unreadable.

"I... I thought you felt it too when I shifted. It was like a hook had caught in my chest. Your scent... it's like nothing I've smelled before. My wolf, he kept whispering that you were ours."

"Our mate?" Lyall whispers.

Past Soren doesn't face his friend when he nods. "I just ruined everything between us, didn't I? Please, Lyall. You do not have to return my feelings. Forget it. Forget I said anything. I am sorry."

Past Lyall stands and goes to the door. My heart sinks. Damn. I guess Past Lyall didn't return our feelings right away. He reaches out and locks the sauna door. Past Soren turns, confusion wrinkling his brow. Before he can say a word, Past Lyall has crossed the room, grabbed Soren's face in his hands, and hauled him into a kiss overflowing with years of desperation and yearning.

I breathe a relieved sigh. "Thought you were gonna reject me for a second."

Beside me, Lyall shakes his head, chuckling. "I'd cut off my leg before I rejected you."

When our past selves start breathing heavily and groping frantically at anything they can reach, I nudge Lyall. "Let's give them some privacy."

Lyall laughs and follows me through the cabin and out into the night.

Congrats, young me, I think to myself as I take Lyall's hand, *you couldn't have chosen a better guy.*

Chapter 15

Lyall

What have I gotten myself into?

Of all the foolish things I could have said, I had to say I was courting the witch my brother is fated to. After spending time with Soren, the very last thing I want to do is pretend to have feelings for another. I'm doing this for Soren, though, so that we can spend time together without raising any suspicion.

I just hope Gunnar doesn't take my head off. Even if he rejected Arlo, it won't be easy to see his fated mate with someone else. Although... mayhap this will be a... what's the word Kieran uses? A silver cloud? I don't remember. Mayhap seeing me with Arlo will be the push Gunnar needs to spend time with him?

Or he'll go berserk and take my head off.

Both seem likely possibilities.

Beside me, Anders growls. "This has to be the stupidest idea you've ever had, brother, and that's most certainly saying something." He pulls up to the curb and unlocks the doors.

I step out after him. "You think I don't know that? I panicked."

"You're an idiot." Anders smacks the back of my head as he passes. "Sometimes I have to question if you've got any brains at all in that thick head of yours."

"Brains?"

"The meatball in your skull that does all the thinking! Or it's supposed to."

There's meat inside my skull? How unsettling... I scowl at him. "It's a simple cover story! That's all. You know I can't tell Wulfric and Gunnar the truth. They'd be furious."

Anders returns my scowl, arms folded over his chest. "I came around, didn't I?"

I shake my head. "Gunnar would lose it if he knew the truth. Wulfric wouldn't forgive me."

"You're making assumptions."

I heave a sigh. "Am I?"

Anders hesitates, chewing his lower lip. "I don't know. It's hard to predict how they'd react. And then we also have the TTA to worry about... I worry about you, that's all."

I try to smile, but I'm unsure how convincing I am. "The TTA won't find out, Anders. I'm not going to endanger our pack."

"Let's hope not." He sounds even less convinced than I feel.

Taking in a breath, I push open the door to Jamie's cafe. The scent of coffee thickens the air, mixing with the pleasant smell of books.

"Morning, Anders!" A woman behind the counter waves. Her hair is bright, the same color as glass when it's been tempered by the sea.

"Morning, Jess."

"Is Jamie coming in?" she asks.

"Later. He's taking the lad to school."

She sighs. "Guess we're stuck with your moody ass." When my brother scowls, she laughs, making Anders chuckle.

Calling Anders an ass would have resulted in a bloodbath not long ago. I'm proud of him. He's settled so comfortably in this timeline, carved out a place for himself.

Will Soren and I ever have that?

Anders goes behind the counter, catches my eye, then jerks his thumb toward the back of the store. Nodding my thanks, I pass through aisles of shelves stuffed with books. Sitting on a sofa is the very witch I'm looking for. Arlo is tall and lithe with glossy golden locks and brown eyes that widen in surprise when he looks up and notices me.

"Lyall! What a surprise."

I offer him a smile. "Greetings."

Arlo sweeps curious eyes up and down my body. "You look like you've settled in nicely. Good. Been spending time with the family here?"

"I have, but that's not why I'm here today. I wished to speak to you."

I haven't seen Arlo for some time. Anders and Jamie told me he visits the cafe often to check in. It worried me at first. Arlo is still an enforcer of the TTA, after all. He hounded Anders for a time until Anders finally registered with the TTA, but he proved himself an ally. I do wonder why he helped Anders stay sane when he was losing himself to berserker rage. I've never asked.

Arlo sets aside his book. There's a handsome, shirtless man on the cover. "Really? Color me intrigued!" He flashes me a grin.

The words are stuck in my throat, reminding me of the time I dared myself to swallow a chicken bone whole to impress my brothers. Father was not impressed.

Why in Odin's name would Arlo ever say yes to such a proposal?

I've got to ask. Anything to keep my brothers off Soren's trail. "Would you like to come over for dinner tonight? My timeline."

Arlo's mouth pops open in surprise. "Oh. Well, I—" He cuts his gaze away, clearing his throat. "Your aunt's cooking is delightful but I'd rather not impose... or see Gunnar."

I wince, wishing I'd anticipated that. "I would not ask if it were not important, Arlo. And this is important. Urgently. I—I need you to pretend that we're... what's the word? Dating."

Arlo spits out his coffee. Coughing, he thumps himself on the chest. "Hold on, hold on! Listen, darling, it's not that you aren't attractive. You're one hundred percent my type. But why in the bloody fuck would I say yes?"

Ah, I'd feared this. "My aunt's cooking?"

"Nope. I'm sorry but not even your aunt's delicious food could tempt me into sitting at a table with your brother after he rejected me in front of all of you. You would have to offer me something truly—" He pauses, eyes going wide. "Wait a moment. This is brilliant!"

Thoroughly confused, I ask, "Aye? How?"

Arlo jumps up and paces, chin in his hand. He murmurs soundlessly to himself, nodding every once in a while. "Yes, this is just what I need." He spins around on his heels to face me. "Fine. I'll pretend to be your date on one condition only."

I don't like the sound of that. What could a witch want with me?

"What is it?"

"You must pretend to be mine as well. My sister is getting married this spring. The whole coven will be there. I'll be your date if you'll be mine at the wedding."

"Is it a custom in this time to bring a mate to a family wedding?"

He huffs. "Just mine. It's essential to my research that I bring a date."

"Your research? What does that have to do with a wedding?"

He shakes his head. "It's a secret. I'd rather not discuss it until I'm certain it's ready. Trust me when I say that my research could benefit shifters greatly—including your family. But that's only if you come to the wedding."

I fail to see the connection between his sister's wedding, my pack, and his research, but my father taught me to always return favors when I can.

"Agreed."

Arlo claps his hands together, smiling brightly. "Oh, marvelous!" He pulls out his phone. "What's your number? Text me all the details, and I'll see you later tonight."

We exchange numbers. Arlo goes back to reading, looking happy as a pig in slops while I'm wondering just what in Loki's name I've gotten myself into now.

The time to meet for dinner arrives. Usually, I love nothing more than gathering with my brothers and their mates for our weekly meal. Between Wulfric and Kieran's duties as Alpha and Alpha-Mate and Anders's duties to work and family, we've had to set aside time for us to gather together. Aunt Helga makes her delicious venison roast, freshly caught by Gunnar. Kieran and Wulfric cook a hearty vegetable stew. Anders and Jamie bring these sweet, delicious things called pastries from their time.

It's a time I always look forward to... except for tonight. I'll be amazed if Gunnar doesn't kill me before the night is over. Arlo is an attractive man, but he can't compare to Soren, and yet I must pretend that we're courting.

Worst of all, I'll have to see Anders and Wulfric doting on their mates, happy and in love, while the only man I truly need is far away in a whole other time.

It hits me that Soren will never be able to sit at our table. I'll have to hide him like some filthy secret, when that couldn't be further from what he means to me. He makes me happy. Even after all these years and the loss of his memories, nothing could take away my feelings for him. My family will never understand how I feel. They'll never accept him.

It breaks my heart and makes me wonder how I'll even manage a smile tonight.

"Yoo-hoo, Lyall!"

I jump out of my brooding. Arlo's way ahead of me, the distant torchlight from the village flickering behind him.

"Coming, darling?"

"Aye. Apologies." I quicken my stride until I'm beside him.

"You know, you never told me why you came up with this harebrained scheme."

A scowl tightens my mouth. "I'm seeing someone my brothers would not approve of."

"Oooh, how intriguing! I don't suppose you'd tell me more?"

I shake my head. "It's not your concern. Let's stick to our arrangement, aye? You help me, and I help you."

Arlo sighs dramatically. "What a tease. Very well."

Mayhap it's unfair to keep secrets, considering he was honest with me. Arlo may have been an ally in the past, though, but he's still an enforcer of the TTA. If he knew it was Soren I was seeing, that I'd exposed him to our world—he'd likely react as poorly as my family. If not worse. He could go to the Council and ruin everything.

Still, who else was I to ask?

As the longhouse comes into view, Arlo suddenly stops. "Hold up a moment. We need a plan."

"For what? It's supper. You grab utensils, eat, drink, and go on your way."

Arlo rolls his eyes. "Freya, give me strength... I *know* what supper is, darling. Believe it or not, I've eaten dinner before. I mean, we ought to have a plan to convince your family that we are dating."

"Can we not just show up and say so?"

"Not if you want to convince them!"

The witch has a point, I suppose. Planning has never been my strong suit. "Fine. What do you propose?"

"Well, for starters, why are we together?"

Good question... Why would I court the man my brother rejected? The answer comes to me. "I was taken with you from the moment I saw you. When Gunnar rejected you, I felt for you and asked if you'd consider being my mate."

Arlo frowns. "So, just so we are clear... you're dating me because you felt bad for me."

"Did you not hear the part where I said I was taken with you before you were rejected?"

Damn. When he puts it that way—

"How about this," Arlo adds. "You sought me out after your arsehole brother rejected me in front of your whole family. I was in a bar, feeling irritable, and you comforted me. Sparks flew."

"Why? Was there a battle?"

Arlo heaves a sigh, raking a hand through his hair. "Goddess, help me. No! We fancied each other. So I dragged you off and rode your cock until dawn."

"I prefer to submit to my lover in bed."

"Whatever! We had sex. It was hot. I used you to get back at your brother."

I scowl at him. "What? Why?"

"Because I was hurt, obviously! But over time we fell for each other. Sort of. It's still new."

It's not a bad plan, aside from the part where he uses me. "It will have to do." So long as my family buys it, then I'll be content.

As we near the front door, Arlo hesitates. "Wait. We should hold hands."

I sigh. "Must we?"

"It would be more convincing."

A good point, I suppose. I take his hand. His skin is soft and warm, lacking the calluses Soren developed from long hours of training. My wolf stirs, making my fangs sharpen. *Mate,* he whines. There's a twist in my gut.

This feels so wrong. A betrayal, no matter how necessary it may be.

"Are you all right?" Arlo asks.

I force a smile onto my face. "I have to be." I lift my fist and knock.

The door swings open, and my heart sinks.

Gunnar looks at our joined hands, then up into my face. His nostrils flare, muscles bunching in his jaw.

"E-evening, brother." I wrestle with the instinct to drop Arlo's hand and run.

Gunnar grunts, shifting his gaze to Arlo's. "Good evening."

Arlo squeezes my hand so hard it hurts. "I suppose it is."

They stare each other down. The air thickens the way it does before a thunderstorm.

"Can we help you?" I ask, my voice like the crack of a whip in the silence.

Gunnar's shoulders tense. "No. I was just leaving."

"Good," Arlo says, holding his head higher. The sour stench of his anger is unmistakable. Tugging on my hand, Arlo drags me past the threshold. He drops my hand like it's a piece of rotten meat. "Jamie! How nice to see you!" He hurries off, eager to be rid of me, no doubt.

I pause, looking back. Gunnar never skips dinner. "Gunnar—"

"No, Lyall. I won't stay. Do what you like with the witch. It matters not." But the stiff set of his shoulders and the way his fur ripples tell another story. One of a wolf full of fury, fighting to come out and take what he perceives as his. How Gunnar fights him back every day he spends away from Arlo, I haven't a clue.

I bite my tongue so I don't tell him to stay, to talk to Arlo, to understand his anger only comes from a place of hurt.

But I can't.

My heart aches as my brother marches off toward the woods. The distance widens between us, and I have to wonder if loving Soren is worth losing the love and respect of my brother.

It aches that I can't have both the love of my family and the man I love. That I must choose. It isn't fair.

But it's my only option.

A life with Soren will be worth any sacrifice.
Won't it?

Chapter 16
Soren

I'm beyond excited to see Lyall. I spent our time apart planning a date for us that I think he'll really like. Once my shift is over, I'll head straight to meet him at Bryant Park. The bell dings and I'm about to greet the customers until I see it's Anders and Jamie. I fold my arms and give them a look.

Jamie smiles sheepishly, waving. "So. The wolf is out of the bag," he says, sitting down at the bar.

"I would have appreciated a warning. 'By the way, the hot guy we set you up with is a time-traveling werewolf.'" It's dead at the bar today. The lunch shift is usually pretty slow, which is why it's my least favorite. But the lack of customers means I don't need to worry about anyone overhearing us. Before Jamie can say something, an apology by the frown on his face, I wave a hand at him. "It's fine. It all worked out. Lyall's a great guy, and I'm glad I'm learning more about my past."

Anders says, "You understand why we couldn't tell you?"

I nod as I pour him his beer. "I think so, but there's one thing I don't get. Lyall told me about what my father did to your pack. He said everyone thought I'd betrayed them. So why did you help bring us together?"

Anders takes a gulp of his beer. "I learned that we were wrong. I'd let grief and rage cloud my judgment of your character. I owe it to my brother to help make things right."

Jamie smiles at me. "It's great things are working out for you guys."

"How'd your dinner go? Lyall said he was visiting."

Anders frowns and Jamie coughs. "It was... fine," Jamie says, not convincing me for a second.

"I wish I could have been there."

Anders shakes his head. "It isn't safe."

There's an ache in my chest at the reminder. I wonder if I'll ever be able to meet Lyall's family or if we'll always have to hide our relationship.

Always. Am I really that far gone for him already?

"There's really no way you can convince the rest of your family that I didn't betray them?" It's not fair that Lyall has to keep such a big secret from his family.

"That would be risky at best and dangerous at worst," Anders says. "Wulfric has let go of a lot of the guilt he carried from that day thanks to Kieran's help. But Gunnar..." He shakes his head, brows furrowing as if just thinking of his brother pains him. "It would destroy him. He would go berserk."

"Berserk?"

Jamie clears his throat. "Wolves from an Alpha bloodline like Anders and his brothers are stronger than most regular shifters, but that power comes at a cost. They can lose control of themselves and be taken over by their wolf if they don't claim a mate."

I'm shocked Lyall didn't tell me this. "Is Lyall in danger of that happening?"

Anders shakes his head. "No. But Gunnar is. I fear if he learned that you two were seeing each other, it would push him over the edge."

"What would happen then? Could he ever be helped?"

The sigh that shudders from Anders's chest is so pained, I wish I hadn't asked. "There are two options a berserker has. The Council can strip them of their wolf. Or their Alpha can kill them."

My stomach twists painfully. "That's it?"

"Aye. So you understand why you must keep things secret, don't you?"

I do, but that doesn't mean it hurts any less, for me or Lyall.

He should be here any moment. My heart races in anticipation, as if it's been months since I've seen him. Whenever we're apart, he's all I can think about, and when we're together, I'm happier than I've been in a long time. How long will these feelings last? Will *we* last?

My worries turn the fluttering in my stomach into painful, nervous cramping. Best not to think about it.

"Soren!" Lyall waves at me as he squeezes through a pack of tourists.

I can't help but grin. I meet him halfway, holding him tight as if we haven't seen each other all week. His shoulders are tense, but as I bring him close, his body relaxes and he leans into me with a quiet exhale.

"Missed you," I tell him, squeezing him. "You okay?"

"I am now. Gods, I missed you too."

I wonder what's been troubling him, but before I can ask, Lyall grasps the nape of my neck and pulls me in for a kiss. I can't help my contented hum as the sweetness in his kiss makes my head spin. Our bodies fit together perfectly, and he kisses me with the familiarity of long-time lovers. Like we've done it a thousand times before.

When he pulls back, it's to rest his forehead against mine. "How are you?"

"After that kiss? Pretty fucking amazing. How about you?"

He chuckles, brushing his knuckles along my cheek. "Better now that you're here."

"Did something happen?"

Lyall drops his hands down to my waist, squeezing. "There's something I need to tell you."

Oh shit.

Taking my hand, Lyall guides me back to the bench and sits beside me. "Everything okay?" I can barely get the words out. Shit. This is it. He's going to break up with me. I can't even blame him, not really. He's risking so much by being with me. But it's happening much sooner than I thought it would. Fuck. This is going to devastate me.

"I feared my brothers were starting to suspect I was seeing you."

Okay, no breakup yet. I exhale slowly. "Okay…"

Lyall frowns down at his lap. "So I lied to them and said I was seeing someone else. Last night I brought him over for dinner."

My stomach churns. "And? Did they believe you?"

"Aye."

That's all? Was he worried I'd be upset? I'm just relieved we're not breaking up.

"So? That's a good thing, right?"

Lyall's jaw bunches. "Aren't you angry?"

"About?"

Lyall heaves a frustrated sigh. "I brought another man to meet my family. I pretended we were together. The whole ordeal felt wrong down to my very bones. I wanted it to be you so badly, but it wasn't."

"Did you kiss him?"

He makes a face. "No."

"Then I'm not upset. Besides, we never really talked about being exclusive." I wonder if it's too early to have that conversation with him.

"Aren't we?" He arches a brow. He makes it sound like it's a given that we're together. That makes sense considering he knows so much of our history.

"Do you... want to be?"

Lyall takes my hand and squeezes. "Of course I do. If that's what you want too."

His sincerity makes me smile. It wasn't long ago I was swearing off relationships. I've been burned so many times. There's something about Lyall that makes me want to swan dive into love with him. "I don't know." I shrug. "Kiss me again and maybe I'll make up my mind."

He leans in with a quiet laugh and does just that. When we finally come up for air, my lips tingle and there's the beginning of beard burn on the corner of my mouth, but fuck it. This sweet, gentle, patient man is worth risking my heart for. "That was pretty good. Your application for boyfriend has been accepted."

At his confused look, I chuckle. Right. I've probably used a ton of words he's not familiar with.

"That means yes, Lyall."

He grins. "Oh. Good." The relief in his voice only endears him to me more. "Just to be clear, you're truly not upset?"

"Not at you," I clarify. I can't deny that knowing someone else got to meet Lyall's family hurts, even though I understand why I can't see them.

Lyall sighs softly and nuzzles his forehead against mine, his breath warm on my lips when he says, "I wish more than anything it could have been you, love."

"I get it. Anders told me about Gunnar, how he could go berserk if he knew. Why? Did I do something to him in the past?"

Lyall shakes his head. "It wasn't you."

Realization makes me feel sick. "My father."

Lyall squeezes my forearms. "Nothing that happened that day was your fault."

A part of me wants to ask Lyall to show me what happened that day. Another part of me never wants to know. "Lyall—"

"Now, where are we going?" Lyall asks, his smile cheery but forced. Guess we're changing the subject.

"It's not far. Just stay close. It's pretty busy today." I take his hand and lead the way.

Bryant Park still has its Christmas market up, and the pathways are flooded with tourists buying overpriced food from vendors. Lyall sniffs the air constantly, taking in the surrounding sights with wonder.

"Do you know what ice skating is?"

Lyall's face lights up. "Aye. Skates are a useful way to traverse patches of ice. It can be fun as well, so long as you avoid weak spots in the ice—" His eyes widen, lips going slack in horror.

I follow his gaze, but I don't see anything unusual. "Lyall, what is it?"

He yanks me close, whispering in my ear, "You know nothing of your past, remember that. We're on a date, nothing else."

Before I can ask, Lyall plasters on a smile and waves. "Ms. Cartwright! A beautiful day, is it not?"

A woman in a black Canada Goose coat looks from Lyall to me with suspicion before she gives us a smile as equally fake as Lyall's. "Mr. Erikson, how are you?"

What the hell? Who is this lady?

"I-I am well." Lyall's hand trembles in my grip. Whoever she is, Lyall is terrified of her, and that alone makes me immediately distrustful of her.

"Who's this?" I ask Lyall, because seriously, who is this bitch and why is he so freaked out?

"Ms. Cartwright, this is Soren."

"How nice to meet you." She couldn't sound less sincere if she tried. "Mr. Erikson, how are your brothers?"

Lyall squeezes my hand so hard, I have to bite my lip so I don't grunt in pain. "They're fine."

A man, British by his accent, calls out, "Lena!" To my surprise, Lyall immediately relaxes as a blond man makes his way over, carrying a tray with two drinks. "Did you find us any seats?"

"No, they're all taken."

The man nudges her. "Want to head back to the office then?"

She sighs. "A shame. It really is a lovely day. Nice to meet you, Soren. Enjoy yourselves, and Lyall, remember what we talked about."

At those words, Lyall's shoulders stiffen. "How could I forget?"

The blond man tugs on her elbow, and they walk off together, chatting.

I round on Lyall. "What in the hell—"

He puts an arm around my shoulders and leads me farther into the park. "Not here."

My heart races as Lyall stops us by the carousel. Obnoxious carnival music plays, and children laugh and shriek as they enjoy the ride. It's noisy, but I suspect that's what Lyall wanted. "That was Helena Cartwright. She's in charge of the TTA's branch in New York."

That's the same agency Fergus mentioned. "They're connected to the Council, right?"

Lyall nods, mouth pinched in a grim line. "Aye. She's the reason I was able to travel to this timeline. Anyone wishing to travel between realms needs approval from the TTA. Unsanctioned time travel is prohibited."

"But I never got approval to travel." My stomach starts to cramp as the realization festers inside me. "Would they erase people's memories if they found out about time travel?"

Lyall sighs. "Aye, if they were ordered to by the Council."

"So... so that woman, Cartwright—she could get us in trouble."

"If she suspected we'd done something wrong, aye, but so far, she's allowed me to see you."

I swallow with some difficulty, throat painfully dry. "Under what conditions?"

Lyall averts his gaze. "That I make no attempts to remind you of your past. Or expose the secrets of the paranormal world."

"But you did both of those things!" I grip his hands, shaking them. "Lyall, if she finds out what you did, what's going to happen to you?"

To us?

When Lyall sighs, his breath warms my cold lips. "It would be considered a violation of traveler law. The Council believes you betrayed us. They think that if you were reminded of your past, you could be a threat to my pack. Your memories would be removed once again. My pack cold lose their traveling privileges."

"But that means we'd never see each other again." No, it's worse than that, I realize, remembering my encounter with Anders and Jamie this morning. "You'd never see Anders again!"

Lyall nods, closing his eyes tight as if the very thought pains him.

I drop his hands, my heart thudding somewhere up in my throat. I knew he could get in trouble with his family, but I had no idea what bigger consequences lay in store for Lyall. He'd estrange himself from his pack in the past, be separated from his twin in the present, just for seeing me.

Nothing is worth that sort of risk.

"I know what you're thinking, love, and I'm stopping you right there." Lyall takes my hands and holds them to his chest. I don't know if I'm shaking from cold or terror. "Anders knows the risks. So do I. Choosing you was not a decision I made lightly, but I've made my peace with it."

My throat thickens. "Are you sure? Lyall, I don't want to be the reason you lose your family."

But selfish as it makes me, I don't want to lose him either.

Lyall blinks fast, eyes damp. "I made my choice. I'm choosing you." Bringing my hands to his lips, he kisses them both, eyes never straying from mine.

"I don't want to lose you." The words tear at my throat, and it terrifies me how true they are. I've only just found him. The possibility of losing him and my memories again makes me weak-kneed with fear.

Lyall smiles, and though it trembles, it gives me hope. "You won't. I can be quite secretive."

I snort. "Says the guy who turned into a big-ass wolf in the middle of a hospital room."

Laughing, he brushes a kiss to my forehead. "Enough worrying, love. I believe you wanted to take me ice skating."

I'd almost forgotten. In the face of everything Lyall shared with me, having fun is the last thing on my mind right now. Instead, I'd rather drag Lyall into my apartment and keep him there where he's safe and hidden.

"Love." Lyall captures my chin in his hand. "Take me skating. Please."

I take his hand, holding on tight.

Every moment we have together feels more precious now than it did before. I don't want to waste a second with Lyall. I never want to forget him again.

But will I even have a choice?

Chapter 17

Lyall

Despite the unsettling start to our outing, the rest of our day together was pure bliss. Soren showed me his favorite parts of the city, from Central Park to the Museum of Natural History. Our day concluded with a feast of burgers and French fries.

With our bellies comfortably full, I accompany Soren to his apartment. "Today was an adventure like no other. Thank you."

He lights up when he smiles. "Think I've earned a kiss."

I sigh heavily. "If I must." We've kissed so many times today, and yet when it comes to Soren, I'll always want more.

He laughs when I tug him into my arms. When his smiling mouth takes mine, a heady rush sweeps through my body. I part our lips so our tongues can tangle, moaning into his mouth at the taste of him. He shifts his hips against mine, his stiffening cock rubbing against my hip.

"Come upstairs?" Soren offers, his voice breathy and low.

My heart swoops. "What's upstairs?"

"Me. You. Naked, if you want."

Gods, I thought he'd never ask. Kissing him, touching him—it's not enough. I need him close, all barriers between our bodies cast aside. "Lead the way."

He grabs his keys. "My granddad is probably asleep by now, but we should still be quiet."

I press myself against his back, desperate for closeness. I rock against his ass, sucking a kiss into the nape of his neck. "No promises. Will he be angry if he sees us together?"

"That's his problem," Soren says, taking my hand and leading me inside. "I couldn't care less what he thinks of you. We're together, and if he doesn't like it, too bad." His fierce defense of our relationship only makes me love him more.

Once we're inside his quiet, dimly lit apartment, Soren leads me to his bedroom. His grandfather isn't anywhere in sight, and I can detect faint snoring from the room down the hall from Soren's. "Asleep," I confirm.

"Thank fuck." Soren shoves my chest, pushing me back against the door.

He takes my mouth in a demanding kiss, teeth nipping my lips until they're hot and tingling. I open for him, and our tongues tangle until my lungs burn for air. We part, gasping, and make quick work of our clothes. Coats, sweaters, jeans, and boots pile at our feet.

Soren leans in for another kiss, but my hand on his chest stops him. "Hold a moment." My throat thickens unexpectedly. "I want to look at you."

Soren's mouth quirks. "Be my guest." He steps back until he's at arm's length but holds my hands so we're still touching.

It's been years since we were naked together. The Soren I grew up with had a body fit for battle. He's different now, his stomach soft where it was once hard, his chest and arms once thick and strong. The way he looks suits the man he is now. Familiar yet different. Once that caused me worry, but now that fear has disappeared. After all these years, we're together again.

"You're beautiful," I whisper, closing the distance between us. I wrap my arms around him and tuck my face into the curve of his neck, breathing in his scent. It's never changed, even when so much else has. Nothing could change the fact that we were meant for each other.

"I've missed you." The words are a choked confession as I squeeze him, rubbing my hands up and down his back.

He's here. He's in my arms. After all this time. I never want to lose him again.

Soren holds me tight, his lips brushing the shell of my ear. "It's weird but... so did I. For so long, something was missing from my life and I think—I think it was you."

His words warm my heart. His soul yearned for mine, even if his mind couldn't remember why.

He's still mine, my mate, in every way that counts.

When our lips collide this time, the rough desperation has mellowed into something else. Soren kisses me deeply, slowly, like we have all night, all of our lives, to do nothing else.

So much has changed as we've grown from boys to men, lovers to strangers, but we've found our way back to each other. This time I'm never letting him go. Not again.

The mattress creaks beneath us as we fall into bed, the sheets soft and cool. Soren kneels between my thighs, eyes dark as he looks me over from head to toe. From the hunger in his eyes, it feels like I'm a feast ripe for devouring.

Inch by inch, he kisses his way down my body. His lips burn like a flame against my skin, and although all we've done is kiss, my cock is so hard it aches. It's been too long. I've wanted him, needed him, with such desperation.

"Wanna suck you," Soren says, kissing my hip. "Let me?"

I bite my lip so I don't beg for just that. "Do whatever you want, love. I'm yours."

The first swipe of his tongue over my sensitive skin has me arching off the bed with a soundless groan. I grab at the sheets, bunching them in my fists. When he sucks on my crown, I see bloody stars. Gods, I thought I remembered how good his mouth felt around me. Nothing compares to having him in bed with me again.

Soren worships every inch of me, sucking me deep into the perfect heat of his throat. Every swipe of his tongue has me writhing. I try to stave off my release, but it's a fight I'm losing. He makes me feel too good, and it's been too long since I've lain with him.

"Close." I gasp out the word as my balls tighten. I don't want this to end. "Come here." Soren pulls off my cock, leaving me wet and throbbing for release. Grabbing his arms, I haul him up my body until he's resting atop me. "Want you close. Just like this."

When we kiss, I taste myself on his tongue. I buck against him, making us both groan as our cocks rub together.

"Fuck, Lyall. Do that again," Soren says, panting against my mouth.

I take his mouth hungrily, swallowing his moans and gasps as we grind against each other. The friction tips me over the edge, and his name spills from my lips. My seed smears our chests and stomachs as Soren thrusts against me, faster and faster, until he's muffling his shout against my neck, spilling hot and wet between us.

We'll smell like each other for hours, even after we've washed ourselves clean.

We catch our breath in the quiet. Our hearts settle and our breathing slows, but Soren never lets go of me. I could lie here in his arms until Ragnarok. When Soren lifts his head at last and our eyes meet, I chuckle at the look of awe on his face. "Enjoy yourself?"

"Nah. No way. I've had better," Soren says, his chest bucking against mine when he laughs.

I snort, giving his ass a slap. "The seed painted on my stomach tells a very different story."

"Shit. That's gonna suck to clean off if it dries. Stay here. I'll get a towel." Soren plants a hearty kiss on my collarbone, then swings his legs out of bed.

I stretch out with a groan, every limb loose and tingling. Gods, it's been an age since I felt so good, so at peace.

When Soren returns, he brings a bottle of water and a cloth. Once we're as clean as we can get, we lie close and take turns sipping from the bottle. Soren rests his cheek on my shoulder. "Today was great."

I nuzzle my nose into his hair. "Aye, it was. Do you mind if I stay here for the night? I don't wish to leave you anytime soon."

He shrugs. "I guess." When I catch his eye, he grins. "Was hoping you'd ask."

When our lips meet, it's tender and slow. I wind my arms around his waist and close my eyes. The gentle touch of his lips and the warmth of his body against mine guide me toward sleep.

"I love you," I whisper. Soren's breath catches. No doubt to him, it's too soon to hear. For me, it feels as natural as breathing. "Does that scare you?" I open my eyes and find him wide-eyed and blinking fast.

"No. Yes. A lot," he admits.

"Why?" I brush sweat-damp hair from his forehead.

Soren looks away. "'Cause every time someone's told me that, they've left. So I've learned not to trust it."

My chest tightens. "Trust me." I take his hand and guide his trembling fingers to my lips. "There is nowhere in this world I would rather be than at your side."

Soren blinks fast, his heart racing in my ears. "I want to believe that. I just... I don't know how."

"You don't have to do anything, Soren. I'll prove it to you by showing up every day. Until there isn't a doubt in your mind that there's no one else in this world for me but you."

"You really mean that? But how could you know for sure?"

I don't know how to tell him that the Norns themselves brought us together. "We're... destined for each other, Soren."

He furrows his brow. "I don't believe in soulmates."

"Understandable. You felt the same way once. It wasn't until you shifted and caught my scent that you understood what we were to each other."

"I don't get it."

"You realized that we were mates. My people call bonds like ours fated. We are each other's perfect match, Soren.

Made for each other. It's why none of your relationships have lasted."

"Because they weren't you..." Soren whispers.

I don't like how deeply he's frowning. "We should rest. You can ask me all your questions in the morning."

"No you don't." Before I can roll onto my side, Soren straddles me and sits on my thighs. "You can't just drop some big bombshell about soulmates and expect me to just go to bed."

I sigh, wincing when he thunks his forehead against mine. "Very well. What do you want to know?"

Me and my big mouth...

The pair of us stayed up late into the night, discussing fated mates, destiny, and other such philosophical topics that made my head hurt. Still, Soren went to sleep more relaxed than when the discussion started, so I must have done something right.

In the morning my growling stomach wakes me. If we were in my time, I'd spring out of bed, shift, and go hunting to feed my mate. I doubt the neighborhood would appreciate my hunting the local pigeon population, however.

Soren stirs beside me, yawning big and wide. Seeing him so soft and vulnerable fills me with a protective urge I haven't felt in years. I nestle closer and pull him into my arms. He sighs, nuzzling into my chest. "Morning, you."

I chuckle and plant a kiss in his mussed hair. "Morning. Sleep well?"

He hums a yes. "Wonder why..." His hands slide down my shoulders and palm my ass. A different kind of hunger awakens as I shift my hips against his. Soren moans softly, teeth pinching my nipple and pulling lightly. Desire shivers down my spine. Licking my palm, I take us both in hand and stroke.

"Fuck," Soren whispers, rocking his hips into my fist. His hardening cock grinds against mine, making my eyes roll back. All thoughts of food fly out of my head as I devote all my attention to pleasuring Soren, squeezing us from root to tip, thrusting hard against him.

When we kiss, it's sloppy with teeth and tongue, only lasting seconds before Soren tips back his head, a groan punching from his chest. His seed spills over my fist and cock, and I use it to stroke us faster. Pleasure tightens my balls and makes my toes curl as I thrust faster against his cock.

Soren kisses me hard just as my release slams into me, muffling what would have been a shout that could have woken the whole building, I'm sure. His lips never leave mine as I shudder through the sweet bliss of my release.

When we finally part, we're both gasping, lips swollen and hot.

My hand is drenched in our seed, and I don't hesitate to rub it into my skin. Soren frowns at me. "Uh. What are you doing?"

"Making sure I smell like you. I don't want to forget last night, or this morning."

Soren chuckles. "You know, we're doing this again, right?"

"Are we?" It pleases me beyond measure to hear him say that.

"Many, many times if I have my way," Soren says, voice low and gravelly. "I'd stay in bed all day with you if I could." Rolling over, he fumbles around for his phone and turns it on. His eyes widen. "Oh shit."

My shoulders stiffen. "What is it?"

"I slept in!" He practically rolls out of bed. "Gotta shower, eat, and go to work."

Throwing off the blankets, I follow him. "I'll join you."

Soren grabs a couple of towels from the closet and wraps one around his waist before handing the other to me. He steps out into the living room and freezes, making me walk into him.

"Hey, Gramps."

My heart drops into my stomach. Fergus sits at the table, a plate of sandwiches in front of him. They smell like ham and cheese and gods, I am *starving*—no, focus, Lyall!

"Good morning. Sleep well?" Fergus's voice is light, casual even, but there's no way he can't smell the sweat and sex on our bodies. And, oh gods, there's the mess all over my stomach and chest.

Kill me now.

"I, uh—we didn't—we were just—"

Soren steps on my toe, making me bite back a curse. "Going to shower and head to work. So we'll just be leaving now."

"Grab a sandwich before you both leave, please. Ham and Swiss, grilled to perfection if I say so myself."

"My favorite," Soren says, laughing nervously. He tugs on my hand. "We'll see you in a sec."

I can't read Fergus's expression. He seems calm and doesn't smell angry, but he could have a shield in place that dampens his scent.

"Oh my god," Soren groans, hiding his face in his hands the second we're behind the bathroom door. "We might as well have just fucked in front of him. Why not!"

"He's an old man, Soren. I'm certain he's no monk."

Soren snorts. "My granddad's had sex. I didn't need to know that. Thanks. That mental image really helps."

I clap his shoulder. "Happy to help!"

From his exaggerated sigh, I don't think he was being serious.

We shower, towel ourselves off, and then throw on our clothes. Soren's shirt is inside out, his cheeks flushed as he finger-combs his hair into something orderly.

"Relax." I kiss his neck.

Soren exhales slowly. "I'm so relaxed."

I take his hand and together we go to join Fergus for breakfast. He smiles and hands us each a plate. I take a big bite to avoid talking, groaning as the sweet flavor of pork and melted cheese explodes on my tongue.

I clear my plate far too quickly, not giving myself any time to decide what I should say. I settle on what feels easiest. "Thank you for the food."

"Of course. If I'd known we were having a guest, I'd have prepared more."

Soren clears his throat. "Well, Lyall's going to be here a lot from now on."

I look down at my plate to hide my massive smile. I love how certain he sounds, the subtle challenge in his words. Soren wants me in his life. He's choosing me.

"I see." Fergus smiles, though it seems fake to my eyes. "Then I'll have to make more sandwiches next time."

"Peanut bubber and jelly?" I ask hopefully.

Soren snorts beside me.

"As much peanut *butter* and jelly sandwiches as you like."

I like the sound of that.

Soren takes away our plates. "Lyall, I'm gonna use the bathroom. Then we're going."

"Sure."

Soren leaves, and I find myself alone with Fergus. He studies me in silence, like I'm a fascinating insect. One he'd like to crush, or one he'd leave alone? I find a thread in the tablecloth to pull on. Why must words always fail me when I need them?

"What are your intentions with my grandson, wolf?"

I tense, not liking the suspicion lacing his every word. Looking up, I refuse to shy away from his narrowed gaze. I'm not going anywhere. Soren's grandfather needs to accept that. "The only intentions I have are to make him feel happy and loved."

"In this timeline, or yours?"

I'd give anything for Soren to be able to meet my family, but I know how that would end. "Here. He has a life in this time. Friends and family and a job. I'm not taking him away from that."

Fergus tilts his head. "You would choose a life here, in this time?"

"I will choose *him*. I will *always* choose him. In the past, the present, the future, in any way he will have me."

We were made for each other. In every lifetime, I would find Soren and fall in love with him. My love for him has no limits, no sense of time or distance. It's as much a part of me as the heart that beats in my chest.

"I'm never letting him go again, so you'd best get used to seeing me around."

"Again?" Fergus repeats, eyes narrowing.

I can't fight my wince. Shit. I didn't mean to say that.

Fergus leans forward, arms braced on the table. "What happened to Soren, wolf? Did you hurt him?"

My lips curl. "I would cut off my hand before I laid a finger on him in anger."

"Then what happened? Why is he here?"

"Don't you know?"

"I was assigned to care for him. The *why* of it was confidential, even to me. I suppose the Council worried that if I knew his past life, I would want to tell him. So they withheld that information."

I fold my arms across my chest. "It isn't your business. All you need to know is that the past will never repeat itself."

"Does Soren know?"

"About what?" I snap.

"That you let him go."

I bite my tongue. Anger heats my face. I despise the accusatory tone in his voice. "Not yet."

"Why not?"

I take a deep breath. "I'm getting there."

"He deserves to know the truth, wolf. Don't keep it from him."

I laugh, the sound coarse as sand in my throat. "You're in no position to lecture me on secrets."

He arches a brow. "I could say the same for you about keeping secrets from him."

"I will tell him when he's ready. It's been hard enough learning what became of his family. I don't want to overwhelm him."

I hate the bitter taste in my mouth. It tastes a lot like lies.

The truth is that I have no idea how Soren will react when he finds out that I chose to let him go. Even if Past Soren had insisted that I stay with my family, it's always felt like an excuse I used to avoid fighting for us like I should have. The Soren I knew had learned the agony of losing his own family, and he hadn't wished that upon me. The Soren I know now has known abandonment and heartache. I've only just convinced him I would never hurt him like the others.

When he finds out why we were separated, will he understand? Or will it only hurt him more?

"Lyall, ready to go?" Soren closes the bathroom door behind him. His face has a pleasant shine to it, and he's trimmed his stubble a hair shorter.

"Aye, love." I force myself to smile as I rise to meet him. He kisses me, tasting of crisp, cool mint. Soren laces our fingers together and lifts our hands in a wave.

"See you later, Gramps."

"Have a good day. Both of you." Fergus smiles, but his gaze never strays from mine.

He's watching, waiting for me to ruin everything.

Chapter 18
Soren

There's still so much I don't know about the day I was exiled to the future. I haven't had the courage to ask Lyall to show me. It was hard enough just hearing about it. Seeing it would be devastating. I feel like we have to, though. It's something we need to move past if we want to have a future together.

By the time my shift is done, I've made up my mind to ask Lyall more about what happened that day. We're meeting tomorrow. Lyall really enjoyed going ice skating, so I want to take him again. When I get upstairs to my apartment, I'm surprised to find Fergus still up. He's relaxing on the sofa, a book in hand. He looks up, glasses crooked on his nose, and smiles.

"Have a good shift?" he asks.

I take off my shoes and put them in the cubby. "Sure. No drama. You?"

He nods, setting his book aside. "Nothing to report. I had a talk with that boy of yours this morning."

A sigh puffs out of my chest. "You're being too hard on him. Lyall's a great guy."

Fergus folds his arms. "I'd believe that if you hadn't shown up in this timeline alone and heartbroken."

"That's not Lyall's fault." It's a struggle to keep my voice even. He's judging Lyall before he's even gotten a chance to know him. "Look, Gramps, I really like him. I know I've made shitty choices in the past, but that's because they weren't *him*. He's..." Shit, what was the word Lyall used?

Fergus sits up with an unreadable expression on his face. "He's your fated mate."

I snap my fingers. "Yes! That's the word."

He sighs, shoulders slumping. "What did he tell you of fate?"

"I didn't really understand most of it. I think the gist is that we were meant to meet and be together forever? Or something like that." Since it looks like we'll be here a while, I pull out a chair from the table and sit down opposite the sofa. "Why, what do you know about fated mates?"

"Wolves and witches can have fated mates. Through worship to our respective deities, we're given great gifts. The gift of change, the gift of magic, and another great gift: the ability to know when we've found our one great love."

"That's pretty convenient. You never have to worry if things will work out." I wish I'd found Lyall sooner. I could have saved myself a lot of heartache.

Fergus hums his agreement, plucking his glasses off his nose. "It's one thing to claim you love someone. It's another to fight to make things work." When he looks at me, his brow is lined with concern. "I'm not convinced Lyall fought for you, Soren."

My spine stiffens. "How do you—"

"Because he let you go. He said so himself."

My throat tightens with a sudden rush of panic, remembering all the men from my past who told me they loved me, only to leave me. I shake my head. "I don't know every detail about that day. I know that Lyall's father was killed, his family village destroyed. The pack turned against me. They chose to exile me."

"So why didn't Lyall follow you into exile?"

"Because—"

Why *had* he let me go? True, he'd searched for me all these years, but if he'd only gone with me, he could have saved himself that pain.

"I don't know," I admit, voice cracking.

"The Norns can only do so much," Fergus says softly. "They guide our paths, but ultimately we are the ones in control of our destiny, Soren. You can still walk away. Fated mates or not, you aren't bound to him."

I'm shaking my head before he's finished speaking. "No."

"You barely know him—"

"I know enough!" I snap. "I know he's the kindest, sweetest person I've ever met. I know he's patient and devoted and loyal. I know that all my life, something has been missing, and I couldn't find it again until I found him. And now that I have, I'm not letting him go."

"Soren, there's nothing stopping him from letting you go again."

Heart pounding, I push to my feet and slam my chair back under the table. "I'm an adult, Fergus. If he breaks my heart, so be it. I'd rather be heartbroken from loving him than go another damn day without knowing him."

And, like an adult, I storm into my bedroom and slam the door. Blowing out a frustrated breath, I undress, and crawl into bed. There's a message waiting for me in my inbox.

I smile at the photo of a white dove perched on a fire escape railing.

He's left a voice message, and my heart skips when I press the play button and his low, deep voice pours from my speakers.

"I asked my brother what this bird was. He said it is called a dove. Like a pigeon but with different colors. Jamie says they mate for life. I also mate for life. I have much in common with this bird."

A laugh bubbles out of my chest, and damn it, I wish he was here so I could kiss him and tell him I—

Whoa, slow down a little. Remember what happened all the other times you thought you loved a guy?

My grandfather's doubts are getting into my head. I don't want to be mistrustful or afraid, not of Lyall. Rather than text back, I call him. He answers halfway through the first ring.

"Soren? Are you well?"

The concern in his voice makes me smile. "I'm fine. Just missed you."

He chuckles, and I don't know when that became my favorite sound in the world. All I know is that I want to hear it all the time, to be the cause of it. "Missed you too," he says.

"I wanna go ice skating with you again," I say.

"That was fun. My ass is still sore where I took that fall, though."

"Mine too."

When he laughs, I can't help joining in.

I need to know what happened that day.

My humor fades, my smile falling from my face. "Lyall?"

"Aye, love?"

I swallow hard, hoping I won't regret this. "Can you show me what happened that day?"

There's an audible hitch in his breathing, and for a long moment, he's quiet.

"Never mind, you don't have to. I just—" How do I ask why he didn't go with me?

"You deserve to know," Lyall says, voice heavy and reluctant.

"If it's going to hurt you, I don't want to."

"Time has stolen much of the pain. What hurts the most is being the only one who knows the truth of that day and not being able to tell my brothers."

His confession makes my chest hurt. "Then show me the truth, Lyall. Tomorrow."

"I will," he vows. "But, Soren..."

I wet my lips, heart skipping. "Yeah?"

"No matter what you see... just remember that I'll always come back for you."

I believe him. I do.

I want to swan dive into love with this man and trust he'll catch me. I'm sick of being scared. No matter what happens tomorrow, I'm not letting him go. A part of me knows he's it. The one I've been waiting for.

All I need to do is let down my walls, and let Lyall in.

Lyall's worried.

I can see it in the stiff set of his shoulders and the furrow in his brow that doesn't disappear even when he smiles at me. It's a ghost of his usual sunny smile, barely touching his eyes.

"Hey," I say, reaching out to him.

He opens his arms and pulls me in, holding me to his chest for several long seconds. I run my hands up and down his strong back. His shoulders loosen when he sighs into the crook of my neck.

"We don't have to do this," I tell him. "You could stay. There's no reason for you to have to witness it again."

Lyall shakes his head. He pulls back and squeezes my shoulders, giving me a smile that softens the worry wrinkling his forehead. "I'll be there, love. Just... can we do something fun first?"

I'm more than up for that. "Sure." There's a vendor selling ice cream nearby. "Ever had ice cream before?" I ask, taking his hand and leading him to the cart.

He gives me a bewildered look. "Ice and cream? How does that work?"

"It's frozen cream and sugar, basically."

"Sounds delicious," Lyall says, and so it's decided.

I buy us each an ice cream, and we find ourselves a bench to sit on. What little snow we had over the weekend melted. It's cold outside, but when Lyall sits beside me and loops an arm over my shoulders, I warm up inside and out. Lyall tears open his ice cream sandwich, gives it a sniff, and takes a bite. I wince just imagining how cold his teeth must be.

Lyall moans his approval and goes in for another bite. "This is brilliant! Frozen cream and... what's this? A cookie?"

His enthusiasm for the most mundane things never fails to make me laugh. "I'm kind of surprised you don't have ice cream in your time. Obviously you don't have refrigerators but it must get pretty cold where you're from."

"It does, aye."

"So, what if you made some cream, put it in a bucket, and I don't know, left it on a glacier or something?"

Lyall's face lights up. "Oh, I get it now! It would freeze, and then I could bring it back to my pack."

I can't help leaning in to kiss him. He tastes like chocolate, so sweet and addictive it's hard to pull away. Lyall suddenly breaks the kiss and steals a big bite of my ice cream.

"Hey!"

Lyall swallows the chunk of ice cream he bit off, and his face twists into one of agony as he grabs his head in his hands. "Cold. By the gods, it's so cold!"

I bark a laugh. "That's what you get!"

"Soren... I think I'm dying..." Lyall groans and rubs his forehead.

I huff and give his shoulder a pat. "You'll be fine."

Once Lyall's recovered from his brain freeze, he decides he's had enough ice cream for the day. When we board the boat, I'm munching on both his and mine while Lyall takes up the oars. That troubled look comes back on his face.

Reaching out, I squeeze his knee. "I'm right here."

The light from the portal whites out Lyall's face, and when it fades, we're rowing toward a familiar island. Lyall gets out, water sloshing around his ankles, and heaves the boat the rest of the way to shore.

Farther down the beach, a crowd has gathered before a pyre. I freeze when I realize that the man resting on top of the pyre is Lyall's *father*. It's Erik. He's dead. I turn to check on Lyall and find his face blank. "This is the day it all ended." There's no emotion in his voice, and it unsettles me.

When a younger version of Lyall steps from the crowd, my breath catches. His eyes are red-rimmed, face grimy with dirt. His lip quivers as he draws a bow taut, flame rising from the arrowhead, and releases it. The pyre goes up in flames, consuming the body.

I look away, stomach churning. "Oh god, Lyall…"

Present Lyall doesn't speak as he turns away from the funeral to face the water.

Before I can reach out to him, a voice catches my attention. "I swear to you all, I will help lead our pack out of this darkness." It's Wulfric. His voice is small, stuck somewhere between a boy's and a man's. God, he looks so young. They all do. Too young for such a terrible tragedy. "We will heal and come back from this terrible loss. I will honor Father's memory and be the Alpha you all deserve."

Gunnar and Lyall go to their brother and comfort him. Anders doesn't. He glares at Wulfric like his brother is to blame for all of this. I search the crowd of grief-stricken faces but don't find my own among them.

"My... my father did this?" My voice comes out as a croak.

"Aye," Lyall says flatly.

I swallow hard, guilt thickening my throat. "Where am I?"

"By this point, you'd been imprisoned. The whole village thought you'd conspired with your father." Lyall's hands clench. "All those years you spent among us, and they turned on you in their desperation for someone to blame." He shakes his head, muscles ticking in his jaw. "Fools, all of them. My brothers too." He turns and marches back toward where the village is.

My heart aches at hearing him so angry. I almost don't want to follow him, dreading what happens next, but he went through it alone and I'm not going to let that happen again. When Past Lyall leaves the funeral and walks the path to town, I follow. Shoulders slumped, he drags his feet through the street, sniffling softly. I wish I could reach out and touch him to let him know he's not alone.

Once Past Lyall arrives at the longhouse, he approaches a cellar door along the side of the house. My stomach churns because I have a feeling I know what's down there.

Present Lyall reclines against a wall nearby. He barely acknowledges me when I come up beside him. Lyall's past self heads down into the basement. Present Lyall grabs my arm before I can go after him. "Are you sure you want to see? It's still upsetting to me, even after all this time."

I make myself nod. "I have to know." Heart thudding, I follow Past Lyall down into the basement.

Chapter 19

Lyall

Will Soren hate me when he knows I let my family chain him up? When he finds out I didn't fight for him, craven that I am, he'll never want anything to do with me. I revisited this memory many times, searching for some way to change things, and it never got easier.

It's strange to witness the worst day of my life from outside of my own body. I'm an observer. I can't feel the same gut-wrenching grief I felt back then. It's as if all these terrible things happened to someone else, not to me. My own voice comes from the basement, broken with grief at seeing his mate chained to a damn wall like an animal.

I should have broken his chains. I should have run away with him.

Why didn't I just go with him?

"Lyall, you're bleeding!"

I jump when Soren snatches my fist and forces my fingers to uncurl. They'd shifted to claws, puncturing my palm. In seconds, the wounds close.

"You saw."

Soren pulls some napkins out of his pocket and wipes away the blood. "I did," he says.

Is that accusation in his voice? Is he already angry with me?

Good. I deserve his hatred.

"Hey." He cups my cheek. "Should we go back?"

I move out of his touch. It's too tender, and I don't deserve it. "You should see the rest." If we're to have any future together, he needs to know the truth.

Soren startles when my past self bursts from the cellar and marches toward the front door. He makes a ruckus as he stomps through the house until he arrives at Wulfric's room. Soren hurries after him.

By the time I've made my way into the room, the fight has already started. Soren puts a hand over his mouth, eyes damp as my brother and I tear into each other. I shouldn't have been so cruel to Wulfric. Had I ever apologized for those words I'd hurled at him?

"Don't make me do this without you, Lyall. Please." Wulfric's broken voice yanks me from my thoughts. We're kneeling on the floor, bloody and bruised, clutching each other. "I lost Father. Gunnar w-won't even speak to us. Anders blames me for everything. I can't... I c-can't lose you, too. Don't leave me alone. *Please.*"

"Damn it, just say no!" The roar tears from my throat before I can stop it. "Tell him no! Tell him you won't stay!"

None of these ghosts from the past acknowledges me. My past self will choose his family over the man he loves and will condemn himself to years of loneliness and misery.

All he had to do—all *I* had to do—was follow Soren into exile.

I should have chosen Soren. I should have.

But my family needed me. They *needed* me.

I can't look at Soren. All I want is to sink into the floor and rest within the earth, like all those who died on this day. He must hate me. How could he not? I hate myself for being too weak to fight for him. Gods, he must be so angry with me.

"Lyall." Soren's voice cracks. He sounds as close to breaking as I feel.

I'm still a coward, even now. I can't face his judgment. "I cannot bear another moment." The words scrape my throat on the way out. "If you want to talk, you can find me on the beach."

I walk out before I can see the disappointment or betrayal surely in his eyes.

Gulls cry as they swoop down over the ocean, tearing fish from the gray waves. One poor bird has been trying to catch a fish and just when he finally catches one, the fish slips from between his jaws and falls back into the sea. I pity him, to have gotten what he wanted only to lose it.

Shoes clack over stones behind me. I close my eyes tight and try to brace my heart for what's coming.

"Lyall? Can we talk?"

My spine stiffens. Gods, here it comes. "Aye." I have to drag the word from my throat when I want nothing more than to run.

"Can you look at me?"

And see the hurt that my decisions have caused him? No.

Soren sighs. The warmth of his body seeps into my side when he joins me, shoulder to shoulder and hip to hip. If he were angry, would he sit so close? Finally, I face him. The anger I expected to see in his eyes isn't there. Instead, they're red and damp.

"I'm sorry." Soren's face becomes a blur through my tears.

He says, "What for?"

What for? He saw the choices I made. Surely he knows I did not choose him.

"You didn't see our talk in the basement after my fight with Wulfric?"

"No, I did," he says.

Then why isn't he angry with me?

"Soren, I let my family exile you. I chose to stay behind. Did you not see that?"

"I did!" he snaps. "What I don't get is why I'm supposed to be angry with you."

He's lying to spare my feelings; he must be. "I abandoned you! I should have followed you into exile. By the gods! You were my mate, and I let you go!"

Soren's lips part on a quiet inhale. "Sweetheart, you'd just lost your father. Your brother was still a child, and he was forced to become an Alpha before he was ready. He begged you not to leave him."

"I shouldn't have—"

Soren leans in, his hands warm as he cradles my face between his palms. "They needed their big brother. I decided to take the blame so your pack could stay together and if I had that choice now, I'd make it again."

I can't speak as my throat tightens and my eyes burn. How can he be so understanding?

Soren's lips tremble when he smiles. "You promised you'd find me. You honored your duty to your family but you never gave up on me. How could I ever be angry with you for that? You found me, Lyall. After all these years, *you found me*."

A laugh shudders from my chest. I hide my face against his palm as a tear spills free. Pressing a kiss into his hand, I say, "I always will."

Soren pulls me into the warmth of his body, and when his lips find mine, he tastes like the ocean. Even after so much time and the loss of his memories, the man he was has never faded. His heart is still the kind, noble one I fell in love with.

Stones press into my back, but I barely feel them when Soren's fingers curl in my hair and we kiss until we're breathless. I pour my devotion, love, and joy into the kiss and pray Soren can feel everything I can't fit into words.

When we finally part, I hold him for several long seconds, unable to let go. He runs his hands up and down my back, pressing fleeting kisses into the crook of my neck as the sun sinks into the ocean.

"What are we going to do?" Soren asks sometime later as we lie on the shore together.

"About?"

"Your family." He tightens his grip on my hand. "The Council. How can we convince them I didn't betray the pack? Could we show them this moment in the past?"

"I wish we could. The Council would not approve of what we're doing here, Soren. If they found out I've been traveling to the past without their approval, I could get in trouble, and so could my pack."

Soren sighs beside me. "So we have to hide for the rest of our lives?"

"The Council made it clear I was not to remind you of your past or expose you to the paranormal world. They made it clear I could have a relationship with you, so long as their terms were met."

"But you've violated all of their terms," Soren says heavily.

"On top of that, my family would never approve of us. So I can't count on their support, either."

Soren's face falls. "So we stay a secret forever. Got it."

It's not what I want either. I can't put my pack in danger. Anders has only just reconciled with our family. It would not be fair for him to be separated from them. "Would you still want to be together, even if we had to keep it a secret?"

Soren rolls onto his side to face me. He guides my hand to his mouth and kisses the back of my hand. "It's not ideal. But you're worth it, Lyall. I don't want anyone to get in trouble because of us. So how do we make this work?"

I heave a sigh. "I don't know. The TTA has a large presence in New York, and I fear Helena Cartwright does not trust me, rightfully, when it comes to keeping secrets from you. So staying in the present with you will be tricky, and bringing you into the past with me is also not an option..." A thought comes to me, making my heart skip. "What if we were to go somewhere the TTA doesn't have a headquarters? Somewhere no one knew us?"

He looks as surprised as I am. I can't believe I'm suggesting such a thing. Being away from my pack would break my heart, but it might be the safest thing.

Soren frowns. "Is there such a place?"

"I don't know, but I know someone who might." If anyone would know, it's Arlo.

"It's a lot to ask of you, Soren, I know. You have a job in the present, friends, your grandfather. I would travel to the future to live with you. You'd have to help me find a job and learn the ways of your time. You would not be the only one making such a big change. We would be in the same boat, aye?"

Gods, it's too much to ask of him. I've overstepped.

"I'll do it," Soren says, and my heart damn near stops. "I'll go away with you, Lyall."

How can he say yes so easily? Has he not considered all that he'd be leaving behind?

"Are you sure? You would not miss your life in the future?"

Soren worries his bottom lip. "Of course I would. Leaving would be hard. But losing you would be harder."

Knowing how deeply he's come to care for me warms me to the depths of my soul. "Soren—"

He leans in for a brief but hard kiss, silencing all my feeble protests. "What about you?" he asks when we part. "Won't it be hard for you, being away from your family?"

I think of Anders when we were pups, crying because he'd scraped his knee. We were young and hadn't yet learned to shift. I'd taken his hand and led him back to the village and had never let go until his cut had been bandaged by our aunt. Holding baby Gunnar for the first time, overcome with an emotion too strong for my young mind to understand. Little Wulfric coming into a world our mother lost her life bringing him into, wailing for our mother's milk and comfort. I'd held him tight as tears fell down my cheeks and whispered, "I'm here. I'm going to take care of you, little Wulf."

Haven't I given enough? Sacrificed enough? Is it finally my turn to allow myself to be happy?

"Lyall?"

My vision is blurred when I open my eyes. Soren's here, his hand warm on my cheek, his eyes full of worry. Blinking away the tears, I kiss the corner of his mouth, mapping a trail of kisses up his jaw to the shell of his ear. "I did my duty to my family. They no longer need me, not as they once did. I will miss them." My throat starts to ache as I think of Wulfric and Kieran, Gunnar, Aunt Helga, Anders and his family… "Greatly. But I surrendered a part of my soul once, and I'll not do it again. Wherever you go, so do I."

Framing my face in his hands, Soren turns my head enough to claim my lips in a kiss that leaves me breathless with how desperately I want him.

I will never let us be separated again. I'm choosing Soren this time, for the rest of our lives.

The desire in Soren's scent is enough to drive me mad. I can barely keep my hands on the oars, running them up his side, curling my fingers in his hair, rubbing his hard cock through his jeans. It's a miracle we get back to the present without wrecking the boat.

When we return to Soren's timeline, he takes my hand and pulls me close. He nips at my earlobe, breath hot on my skin when he says, "There's a hotel nearby. Want to stay the night?"

"Why not go to your home, though?"

"Because I don't want anyone but me to hear you screaming my name all night."

I don't think I've agreed to anything faster in my life. This hotel Soren spoke of isn't far at all, but he does stop briefly to buy some supplies for our night together.

It's not long before we've made it to our room. There are stunning views of the river from our windows, but I'm far more interested in the large bed. Soren tosses the bag of supplies on it and then takes my hand in his. It's only a few feet to the bed, but in that time, we manage to get out of our clothes. The sheets are as soft as clouds look, puffing up around me when Soren pushes me onto the mattress.

I spread my legs wider to accommodate him when he drapes himself over my body. "Fuck, Lyall. It hurts to look at you."

I frown. "What? Why?"

Soren's eyes widen, then he laughs, pressing a kiss to my forehead. "Sorry. Not literally. I just meant—ugh. You're hot. Okay? Really, really hot."

"I feel quite cool, actually."

Soren doubles over with a snort, laughing into the crook of my neck. "I can't with you."

"Enough talk." I roll my hips against his waist, breath hitching as our cocks grind together. "Gods. Soren. I need you."

He claims my mouth, teasing the seam of my lips with his tongue. I part for him, groaning past his lips when his tongue teases mine. As we kiss, Soren grinds relentlessly against my cock until I'm reduced to whimpers and gasps. I need this man with an urgency that makes my very bones ache.

"Tell me what you need, sweetheart," Soren rasps. He kisses his way down my chest, stopping to scrape his teeth over my nipple. I thrust up against him, fingers bunching the sheets.

"Need you inside me." It's been so long since we were joined so intimately. I can't wait much longer.

Soren's lips form a smile against my skin. "Whatever you need." Reaching down, he takes my cock and strokes. His touch is slick and perfect, and I can't stop myself from bucking into the tight sheath of his fist.

Hot lips trail kisses and love bites down my skin. Soren takes me into his hot, wet mouth and sucks from root to tip. I can't stop the cry that tears from my throat, grabbing his hair to urge him on. "Gods, love, don't torture me like this!" His mouth feels incredible, but it's his cock I want more than anything.

Soren chuckles around me. There's a click followed by a spurting sound, and then slick fingers rub circles over my hole. My breath hitches in anticipation, my hips rocking back against his fingers of their own volition.

A thick finger slips inside, making me gasp at the sensation. When Soren adds another finger and curls them inside me, sucking hard on my cock at the same time, it takes everything I have not to spill down his throat. As amazing as he's making me feel, what makes it all the better is knowing he's the one I'm sharing our bed with.

Soren's fingers slide in and out, stretching me open. He pulls off my cock with a gasp. Before I can growl my disappointment, his tongue is inside me, and I can do nothing except moan his name. Gods, he's too good to me. He was always a generous lover. That hasn't changed, not even now.

"Soren. Love, you're going to drive me mad."

He flattens his tongue and licks from my hole to my balls, sucking on one. "Ready for me?"

I groan, thrusting against his fingers so they slide in even deeper. "Been ready, love. For so, so long."

Soren's face twists into something bittersweet. "Fuck. Me too."

Sitting up, he grabs the backs of my knees and pushes them up toward my chest. "Hold yourself open for me, sweetheart." I do as he says, holding my knees in place. Soren bites his lip as he pumps his hand up and down his shaft until he's slick. He sinks inside me slowly. The stretch and burn makes me hiss in discomfort that fades slowly into pleasure as my body adjusts.

Soren moves slowly, eyes heavy-lidded, lip between his teeth. "You feel so fucking good, sweetheart."

My legs wrap around his waist, bringing him closer, deeper. I feel my way across the sheets until I've found his hand, grabbing hold and squeezing tight. Our foreheads touch. Soren's breath gusts against my mouth in shuddery gasps, his skin feverishly hot and slick with sweat. He goes slow at first, likely afraid of causing me pain, but I roll my hips to take him in deeper, faster.

The memories of all those agonizing years we spent apart will never fade, but as Soren presses kisses into the nape of my neck and his hand grips mine, they hurt less and less. I throw my arm around his shoulders, clutching him to me. I never want to lose him, not again. Soren took my heart with him when he left, and now that I'm finally whole again, I never want to go another day without him.

When I come, it's with a cry of his name.

"I'm right here," Soren says against my neck. "Right here, Lyall. I've got you, sweetheart." He shudders in my arms, gasping through his release. There isn't a part of me that won't smell like him, like us. I despise knowing I'll have to shower thoroughly later so no one in my time can scent him. Scent fades, but my memories won't. Soren is here in my arms, his cock softening inside me, his body warm as sunshine in my arms.

I will never go another day without his light, even if it means leaving the life I know behind for another.

Chapter 20
Soren

"This is delicious," Lyall says through a mouthful of hamburger. Neither of us had wanted to leave the bed, so I'd ordered room service.

"Don't let the fries get cold." I pick one up and hold it out to him, grinning when he plucks it from between my fingers with his teeth. I could watch Lyall eat and never get bored with his reactions. So much of this time is new and exciting to him, even things as mundane as burgers and fries.

"That reminds me, I'll need to teach my brothers how to make these fries," Lyall says.

I take a bite of my fried chicken sandwich. "They'll love them."

Lyall doesn't reply. He lowers his burger back into the take-out carton, a frown erasing the excitement on his face. I don't need to ask what's wrong. I know, and it makes my heart hurt for him.

"Lyall... we don't have to do this. We can try and keep our relationship a secret."

He shakes his head. "No. I can't continue going behind my brothers' backs, watching them be happy with their mates while I'm denied that same happiness." His jaw tightens, his eyes going glassy. "I will miss them."

I wipe my hands on my napkin and then reach over to pull him against my shoulder. He settles with a heavy sigh, his beard scratching my skin when he kisses the crook of my neck. "I'm sorry, sweetheart. I wish things could be different." It's not fair that he has to choose between me and his family. He's given enough already.

Lyall doesn't reply, but he takes my hand and laces our fingers together.

"If we're going to leave together, we need a plan," I say, feeling Lyall nod his agreement. "We've got to decide where we're going, and moving out will take a while. I've got to give my manager my two weeks' notice. Say goodbye to Frank and Tom. And Fergus..." My throat thickens, making it hard to swallow. "Fergus will be gutted."

Lyall squeezes my hand, offering his support. "Will he try to stop you?"

I snort. "No. He'll be a mother hen about it, for sure. Don't worry. I'll tell him how happy you make me and he'll come around. That's all he really wants, for me to be happy."

Lyall tilts his head to look at me, one corner of his mouth hooking up. "I make you happy, hmm?"

I pout at him. "Shit. I must not be a good boyfriend if you don't know how happy I am when I'm with you."

Lyall shrugs. "There are... certain areas where you could improve, aye." His teasing tone has me fighting back a smile.

Hunger for more than food stirs in my stomach as I lean into his space for a quick but hard kiss. "Yeah?" I nip his bottom lip. "Tell me and I'll be better for you."

Lyall's breath hitches, his eyes darkening. "For starters... I believe you said you would make me scream your name. Did it sound at all like I screamed to you?"

Fuck, this man drives me crazy.

"You wanna scream, sweetheart? You'll be hoarse by the time I'm done with you."

Our food is forgotten as I set the containers on the nightstand. I tug Lyall into a hard kiss, my tongue demanding entrance. He lets me in, whimpering when I reach between us and grab our cocks. It only takes a few strokes before we're both hard and grinding against each other.

It's only been a little over two hours since we made love, and I still haven't had my fill of him. I need to hear more of those desperate sounds he makes when he's lost in pleasure, need to lose myself in the heat and tight grip of his body.

I just need *him*.

If our plans fail and I lose him... Fuck, it hurts just thinking about it. I shove my fears down and focus on kissing the man in my arms, making him feel good.

"Turn around and grab that headboard, sweetheart," I order.

Lyall obeys, gripping the wood so hard it creaks. He slides his hips back, presenting his amazing ass, round and muscular and perfect. Opening the lube, I slick my fingers and my cock. "Does this hurt?" I ask when I slip a finger inside, swirling it around.

Lyall's back arches, and he groans. "Nothing's ever hurt less," he assures me, rolling his hips back to ride my finger. "I'm ulfhednar. We heal fast, and we have plenty of stamina to spare." He throws me a cocky grin over his shoulder, biting his lip when I crook my finger against his prostate. "Now, stop holding back. Take me hard, love. Make the whole building know how good you make me feel."

Fuck, if that doesn't get me moving, nothing else will.

Grabbing his hips, I pull him down onto me. As his walls grip me, I squeeze his ass hard, dimpling the skin. "Fuck, sweetheart, you feel so damn good." I rock my hips a few times, working him open on my cock. Lyall groans low in his throat, knuckles whitening against the headboard.

When he begins to thrust back against me, taking me in deeper and faster, I stop holding back. Plastering myself to his back, I hold on tight to his hips and fuck him like I'll die if I stop.

"Gods, yes!" Lyall shouts. His head falls back against my shoulder, and I kiss and nip every inch of exposed skin. Nothing has ever felt as right as this. Whether we're out having fun or fucking our brains out, when I'm with Lyall, I know I'm exactly where I'm meant to be.

That's why I know that going away with him is the right decision. No matter how much I'll miss my friends and family or the life I've made here, I'll miss Lyall more if I let him go.

"That's it, Soren. Gods! Don't stop. Give me more," Lyall demands. His cock is leaking a river between my fingers as I stroke him. He's close, but so am I. I'm not letting myself come yet, not until I've made him do it first.

I nip the spot between his neck and shoulder. He gasps, cock jerking in my fist. "Do that again," he says, and the desperate plea in his voice is one I could never ignore. I'll give him anything he needs if it makes him feel happy and treasured.

I bite down hard enough so he feels it but not enough to break the skin.

A shudder racks Lyall's body, and he spills all over my hand with a roar worthy of a wild beast. A few thrusts later and I'm coming as well, collapsing against his back. I grind into him, riding out my release until I'm too spent to move a muscle.

I pull out carefully, and Lyall wastes no time in turning around and taking me into his arms for a slow, tender kiss.

"What... was that?" I ask once I can speak.

Lyall chuckles. "I asked you to bite me where ulfhednar claim our lovers when we mate. That spot is... quite sensitive."

"Is that what this is?" I run my thumb carefully over the scars of teeth marks. My chest hitches. "Are these marks..."

"Aye. They're yours, love."

My throat thickens as I run my fingers over the scars, a reminder of the love we shared that hasn't faded.

"You have them too."

That draws me out of my thoughts. "Huh?" I'd have noticed if I had teeth marks in my shoulder. "Where?" I check each shoulder even though I've seen them thousands of times by now.

Lyall runs his fingers over the spot between my neck and shoulders on my left side. "They should be here." Sadness pulls at his brow. "I think the Council took those away as well."

Of course they did. Motherfuckers.

"Oh..." I don't know how it's possible to grieve for something I can't remember having. I hate that so much of my life with Lyall was taken from me.

"I could always give them back—if you want," Lyall adds hastily. He looks away, uncertainty on his face. Does he think I'd say no? Even though it will hurt, I want it more than anything. I want to be marked by him. I need it on a primal level I can't comprehend.

"I want that," I say, grabbing his hand and holding tight. "So much. I don't even know why, or what it means. Not really."

Lyall exhales softly, smiling. "Even now, there's still a part of you that recalls our bond. They couldn't take that from you, no matter how hard they tried. When ulfhednar exchange bites, it completes the mating bond. It means sharing in your joy and your struggles and being connected in our hearts and minds. It's... a feeling like no other." Lyall leans in to rest his forehead against mine. "I have missed that connection to you, Soren. So much." The pain in his voice makes my eyes sting.

I take his face in my hands. "I'm here, sweetheart. I'm not going anywhere. I want everything you just described, but not yet. Not until I know we're both safe."

Lyall touches his lips to mine. "I'll wait for you as I always have, Soren. Time has taught me that you're worth it."

I pull him close and kiss him until I'm breathless, never wanting to stop.

Soon we won't have to hide. We can start our lives somewhere new, and we'll never be separated again.

Lyall called a friend of his before we fell asleep, Arlo, and Arlo confirmed that the TTA doesn't have a headquarters in San Francisco. Which is perfect because my friend Tom owns a chain of restaurants, one of which is in San Francisco. I'll ask if he can get me a job at his SF location. If he agrees, then I'll start looking for apartments there.

It'll be a big change, moving across the country. I'll be so far away from Fergus and my friends. If someone had told me I'd be uprooting my whole life to be with a guy I'd only just met, I'd have laughed in their face.

But it feels right. Lyall is it for me, and there's nowhere else I'd rather be than with him.

All I have to do now is fight for us. It won't be easy, but Lyall is worth it. I'm not the only one making sacrifices. Lyall will be leaving his world behind. He'll have even more to adjust to than I will. It will be a difficult transition, but we'll have each other.

Once I'm at work, I begin the first phase of my plan. Franklin and Tom arrive within the first hour of my shift, and while I prepare their drinks, I try to piece together what I'm going to say.

"You okay?" Tom asks when I set their drinks down.

I force a laugh. "I'm fine, just been thinking it's time for a change."

Franklin sips his cocktail. "Oooh. Interesting! You gonna grow a mustache? No, wait! You're getting a tattoo!"

I snort. "No, and hell no."

Tom chuckles and pats his partner on the back. "How about we let him tell us the big news? Besides, he's obviously going to get a Prince Albert."

I wince and cover my crotch. "God, no! I... I'm moving. Possibly. It depends."

"No!" Franklin gasps dramatically and takes my hand. "Where? Why? With who?"

"I'm thinking San Francisco, and my boyfriend's going with me."

Tom shoots me a quizzical look. "The guy you just started dating?"

"I know. It's fast but I've got a good feeling about Lyall."

Franklin frowns. "Didn't you have good feelings about all the other guys you dated?"

I get his concern. It wasn't long ago that I was swearing off relationships. "This is different. He's different."

Tom adds, "Why San Francisco?"

"Well, I was hoping a certain silver fox could help me and my boyfriend get a job at one of his restaurants..."

Franklin elbows Tom. "He was using us this whole time!"

He barks a laugh. "With all the money I've given you, I'm practically your employer already. Sure. I'm happy to help."

How can I argue with that?

Step one of the plan, complete. The rest of my shift is pretty slow after Franklin and Tom head out, so I spend my time on my phone looking at apartment listings. SF is an expensive city, but I've done the math by the time I get home, and I'll be able to afford it. Plus I'll have Lyall with me. He doesn't have a degree of any kind, so I'll help him find a job at Tom's restaurant. What skills could a Viking from the past bring to the present?

I hesitate with my key in the lock when I hear Fergus washing the dishes. My heart sinks. Telling Fergus will be difficult. There's no telling how he'll react. Will he be angry? Hurt? Too bad. I'm an adult, and I can make my own decisions.

Squaring my shoulders, I head inside.

Fergus smiles at me. "Hello. Did you have a good shift?"

"Yeah. Sure." I lean on the counter, tapping my fingers. Drawing in a breath, I let it out slowly. "Gramps, can we talk?"

"Certainly." Fergus sets the last dish in the dishwasher and turns to face me, drying his hands on a dishrag. "Are you all right? Did something happen at work?" His eyes darken. "It's the wolf, isn't it?"

"No. Lyall's great. We're great." Fergus still mistrusts Lyall. There's no way he'll approve of my decision. "Gramps... is there any chance that the Council will let us be together?"

Fergus sighs. "The Council made it very clear to me that you were never to learn the truth about your past. They feared you would endanger the Erikson pack. I imagine they gave Lyall similar instructions. So long as the Council believes you are unaware, there shouldn't be any issue, but..."

He trails off, leaving me to imagine all the horrible scenarios where our secret's discovered.

"They'd take my memories again, right?"

"Most likely, yes. Lyall would also be punished, and his pack would face dire consequences. Lyall could be forbidden from traveling. The whole pack could lose their ability to travel."

"I know, he told me." My stomach churns. "Could the Council find out that Lyall told me the truth?"

Fergus is quiet for a moment, rubbing the stubble on his jaw. "I would never put it past them. They take protecting the secrets of time travel and the paranormal community very seriously."

I wet my lip, sensing my opportunity. "And what if we went somewhere they couldn't find us?"

Fergus's brows furrow. "How exactly would you do that?"

"What if we moved somewhere they don't have a headquarters?"

"You're leaving?" The shock in Fergus's voice makes my heart sink.

"It's just an idea. I was thinking we could go to San Francisco. Lyall mentioned they don't have a headquarters there. Plus one of my customers owns a restaurant there, and he can get me a job."

Silence stretches between us. I tighten my jaw to hold back the sudden urge to apologize, to tell Fergus I'll stay. He's done so much for me, and I hate disappointing him.

"Soren," Fergus says at last, a quiver in his voice I was dreading. I've hurt him. Damn it, that's not what I wanted. He clears his throat. "You barely know the wolf."

"Lyall," I say. "He has a name. And I know enough."

"But he abandoned you!"

"He didn't. Lyall may have chosen his family, but he never gave up on me, Gramps. He searched for me for years. He promised me he'd find me, and he did. When he told me we were fated mates, I didn't understand, but I do now. Some part of me knows that he's who I'm meant to be with. If I left with him tomorrow, I wouldn't regret it. The only thing I'd regret would be losing him again."

I mean every word. Lyall isn't just a part of my life; he's my future too. I've never felt this way about anyone.

"Well then. Who am I to come between you and the one destined for you." He doesn't sound hurt or judgmental, but resigned. I look up, startled to see tears lining his eyes.

"Gramps—" I want to tell him I'll stay in touch, that just because we'll be apart doesn't mean we won't be family. That it's not personal.

"Don't, Soren. Don't mind me." Fergus rubs his damp eyes. "It's all right. It's a grandfather's job to care for his grandchild, not to hold him back from the life he wants. But that's exactly what I did when I kept you and Lyall apart. For years I denied you happiness. I won't make excuses for my actions. It wasn't right. I can see that now."

"So... you're not upset?"

Fergus's lips tremble. "You look happier than I've ever seen you. All these years, I watched you be heartbroken. If I had let you both meet sooner, I could have spared you so much pain. I'm so sorry, Soren. Truly." Tears spill down his cheeks faster than he can wipe them away.

My throat thickens as I go to him and pull him into a hug. "It's okay, Gramps. I'm not angry anymore. I'm gonna miss you." My eyes sting at the admission.

Fergus holds me tighter. "I'll miss you, too."

Chapter 21

Lyall

Toward the end of the month, Soren makes plans to fly us out to San Francisco to visit apartments. He says it's all the way on the other side of the country. We'll have to ride in this thing called a plane. It flies high in the sky like a bird. He's pointed them out to me a few times on clear days.

I can't say I'm looking forward to that, but it will be worth it to spend the rest of my life with Soren, somewhere we don't have to hide from the TTA.

But the closer the day of our departure draws, the heavier my heart becomes. I go back and forth between my time and Soren's, but I find myself spending more time in the past with my pack. It hasn't set in that soon I won't see them again. Anders and Jamie can visit, certainly, although I won't see them as often as I do now after we move; Wulfric and Gunnar will not be able to visit. It's not a risk we can afford.

How will I explain it to them in a way they'll understand while also keeping my secrets?

The day arrives before I'm ready. My last day with my family. A part of me wants to just tell them the truth and leave, so they at least know why. So they don't believe I left out of spite or because I didn't care.

Kieran has grown into himself as Alpha-Mate and cares for our pack as if he were born into it. Wulfric watches him with pride as he teaches a girl to use a bow. Jace runs and plays with the other children, beside himself with excitement when one of the older whelps shifts into a wolf. Anders and Jamie bring back pastries and coffee from the cafe. Aunt Helga makes her beloved stew, made with beef from a cow Gunnar butchered himself.

It's going to be an evening both bitter and sweet.

"Come inside, everyone!" Helga calls from the front door. "Supper is ready."

"Finally, I'm starved!" Jace races past us and into the house.

"Make sure to thank Aunt Helga!" Jamie calls after him.

"I hope you left room in your belly for a proper meal," Anders says, elbowing me.

I brush croissant crumbs off my shirt. "I always have room for Aunt Helga's beef stew."

My family heads into the house, but before I can follow, a hand grips my shoulder. Claws dig into my shirt and dimple my flesh. "How's Arlo?" I barely recognize my brother's voice. It's harsh, scraping against his fangs with every word.

My mind goes blank. "Arlo?"

Gunnar's claws bite into my shoulder, making me wince. "Did he leave that mark on your skin?"

"What mark—"

Oh shit.

Gunnar's eyes are blazing wildfire as he glares at the spot on my neck Soren nibbled and kissed this morning. I haven't worn my furs since I arrived, so the mark hasn't healed.

"A-and what of it? We're together, brother."

Gunnar's nostrils flare, his lips curling away from his fangs. "Then why have you scrubbed his scent from your skin? If he were mine, I'd want the whole world to know it!"

My heart's hammering, and surely he can hear it. I've got to keep my composure. Like when I first learned to draw a bow. I was scared I'd miss my shot, that we'd go hungry. Father had squeezed my shoulder and said, "Breathe, boy."

Drawing in a breath, I turn to face Gunnar, taking his hand off my shoulder and holding it tight. It pains me to see him like this, the line between man and beast as thin as a blade's edge. "I didn't want you to have to smell him on me. Do you really think me so cruel that I'd taunt you in such a manner?"

Gunnar's breath hitches. His hand curls around mine hard, claws biting into my skin. Hot blood drips down my palm, and I grind my teeth against the stinging pain. The scent of blood fills the air between us. Gunnar wrenches his hand away, panic spiking his scent. "Apologies," he says in a breathless whisper, then shoves past me into the house without another glance.

I exhale, my heart racing hard enough to burst from my chest.

It's a good thing we're leaving soon. If Gunnar found out who I was truly with, it would drive him into a rage. I've hurt him enough with my lies.

Inside the house, everyone has already gathered at the table. I linger at the threshold, wishing I had my phone so I could capture this moment of my family whole and happy like we haven't been in years. All but Gunnar, who doesn't react to anyone and focuses on filling his plate.

Once I'm gone, will Gunnar lose himself completely to his wolf? What if my absence pushes him over the edge? I've got to find a way to let them know that my reasons for leaving aren't callous.

I join them at the table and smile at my aunt. "Thank you for the stew."

"I made it just for you, lad." Her smile is soft and so full of love it hurts to look at her.

My chest tightens. Helga knows it's my favorite. Gods, why does it feel as if I'm betraying them? I'm not. I deserve to be happy. They will survive without me.

"Thank you," I croak, lowering my gaze to my food. I take a sip of the stew, savoring the flavorful broth and tender chunks of meat. I will miss her cooking, miss *her* more than I can say. My eyes sting, and I force the melancholy thoughts down. I can't break. My family will know something is wrong. If this is my last evening with them, let it be a joyful one.

"How was your day, Alpha-Mate?" I give Kieran a teasing smile, knowing how the title makes him blush.

He gives me a withering look but laughs softly. "Pretty good. I've started teaching the kids how to play instruments."

Wulfric rubs Kieran's back. "You should start a... what's that word? A band."

Kieran barks a laugh, squeezing Wulfric's hand. "I'll make a Viking version of the Jackson Five!"

"One of those pastries you brought was new," I say to Anders. "It tasted like apples."

Anders nods. "Aye, it's called an apple turnover."

Jamie gulps down some mead. "They're good, right?"

"Delicious," I say. I hope they have these apple turnovers in San Francisco. "How are you, Aunt Helga?"

"I'm quite well, dear. The garden is thriving. Our village is safe. My lovely nephews are happy. I could not ask for anything more." She pats my hand, her touch soft and warm.

I'm almost afraid to speak to Gunnar, but it's only fair since I've asked after everyone else. I clear my throat and force myself to look across the table at Gunnar. "And you, brother?"

Gunnar doesn't reply right away, draining his whole mug of mead. His beard glistens, and he flicks his tongue over the pointed edge of his fang. His narrowed eyes dart from face to face, his shoulders hunching up toward his ears. "Stop looking at me like that. I'm not some deranged beast yet."

Jamie coughs. "We weren't—"

"Aye, you were. I've still got my sanity. You needn't look at me with fear nor pity." Gunnar spits the words out through his fangs.

Wulfric clears his throat. "Apologies, Gunnar. That wasn't our intention. How did the hunt go?"

Gunnar jerks a shoulder. "I caught it, killed it, butchered it. Nothing to tell."

Wulfric hums, frowning down at his bowl. Kieran rubs his shoulder. "Thanks, Gunnar. You're one of the best hunters we have."

Gunnar answers with a grunt, eating more stew.

Time flies after that, the tension fading like mist when Kieran offers to play a song he learned on the lyre. His music lightens the mood and makes the evening a memorable one. I couldn't have asked for a better farewell than this.

Before I'm ready, the time comes for us to part ways. Emotions thicken my throat, but I smile through them as I pull Wulfric into a hug. He grunts, arms stiff and awkward at his sides. "Uh... Lyall?"

I squeeze him, savoring the warm thrum of the pack bond between us. "You've become a fine Alpha, little Wulf. Father would be proud." Wulfric's breath catches, then his arms come around me, holding me tight for a few seconds.

"Thank you. And don't call me that," he grumbles, face red and eyes glassy.

I tousle his hair. "Not so little anymore, are you?" I'll never forget the first moment I held him in my arms. Sometimes I look at him, and it takes my breath away to see the man he's become.

Wulfric bats my hand away, wrestling back a smile as he goes to stand by Kieran.

I wrench Kieran into a hug, making him squeak. "And you! I knew you'd make a great Alpha-Mate!"

Kieran wheezes. "Suffocating... in your armpit... Can't... breathe!" Snorting, I let him go and find him smiling. "You know, I'm only as good as the pack who taught me."

Anders and Jamie will head back with me, so we don't have to say our farewells yet, thank the gods.

Gunnar grips my shoulder. There's a knowing look in his eyes that makes my heart skip. He pulls me close for a one-armed squeeze. "Something is off with you tonight, brother."

"Is it?" I laugh to hide my rising nerves. "You know family gatherings make me emotional."

He grunts, not sounding pleased, but he doesn't push for me to open up, thankfully. I hold him to my side for a moment longer, closing my eyes tight.

Please, gods. Let him find happiness after I'm gone. Bring him and Arlo together. Teach him to open his heart once more to love.

It's hard to let him go. All I want is to hold on to him and keep him in my sights, but I can't draw any more attention to myself. I force myself to drop my arm to my side, to not look back at my family as I step out the door. It closes behind me with a finality that makes my throat ache. I pray I can hold it together long enough to say goodbye to my aunt.

She's sitting outside on a bench, looking up at the stars. Anders looks back at me, but I motion him on ahead. When I take a seat beside my aunt, she puts her hand on my knee. "Do you remember when I taught you to navigate by the stars?"

Above, the stars are countless, glittering like gems in the night sky. "Aye. How could I forget?" I point to the North Star, shining bright. "And the ones that look like a big and little spoon."

She laughs. "Ready to dip into the ocean and scoop up all the fish! You were so upset when I said that."

"Aye. Those are our fish!" I lean my cheek against her soft silver hair.

"Does the present have these same stars, lad?"

I nod. "Aye. They're not as visible in the city, but on a clear night, I see them and I think of home, of you and my brothers."

The scent of salt hits my nose, and my heart sinks when her shoulders tremble. "Then promise me that no matter how far you go, you'll look up at the stars each night and remember us."

I try to laugh, but it gets stuck in my throat. "I... I'm not going anywhere."

She takes my hand. "Don't try and lie to me. Last night the gods showed me a vision. You've found him, and you're going away with him."

I don't know what to say. Guilt and grief take me by storm, making tears flood my eyes. I hang my head, grinding my teeth. "Aunt Helga, I'm so—"

"Don't you apologize to me, lad." Warm hands frame my face, tilting my head. Tears shine in Helga's eyes. "What happened that horrible day was not as it seemed, was it?"

"What makes you say that?"

"Because if Soren had truly betrayed us, you would not be leaving with him."

I place my hand over hers. "It's true. He never betrayed us. He lied so I would not take any blame for the attack."

Helga breathes in slowly, wiping away her tears. "And it's because of that lie that our pack was able to stay together."

"Aye, Auntie. He did it for me, for our family."

Her eyes are watery, but her tone is steady and sure when she says, "Then we failed Soren, and we failed you, and for that I beg your forgiveness."

I shake my head. "No. There's nothing to forgive. I made the choice to stay, and I don't regret it. It all worked out in the end, did it not?"

Helga's lips tremble when she smiles. "You have given enough to our pack, lad. You've honored your father's wishes. Go now and know that he would be so very proud of you."

"Would he?" A tear spills down my cheek, and Helga wipes it away with her thumb.

"Of course, and so would your mother. You deserve all the happiness in the world."

I pull her close, hiding my face in her neck. I take a few deep breaths, trying to hold myself together. "I love you, Auntie."

"I love you too," she says, holding me tighter.

I never want to let her go, but now that she's given me her blessing, I can forge a future with Soren free of guilt.

"Thank you for everything," I say, brushing a kiss over her palm.

"Be well, Lyall. Be happy. That's all I ask."

A grin spreads over my face. "With Soren by my side, that will be all too easy."

Despite the ache in my heart, a burden has fallen from my shoulders. Each step feels lighter, the air a bit sweeter.

Jamie and Anders wait for me by the boat. Jace hurries up to me. "Are you okay, Uncle Lyall?"

Smiling at his concern, I tousle his hair. "Aye, lad. I will be. But you have to promise me something?"

He straightens up, serious as can be. "What?"

I point to Anders and Jamie. "You look after those two for me, aye?"

He salutes me, making me laugh. "You got it! Have fun with Soren, and..." He swallows, eyes bright. "And we'll see you two a lot, right?"

I tug him into a hug. "Of course you will."

"Ready to go?" Anders looks me over, no doubt scenting the tears still drying on my cheeks.

"I am."

He swings an arm around my shoulders and leads me to the boats. "Then let's not keep your mate waiting."

"How'd it go?" Soren's hand is warm in mine. Central Park is busy even in the evening. Folks walk the trails together, laughing uproariously and talking far too loudly. The setting sun casts its reflection over the lake, where ducks paddle and dive for food.

"Hard," I say with a sigh. "I wanted to tell them so badly. My aunt knew. She had a vision that I was leaving."

Soren's fingers grip mine. "Was she angry?"

I give his hand a reassuring kiss. "No. She wished me well."

"Are you feeling okay?"

I don't know how to answer. My heart aches, and telling it this is for the best doesn't help. "I just need time."

Soren's quiet, picking at some peeling paint on the bench's armrest.

"Listen to me." I take his chin between my fingers and make him look at me. "I love them, and I'll always wish things could have been different. No matter how much it hurts, I would make the same choice I made tonight again if it meant being with you, Soren."

He blinks, eyes damp, lips curling into a smile. "I love you."

I knew love could hurt, but I never knew it could hurt so achingly sweet as this.

Tears sting my eyes, so I close them tight. For a moment, I can't speak, overcome with too many emotions to name. Framing his face, I press my forehead against his. "I love you too." The words come out on a ragged gasp, and I can't be sure if I'm laughing or crying.

Soren chuckles before he pulls me into a kiss, sweeter than the finest mead and just as intoxicating.

This is it. We will never be separated again. This is the start of our beginning together.

There's a flash of light behind my eyelids. Suddenly, fury slams into me, burning my lungs so pungently I can taste it. It's Gunnar's pack bond, but it burns in my chest like fire.

No, no, no!

I'm on my feet, throwing myself in front of Soren. "Please. I can explain."

I barely recognize Gunnar as his bestial rage twists him into something inhuman before my eyes. Fur crawls over his skin, fangs glistening in his mouth. The portal shimmering over the lake slams shut behind him as he wades onto shore.

"You *lied*," he snarls, the words grating over jagged fangs. "All this time, you fucking lied!"

"Lyall, let's go!" Soren grabs at my shoulder, but I refuse to move. My brother's wolf is riding him hard, and I fear running will provoke his prey drive.

"Gunnar. Please. Sit down, we can talk about this. There's so much you don't know. Just listen—"

"You've been meeting with this traitor, all this time!" Gunnar roars, sending birds flying from the trees. People passing through the park gasp, throwing worried looks over their shoulders.

Run, run, run. I wish I could scream the words at them.

"It's not like that!" Gods, he must hear me out.

Gunnar grows taller, muscles bulking up. His shoes split as clawed feet puncture the material.

"What the fuck?" Soren whispers, voice thin with terror.

"He killed Leif," Gunnar snarls, panting harshly as his clothes tear, body twisting into that of a beast. "T-took my little Bjorn from me." Grief thickens his voice. "He was just a baby. Because of *him*, my family is gone!"

It's hopeless. Gunnar has finally lost himself to his berserker, and it's all my fault.

"Lyall—"

Whirling around, I shove Soren in the chest. "Run! I'll hold him off!"

I have no fur to aid me in my shift. If I go up against him in this form, he'll tear me apart. But I have no other choice. No one is taking Soren from me again.

A roar shakes the ground. People scream in shock and terror. The air wheezes from my lungs as Gunnar slams into me, throwing me onto my back. I brace, hands over my face, but he doesn't waste a second on me.

No, he goes straight for Soren, and my worst nightmares are made reality.

Soren screams in agony when Gunnar's fangs drive into his shoulder. The scent of his blood turns my world upside down.

"No!" I charge at my brother, leaping onto his back. I grab his arm, trying to pull him off.

"Gunnar, stop! Please!" a voice cries. A familiar one.

Gunnar freezes, fangs still buried in Soren's flesh, eyes wild with rage.

Arlo and several other men and women emerge from the shadows of the park. The scent of their magic burns my nose. Golden torcs around their necks glint in the light from the streetlights.

Witches.

My heart sinks. They must have been nearby this whole time, watching us.

Oh gods. This can't possibly get worse.

Arlo holds out his hands. "Easy there, stud. Let him go. Please, don't make this worse for yourself."

The rage burning in Gunnar's eyes sputters out. He pulls his fangs from Soren's flesh. My mate cries out and crumples to the ground.

"Now!" one of the witches snaps, and then the world around me falls utterly still and quiet. Soren's face is twisted in agony—that image will come to me in my nightmares—but he doesn't make a sound or even twitch a muscle. I shake Gunnar, but he's stiff as if he's turned to stone. The people around us are motionless, even those who were fleeing. Their bodies are frozen in the act of running or hiding. One fool was even filming the attack on his phone, his face stuck in an expression of awe and terror.

I collapse the moment I'm off Gunnar's back, trying to stay calm as the witches close in.

How could things have gone from bad to worse so quickly? It took only minutes for my fantasy to warp into my worst nightmare.

"Hands over your head, now!"

I do as he says, never taking my eyes off Soren's agonized face frozen in a silent scream. "Please. Help him."

The witch ignores me, barking orders to his companions. "Initiate containment protocol!"

"Yes, sir!" a witch says, lifting her hands to the sky. A tear slashes across it and black blurs shoot from the void. Ravens caw as they descend upon the park. They land on the shoulders and heads of frozen citizens and peck... something from their skulls. Not flesh, but nothing I can see.

They remind me of Odin's ravens, Hugin and Munin. They fly around the world and gather wisdom and knowledge for the Allfather. Could these ravens be taking *memories*?

A witch, terrifying in her familiarity, moves to stand in front of me, obscuring my view of the birds. Helena's mouth twists into a smirk. "Mr. Erikson. I think you have some explaining to do."

How could things have gone so wrong so fast?

Chapter 22
Soren

When I open my eyes, I'm back in my apartment, like I never left. My shoulder throbs, making me gasp.

"Easy, boy." Fergus leans over the bed, settling his hands on my arm. "Be still. The pain will fade in just a moment." Warmth spreads from where he touches me. The puncture in my shoulder stops throbbing and closes before my eyes.

"Where's Lyall?" *Please, let him be okay.* I don't know how I got back home. The last thing I remember is being rushed by Lyall's brother, who'd turned into a monster straight out of a horror movie. He'd bitten me, and I don't remember what happened after that.

"The TTA has him in their custody."

Bile burns the back of my throat, and I struggle hard not to be sick. Our plan failed. We were caught. "What's going to happen to him?"

Fergus squeezes my arm. "I don't know. That's for his Alpha to decide."

"His Alpha is his brother, and he believes I betrayed them all."

"I know."

Is this it then? Is this how we end, before we even had a chance to start?

I grind my teeth against the sudden burn of tears, squeezing the blankets in my fists.

"Soren, talk to me."

I suck in a gulp of air that burns my lungs. "I'll never see him again."

Fergus runs his hand up and down my arm. "You don't know that. Nothing has been decided yet. The TTA will want to speak to you once you're well. They've issued a summons for this Tuesday."

I sit up, rubbing my eyes hard. "Why? What do they want with me?"

"I imagine they'll want to question you."

"Will they erase my memories?" I won't let them. I never want to forget Lyall again.

"Not yet. As this is a pack matter, they'll want to get approval from Alpha Erikson."

Then my chances of keeping my memories look like absolute shit.

"I have to do something. Can I go back in time and stop this?"

Fergus shakes his head. "Imagine how different the world might be, for better or worse, if we had the ability to go back and change things. The witches have measures in place to prevent tampering with the past or future, and even if anyone found a way past those, manipulating timelines is a grave offense."

"So what can I do?" My chest tightens, making it hard to breathe. I can't lose Lyall, not again.

"Breathe, boy." Fergus rubs my back. "If you truly are fated, then this is not where your story ends. You will find your way back to each other, but not if you give up."

He's right. I've got to stay strong and fight for us the way Lyall did. No matter how much time passed, he never gave up on me.

I'm not about to either.

Apparently, I'm under the equivalent of house arrest. I found out when I tried to leave, despite my granddad's warning, and walked into a wall of muscle on the other side of the apartment door. The TTA enforcer had ordered me back inside. I'd obeyed and cursed him out before slamming the door on his ugly mug.

I'd had to call in sick to work and missed a whole day. When I can finally leave to go to the meeting, the enforcer drives me to a big office building across from Bryant Park. It doesn't look like anything special. The lobby's full of normal-looking people in business attire going about their lunch break.

The elevator takes us up to the very top floor, and that's when things get weird as shit. We pass people dressed in all sorts of odd clothing lined up to get passports and IDs. There's a guy dressed like a pirate. A knight in full plate armor. A woman who looks like she walked off the set of a Jane Austen movie. I feel like I just walked into a supernatural DMV.

The enforcer leads me to a quieter hallway full of cubicles and then to some private offices. He opens the door for me, revealing a small sitting room. As far as interrogation rooms go, at least it looks cozy.

"Have a seat. Ms. Cartwright will be with you shortly."

I've only been seated five minutes when the door opens, and recognition slaps me in the face. It's her! The woman Lyall and I encountered when we went ice skating. She smiles at me and it's polite enough, but my shoulders still stiffen with apprehension. "Soren. How good to see you again. How are you feeling? My enforcers told me you had been bitten."

"I'm fine. Ms. Cartwright, please don't take my memories away again."

She sits down opposite me. "Unfortunately, that decision is out of my hands."

"Then can I talk to whoever makes that decision and tell them I don't consent to having my memories ripped out?"

"How much do you know of your past?"

"All of it."

"And how did you learn about it?"

I wet my dry lips. "Lyall took me back in time. We didn't tamper with anything. He showed me my history, and I didn't betray the Erikson pack, Ms. Cartwright. The pack thought Lyall had been in on the attack. I lied so he wouldn't be punished."

"Do you have proof to back up your claims?"

"Yes! Can someone, I don't know, look at my memories? Is that a thing?"

Ms. Cartwright waves her hand dismissively. "We already reviewed your case. Your memories showed that you had betrayed Alpha Erik and his pack. There is nothing more to discuss." "That's not true!"

"It's what we have on file—"

"Then whoever reviewed my memories did a piss-poor job because that is not what happened!" I unclench my fists and force in a slow breath to calm myself. "I want my case reopened and all the evidence reviewed properly."

"That is out of my hands. You would have to schedule a meeting with my superior, Kirsten Harding. She's the head of the Travelers Council."

I exhale slowly. I'm getting somewhere. "Tell me how."

Ms. Cartwright looks me right in the eye. "No. I don't think I will."

The hair on my neck stands up. "What? Why?"

She stands, sending her chair screeching back from the desk. "I won't let you and that animal undo all my hard work!"

My heart drops into my stomach. I scramble out of my seat and make for the door. The knob freezes to a chunk of damn ice seconds before I can grab it. "Let me out!" I pound on the door, but nobody answers.

"They can't hear you," Ms. Cartwright singsongs, lips stretching into a smile that only widens when I press myself flat against the door. "This room is sound-proofed. Now, stop kicking up such a fuss. It will only make the procedure hurt worse. I'd hate to hear you scream so loudly. Again."

She did it. She's the one who took my memories, and she wants to do it again. Fuck! I can't let this happen. I've got to see Lyall again. We're supposed to have a future together.

"Please. Don't do this. We've never even done anything to you!" I speak loudly, hoping someone, anyone, will hear me despite whatever spell she's cast.

Ms. Cartwright's lip curls into a sneer. "You haven't. But your father did." Her voice thickens, and tears fill her eyes. "He killed my son. My Gerard."

As scared as I am, I can't help but feel her pain down to my core. I hate that my father caused so much suffering. "O-oh. I'm so sorry."

"He was visiting some wolf bitch he was sweet on the day your father attacked the village. I told him, I *warned* him, that those animals were beneath us, but he wouldn't listen!"

And there goes my pity. Fuck her and her bigoted ass. "I'm sorry for what happened to your son, Ms. Cartwright. I am. But you've seen my memories. You know I had nothing to do with the attack, so just let me go."

She shakes her head, curls flying around her face. "Someone has to pay for what your father did." Chest rising and falling fast, she thrusts out her hand. "Come here, boy. This will be quick and painless, but only if you don't struggle."

Fear and despair thicken my throat. She's smaller than me in height and build, but her magic gives her the advantage. No matter how hard I fight, she'll likely win. I've got to try. For Lyall.

I lift my fists and channel every ounce of desperation and terror into a shout as I rush her. My feet leave the ground, pressure clenching at my waist. The room spins around me, and I slam into the wall so hard, the breath goes out of me.

She scoffs as she kneels before me. I try to struggle, but I can't lift my arms or legs as freezing cold paralyzes my wrists and ankles. They've been frozen into blocks of ice. Ms. Cartwright places her hand at the base of my skull.

There's a tingling in the back of my head, and a wave of dizziness makes the room lurch.

I'll never see Lyall again. She'll take away the truth and leave behind nothing but lies. Lyall's pack will be torn apart. I'll go through the rest of my life with a hole in my heart, never knowing the love that's been stolen from me.

"Don't do this." Tears spill down my cheeks. "Don't take him from me. Please—"

A flash of light sears my eyes. My ears ring as an explosion rocks the room. It takes several seconds of blinking before my vision finally clears. Someone's kneeling over me, but they're wearing trousers, not a knee-length skirt.

"...ren? It's... right... safe, darling."

That English accent is familiar. I've heard it somewhere before, haven't I?

"Soren?" Warm hands touch my face.

No!

I thrash, trying to bat them away. "Get off me! Get away!"

"Helena's out cold. You're safe. I'm not going to hurt you."

The man leaning over me has brown eyes and hair the color of polished gold. He's undeniably familiar, and then it hits me. "You. Lyall knew you. You were there in the park."

Arlo winks. "Memorable, aren't I?"

I huff a laugh and slump back against the itchy carpet. "After that entrance, yeah, damn right you are."

"I love to make a scene. What can I say?" There's a flare of heat near my ankles.

I look down and nearly lose my shit when Arlo melts through the ice binding me with a freaking live flame in his hand.

"Don't move!" Arlo snaps, like my reaction to having fire inches from my bare skin is completely unreasonable. "Unless you want to lose some leg hair?"

I close my eyes, dreading the moment he'll slip up and roast me, but it never comes.

"Thank you," I say, exhaling in relief. "I thought nobody could hear me thanks to whatever spell she cast."

Arlo makes a disgusted face. "I couldn't. But I had my suspicions about her since our meeting in the park. She ranted for almost an hour about you and Lyall."

"Really? What did she say?"

He waves a hand. "Nothing worth repeating. That was bad enough, but she's been hiring witches to shadow the pair of you."

My blood run colds. "Really?" The TTA has been spying on us for days. Talk about creepy.

"It's why they showed up at the park so quickly when Lyall's brother went berserk. I had no part in it, I promise." He grimaces. "I just happened to be nearby on a job at the time. I felt her use her magic just now, and I knew something was up."

"Come to my bar sometime. You'll have drinks on the house for the rest of your life."

Arlo oohs excitedly as he crosses to the massive hole he blew into the wall by the door. I blow on my fingers, trying to warm them while Arlo motions some witches into the room. Ms. Cartwright groans as they put her in cuffs but appears too dazed to fight as two witches march her out of the room.

An unsettling thought strikes me. "They won't think I attacked her, will they?"

Arlo scoffs. "No offense, darling, but no. She'll be interrogated. You will too, I expect."

I swallow through a dry throat. "Then what?"

Arlo grins. "Then I think a little justice is finally in the cards for you and your wolf."

Chapter 23
Lyall

The sun has risen and set. I have not been allowed to leave my home once since the TTA detained me and brought me back to the past. Left with my own thoughts, all I can do is torment myself with worst-case scenarios all night. No one has come to visit me.

There's been no word of what's become of Gunnar. He violated the Council's most sacred rule when he shifted to his berserker form in front of countless witnesses.

There's no telling what will become of him. The Council could rule to strip Gunnar's wolf. He could lose the ability to shift forever. But what if he hasn't shifted back? What if seeing me with Soren tipped him over the edge?

The Council would have to put him down. Once a wolf goes berserk, there's no bringing them back. If by some miracle Gunnar is still sane, then he could agree to be stripped of his wolf. Only, I cannot imagine him agreeing to have such a vital part of his identity ripped from him. And if he refuses to let his wolf be taken, then the Council could rule to execute him.

My brother could die because of me.

Fury and anguish tear into me. I grab a plate off my table and hurl it across the room with a roar that shakes the windows. Another plate shatters against the wall, and another as I drown in a red haze.

I was so close to having everything I've ever wanted, and instead I've destroyed my family and endangered Soren.

Father, I'm so sorry. I tried to keep my promise to you.

Tears flood my eyes, turning the surrounding room into a blur. My knees buckle and I fold in on myself, trying to make myself small, invisible. I sob like I haven't since the days after losing my father and Soren. Time blurs as I lie there on the floor. My head aches, and my throat is hoarse. It feels like I'll never be able to stand again.

Someone pounds on my door, making me jump. "Are you quite done being sorry for yourself?"

I choke on a gasp. Wiping my eyes, I bolt to my feet. "A-Anders?"

Thank the gods! Someone's come. *Please let him bring good news...*

"I'm coming in."

"Yes, hurry!"

The lock rattles, and Anders steps into the room. His shoulders are slumped, eyelids heavy like he's been up all night. "Before you ask, I don't know where Soren is or what's become of his memories."

Not knowing what's become of my mate makes me feel sick. "And Gunnar? Brother, please tell me he's all right."

Anders raises both hands. "The Council sent a representative to speak with Wulfric and Kieran. They're in talks now. They only told us that Gunnar's been detained. They'll need the Alpha's approval before they do anything."

"Gods damn it, brother! Is there anything you *do* know?"

At Anders's flinch, I nearly break apart all over again.

"I'm sorry," I croak, blinking back the fierce burn in my eyes. "I'm just... I'm so damn scared. For Soren. For Gunnar. If anything happens to either of them—"

Scowling, Anders marches across the room and wrenches me into a hug so tight, it's almost painful. "If you try and blame yourself, I'll whack you upside the head. Soren made the choice to learn more about his past. Gunnar made the bloody foolish decision to follow you to the present. None of this is your fault."

I gulp hard around the lump in my throat, hands gripping at my twin's shoulders. "Then why are you here?"

Anders pushes me into a chair, then uncorks the barrel of mead in the corner of the room. He pours us both a cupful, then shoves mine into my hands. "I spoke to Wulfric on your behalf. Told him what you shared with me about Soren and what really happened that day." Anders's jaw twitches, his lips thinning. I can only imagine he's remembering the horrible events of that day, wounds he's only just started to heal from, but he's torn them wide open for me. "He didn't believe me. Kieran promised to speak with him. He's always been good at breaking through Wulfric's walls to the heart behind them."

If I know my little brother, he will find it hard to accept. Not only because it means letting go of his anger, but because he'll be forced to acknowledge that he was wrong. If anyone can get through to him, it's Kieran. He's helped Wulfric let go of so much grief and guilt. I have to believe he can guide Wulfric through this as well.

More pounding on my door jolts me from sleep. I lift my head from the table, rubbing sleep out of my eyes. The sun has risen, brightening the sky beyond the windows. I can sense who it is before they speak.

"Hey! It's Kieran. Can we chat?"

My heart settles at his voice. Kieran will be easier to speak to than Wulfric right now. He knew about my trips to the present before anyone else. I walk around Anders, who passed out on the floor sometime during the night. Having him nearby was a comfort I am ashamed to admit I needed.

Kieran smiles, but his eyes are baggy. "Morning."

"Did you get any sleep?" I ask, stepping aside so he can enter.

"Nope. Wulf and I stayed up all night talking."

My heart thuds hard against my ribs. "And what of Gunnar? Is he—"

Kieran raises both hands. "He's okay and he's shifted back, but the Council has him detained until he calms down."

A weight falls from my chest, and for the first time in hours, it feels like I can breathe again. "Thank the gods..."

Kieran rubs my shoulder. "Wulfric wants a pack meeting as soon as possible."

Anders yawns behind us, sitting up from the floor. "Can his royal Alphaness wait until we've broken our fast and pissed?"

"Helga's got breakfast at the house. But yeah. For sure do the other thing on your own time and *not* during the meeting." Kieran grins when Anders scowls.

"I'm not an untrained puppy," Anders grumbles, getting to his feet with a wince, then cracking the muscles in his neck.

Kieran waits for us to empty our bladders of all the mead we drank last night, and then we follow him to the longhouse. Curtains part from the windows of houses we pass, suspicious faces watching my every move. "Do our people know?" I ask, unsure if I want the answer.

Kieran shrugs. "They know something's up, yeah, but Wulf and I haven't shared any details."

As we near the house, the scent of sausages hits my nose. I never turn down a meal from Aunt Helga, but my stomach is far too nervous about the talk with Wulfric.

"Just in time!" Aunt Helga says, setting a pan of sizzling sausages on the table. "Have a seat, dears!"

When I catch Wulfric's eye, my heart jumps into my throat. His jaw is tense, hands in fists against the table.

Throat thick, I hang my head and sit down beside Anders. Kieran takes his seat beside Wulfric, and Helga settles in on my left, her hand warm on my shoulder.

"Jamie made coffee," Helga says, her soft voice loud in the silence. "He had to work, so he couldn't stay."

No one says anything.

Kieran clears his throat. "I'll have some."

Anders passes him the pot, and Kieran fills his mug. He hands a mug to Helga, then another one to me. No one speaks as he fills our cups. My heart pounds in my ears as I wait for Wulfric to break the silence.

Wulfric sets down his mug of coffee and takes in a slow breath. Every muscle in my body tenses, bracing for impact.

"The Council have asked me to make a decision concerning the future of our pack," Wulfric says. "Lyall, you and Gunnar violated traveler laws. You, when you went back in time without approval, and when Gunnar went to the present. Not only that, but Gunnar exposed the paranormal world to the mundane, and Lyall, you told Sor—*him* about his past when you were forbidden from doing so." Anger thickens his voice, and it takes everything I have not to hang my head in shame. I disappointed my brother and lied to my family, but I had very good reasons for doing so.

Kieran frowns. "But hang on. I was allowed to go to the present, and Helga sent me back to the past. Why didn't we get in trouble with them? I mean, Helga gave me the wooden wolf and that caused a whole freaking shipwreck."

"Which was not my intention!" Helga clarifies hastily. "The Council arrived shortly after to ensure the safety of the passengers."

Wulfric clears his throat. "Helga, behind my back, had obtained permission from the Council. They only approved her request to send you to us because you're my fated mate. I had also gotten permission from the Council before sending you to the present. They had placed wards around the lake you appeared in so no witnesses would question your sudden arrival. What Lyall and Gunnar have done is very different. Explain yourself, Lyall. You have been keeping secrets and lying."

I have to take a gulp of water to ease the dryness in my throat. "I have been, but I assure you it was for good reasons." My lungs shudder on a short gulp of air. "It's exactly as Anders says. Soren *never* betrayed our pack. He knew nothing about his father's plans to attack our village. He lied to preserve my image so you would not be forced to exile me. He did it to keep our pack together, no matter the cost he had to pay." My voice shakes so badly I can hardly get the words out as they spill free, almost faster than my mind can produce them.

Year after year of keeping these secrets close to my heart and at long last they're free. Even though my knees shake and my breaths are woefully short, it's worth the fear to finally tell the truth.

Wulfric is quiet, frowning down at his plate.

Helga breaks the quiet. "His reasoning never did sit right with me. We raised him. He became one of us. That boy loved you so much, Lyall. How could he have betrayed us?" She dries the corner of her eye, sniffling. "I was so lost in grief. I let it blind me to the truth." She takes my hand, eyes shining with tears. "I will never be sorry enough, dear. I should have fought for you, for Soren."

I squeeze her hand. "It's all right, Auntie."

Anders shakes his head, squeezing his eyes shut. "I could never have let myself be separated from my mate. I can't even imagine being that selfless..."

"Lyall is," Wulfric says, surprising me. "Nothing was stopping Lyall from following Soren into exile. He made the choice to stay." He pauses, throat bobbing. "And I have never thanked you for it. Never made it clear how much your sacrifice meant to me." When his eyes begin to glisten, it's an effort to hold back my own tears. "I never once thought about how painful it must have been, how losing Soren must have torn at you. I didn't know. I do now because if I ever lost Kieran, it would break me."

Kieran rubs his shoulder. Wulfric leans into his touch, taking in a steadying breath. He never takes his eyes off me as he says, "You have always been honest with us, Lyall. You're loyal to the core. The very fact that you felt you had to go behind our backs, that you believed you couldn't trust us with this... it tells me all I need to know."

I swallow hard. "And that is?"

Wulfric takes Kieran's hand, kisses his palm, then rises. Heart racing, I stand to meet him as my little brother comes to me. He puts his big hands on my shoulders and looks me in the eye, man to man, brother to brother. "I was wrong. In my grief and guilt, I wanted someone to blame, anyone but myself."

"It wasn't your fault," I say, gripping his arm.

Wulfric nods. "I know that now. But I pushed all of my guilt onto Soren. I allowed you to be separated. It wasn't right, and I'm sorry, Lyall, for all the pain I caused you."

I can't believe I'm hearing my brother not only own up to his mistakes but apologize for them.

Wulfric cups my cheek, wiping away a tear I hadn't realized had fallen. Then he grips the back of my neck and pulls me close, bumping his forehead against mine.

"I wasn't there for you, but I am now. I'll speak to the Council and tell them to reopen Soren's case."

I suck in a gulp of air, gripping his arm hard so I don't collapse. "Y-you will? Truly?"

Wulfric claps my shoulder. "You've fought for us. It's about time I fight for you."

Never in my wildest dreams could I have imagined such support, such warmth. My knees hit the floor, and Wulfric goes down with me, holding me close as I fall apart in his arms. My broken heart is fuller than it's been in years. No more secrets. No more lies. With my family's support, I'll be reunited with Soren.

I'm no longer fighting alone. I never had to. We've changed in so many ways since meeting our mates. Anders has let go of his rage, Wulfric of his guilt. Mayhap I can finally relinquish my own pain.

I take a few breaths to compose myself, laughing against Wulfric's shoulder. "Thank you, brother."

Chapter 24
Soren

The Travelers Council has a headquarters only a few blocks up from their Bryant Park location. My stomach spins like a washing machine as our cab pulls up to the curb. Fergus steps out behind me, resting his hand on my shoulder. I'm grateful for his company. I need his support today.

After getting my account of what happened and Cartwright's confession, the Council has agreed to reopen my case. I hate that my future with Lyall rests in their hands, especially after how it was handled last time.

"Breathe, boy," Fergus says as the elevator carries us to the thirtieth floor.

"I'm trying." My heart's racing like a damn racehorse. I skipped breakfast this morning, too worried I'd get sick with nerves.

"You have nothing to hide. Cartwright is gone and you still have your memories. They'll review the evidence, and the truth will come out."

He's right. Of course he is. I'm just scared of getting my hopes up. What if Cartwright wasn't the only source of corruption? Can I really trust these witches to try me fairly?

The doors open, and we step out into a waiting room where a small crowd has already assembled. Recognition slams into me, halting me in my tracks. Anders dips his head in acknowledgement while Jamie grins and hurries over.

"Hey. What are you guys doing here?" I let Jamie pull me into a hug, grateful for the support.

"To support you and Lyall."

My heart trips over itself. "Is he here?" Over Jamie's shoulder, I notice a few other people, surprised I recognize them. One of them is big and blond with a rugged beard. That has to be Wulfric. Beside him is a slightly shorter man with ginger hair. He takes Wulfric's hand and leads him over.

I force myself to breathe as the pack Alpha who exiled me stops only inches away. I always thought I was tall, but Wulfric is huge, and the sour expression on his face is far from welcoming.

"Soren?" the shorter man asks with a friendly smile. I nod, and he extends a hand. "Nice to meet you. I'm Kieran. This is—"

"Wulfric," I say, reaching out slowly to Kieran. "I recognize you."

Wulfric looks down at my hand, like he isn't sure if he should bite it off or not. Kieran elbows him, and Wulfric clears his throat. "And I, you." I shake Kieran's hand, then Wulfric's, pulling away more quickly than is polite.

Wulfric's brow furrows. "I... know what you must think of me."

"Do you?" Anger snuffs out my nerves, making my nails bite into my palms.

Wulfric rubs the back of his neck. "I won't excuse the choices I made. There were many ways I could have handled what happened. What I did wasn't fair to you or my brother."

His solemn tone is pretty convincing. It will take time for me to trust him, but at least he seems sincere. "Thanks. I appreciate it."

There's a low growl nearby, and I freeze in panic when Gunnar approaches, flanked on all sides by men and women. His arms are bound behind his back, and a muzzle is strapped to his skull. Wulfric puts a hand on my shoulder and urges me closer to him and Kieran as the guards escort Gunnar past us. Just before they enter the big double oak doors, Gunnar looks over his shoulder at me. Wide silver eyes, narrowed in rage, find mine and then the door slams and conceals him from sight.

Wulfric exhales beside me. "I hope Arlo will be able to help him..."

The name is oddly familiar.

"Soren?"

At the sound of that voice, so small and hopeful, the noise in my head just stops. Throat thickening, I look up and Lyall's there, two cups of water in his hands. Tears fill his eyes, his face a mirror of the joy and sheer relief coursing through me.

The cups of water hit the floor, soaking into the carpet when I pull him into a hug so full of desperation, it makes my chest ache. Lyall's arms fly around me, holding me to his chest. "Gods, I missed you," he says, cradling the back of my head.

"I'm here. Not going anywhere," I say into his shoulder.

Lyall's here. He's okay. We're together, and I'm going to do everything I can to make sure it stays that way. This man is my forever, the big damn love story I've been looking for, and I'm never letting him go without a fight.

Taking my face between his hands, Lyall presses his lips to mine in a kiss so hard and fierce, it takes my breath away. We're both breathing hard when we break apart for air. Lyall nuzzles his forehead against mine. "I'm so sorry," he whispers, tears lining his lashes. "I should have—"

"It's okay, sweetheart. I'm here. I'm all right. We both are." For the first time in the days since we were separated, I feel hopeful. I take his hand and kiss his palm. "We're together. All we need to do is speak our truth to the Council, and then we'll have our whole lives together."

Lyall's lips tremble when he smiles. "Aye. Together."

"Erikson Pack? Fergus and Soren?" An older woman in a business suit enters from the double doors.

"Present," Wulfric says.

She holds the doors open wider. "I am Councilwoman Harding. Please come inside and take a seat."

Just like that, my nerves come rushing back. If they didn't give me a fair trial last time, who is to say I will get one this time?

Lyall squeezes my hand. "Whatever happens, Soren, I'll find you again."

A lump rises in my throat. "I know." I hold his hand, never wanting to let go.

Inside the room are several benches facing a tiered stand. There are at least ten council members seated in the stands. I take a seat beside Lyall with Fergus to my left while Lyall's pack find seats around the room. Gunnar is already seated in the back between two guards, muzzle removed but arms still bound.

Councilwoman Harding bangs her gavel. "This meeting is in session. Do you consent to share the memories of the events that occurred prior to your exile with the Erikson Pack?"

How will they react? Wulfric seemed remorseful, but that doesn't mean he'll believe my side of the story. Lyall puts his arm around my shoulders, and I lean into the comfort offered.

"I do, Councilwoman."

She motions to the empty seat beside her. "Then be seated."

Knees a little shaky, I approach the chair and lower myself into it. When a man wearing a golden torc like all the other council members approaches my chair, I grip onto the armrests until my knuckles whiten. What if this is a trick? What if they take my memories all over again?

"Relax, please," the man says. "I'm going to touch the back of your head. You'll feel a slight tingling sensation and some lightheadedness. This is all normal."

I look at Lyall and exhale slowly. "Go for it."

The witch's hand clasps the back of my skull. A tingling feeling spreads from where he touches me down to my toes. My instinct is to bolt, but a wave of dizziness hits me, making me close my eyes as the room tilts.

"Traitor!"

My eyes fly open. Men and women in antique clothes form a circle below the stands. They're transparent, like how ghosts look in movies.

"I-It's true," says a voice. My voice. In the center of the circle is my past self, hands raised as the crowd advances on him. "I used you filthy beasts! All of you. I was never your pack. My real family was always the one Alpha Erik stole me from!"

"No... this isn't true! It can't be," says a much younger Wulfric, shoving through the crowd to face my past self. "Tell me you didn't do it, Soren."

"I did, and I did it alone. Lyall had nothing to do with it. He's always been weak. Soft. I knew if he found I was meeting with my father, he'd rat me out."

I wince at the harshness in my own voice. It's no wonder the pack believed me. I'm not making a good case for my own innocence.

Wulfric shakes his head, chest heaving. "So... all this time you were just pretending?"

My past self barks a laugh. "I did what I had to in order to survive until my real family could rescue me. As if I could ever live side by side with animals."

Wulfric stumbles back, one hand going to his stomach.

"My family is dead because of you!" a younger Gunnar shouts, lunging forward, only to be restrained by his aunt and another pack member. "Let me go! I'll rip the flesh from his bones!"

"Kill him!" another roars. The crowd erupts into chaos, running at my past self, shouting curses.

Wulfric puts himself in front of me and brings the pack to attention with a roar that rattles my eardrums. "Enough! Anders, put him in the basement. Make sure he can't escape. I will decide what to do with him."

Anders grabs my past self by the scruff of his neck and hauls him out of view.

That was hard enough to watch, but I know the worst is yet to come. There's an unpleasant numbing sensation at the base of my skull as the memory plays on until we arrive at the moment Lyall finds me in chains. It breaks my heart all over again to see the pain in his face as my past self explains what I've done. I glance at the faces of the council members, trying to tell by their expressions if they believe what I told Lyall.

It's hard to tell. Many of them watch the memory play out as if they're watching a dull documentary. Some take notes. I'm relieved to see at least one council member dab her eyes with her sleeve.

"I think we've seen enough," Harding says, hands laced on her desk.

The witch removes his hand from my head, and the irritating tingling sensation finally goes away, leaving behind a dull throb that isn't much better. In the seat below, Lyall watches me, hands in fists, eyes full of desperation. Behind him, Wulfric has his head hung low, Kieran's hand on his shoulder. Gunnar catches my eye, but the anger I was expecting isn't there. There's a slump in his shoulders, a bitter twist to his lips.

"I want to clarify that the council has never seen this portion of the memories." Harding clears her throat. "During her interrogation, Helena Carwright confessed to tampering with the evidence to show only Soren's confession of guilt. Yours was not the only case she had skewed against shifters. I am deeply sorry for the turmoil her actions have caused your pack."

Angry growls rumble from Lyall. Anders leans over the bench and squeezes his shoulder.

"Alpha Erikson. After reviewing this evidence, has your belief in Soren's guilt changed at all?"

The bench creaks as Wulfric rises, but he doesn't look at the councilwoman. He looks right at me and says, "Aye. It has."

"And what is your verdict?"

Wulfric's throat bobs, his voice shaky when he says, "Soren sacrificed himself to keep our family together, out of love for my brother. He is innocent."

"And what of the rest of the pack?" Harding asks.

Helga rises, eyes glassy. "Innocent. Soren, you will always be welcome in our home."

Relief threatens to bring tears to my eyes.

Anders says, "I misjudged your character greatly. Even when we turned against you, you kept our family together. Soren is innocent and just."

A long silence falls as everyone waits for Gunnar to speak. He lifts his head, exhaling the tension from his shoulders and jaw. "Innocent."

Harding says, "And what is the judgment of this council?"

One by one, the council members say, "Innocent," while two abstain.

Harding announces, "All charges of treason are dismissed. For violation of time travel law section 3a, you are barred from traveling until you report to the TTA for proper documentation, after which you must return to the council and present proof of documentation."

I nod so hard my head throbs. "Understood!"

"I will help him," Lyall says.

Harding says, "Mr. Erikson, for exposure to the paranormal world and unauthorized time traveling, you will have your traveling privileges revoked for six months. You may only travel if there is another person with you, and they will be expected to report in once a month. If after six months there have been no further violations, you may travel freely again."

Lyall looks up with hopeful puppy dog eyes. "That's all?"

I gesture wildly at him to shut his sexy mouth. "They're letting us off easy! Don't question it!"

Harding replies, "The penalties are normally more severe but given the unconventional nature of this case, we're dropping the more serious charges. I trust you won't make me regret it?" She arches a shaped brow.

Lyall slaps a fist to his chest. "You have my word!"

I slump in my seat, unsure if I'm feeling faint from the magic in my head or from relief.

The doors at the back of the room creak open. "Ahem." Arlo pokes his head into the room and waves his fingers. "Pardon me. I hope I'm not interrupting."

"Not at all. You're right on time," Harding says. "Lyall, Soren, and the rest of the pack, you may leave. Gunnar and Arlo and Alpha Wulfric, please stay. There are matters we need to discuss."

"Come on, stud. Let's do this," Arlo says.

Gunnar grunts, glowering at the floor.

Arlo walks to the front row of seats, and Gunnar trails after him.

I spring off the bench and throw my arms around Lyall. He holds me so tight it's almost painful, and he laughs in my ear. We did it. We *won*. No more hiding from Lyall's family, no more secrets. When Lyall claims my lips, I lose myself in his taste, the rasp of his hand over my cheek.

"I love you." The words are out the second our lips part.

Lyall's smile makes sunlight look dim by comparison. "And I you, until we're nothing but ash in the earth."

I chuckle. "A bit morbid but yeah, same."

"Does this mean we are not moving to San Francisco?" Lyall asks, tilting his head.

"We don't have to. I haven't said yes to the apartment yet."

Lyall takes my hand and leads me from the room. Anders and Jamie follow. "Do you want to go?"

The idea was exciting once I adjusted to it, but now that we aren't being forced to leave... I squeeze his hand. "Your family is here. So is mine. Let's face it, they couldn't function without us."

Tossing back his head, Lyall laughs. "Nay, I don't believe they could."

"Heard that," Anders growls, elbowing Lyall in the head.

"Congrats, you two!" Jamie says, slapping my back as he passes. "We should have dinner sometime. Our place."

"Sounds good," I reply, loving the sound of an evening with Lyall's family.

"Anders." Lyall tugs on his twin's arm, taking him aside. He whispers something too low for me to catch. Anders hands him a duffel bag, which Lyall slings over his shoulder. I wonder what that's all about?

Once we're downstairs, we say goodbye to Anders and Jamie. It's a beautiful day, even if it is freezing. It snowed recently but the streets have been salted and shoveled. The sky is clear and blue without a threat of more snow.

"Wanna walk around a bit?"

Lyall puts his arm around my shoulders. "You lead, and I'll follow."

We spent the rest of the day walking along the Hudson River, stopping for some beers at a bar. My feet ache, and I'd love nothing more than to crawl into bed and sleep next to Lyall, but he insists on a trip to Central Park. "There's a spot there where we're allowed to shift. The witches have glamoured the area so humans won't notice."

I yawn into the back of my fist. "Okay, but I'm not chasing your fluffy ass around the park."

A quick train ride later, and we're walking beneath the canopies of green leaves. Lyall stops outside Sheep Meadow. It's a huge open space, perfect for wolves to run. Lyall examines the trunk of a tree, running his fingers over a symbol carved into the wood. "Should be the place." He sets his duffel bag down and pulls out his white fur cloak while I find a spot beneath a tree to sit.

"Have fun, sweetheart."

The white fur catches the sunlight when Lyall throws it over his shoulders. "Sure you don't want to join me?"

I snort, resting my back against the tree. "As if I could keep up with you."

Lyall grabs something inside the bag. "With this, you might." He pulls out a thick pelt of fur. One I vaguely recognize.

"Is that..." I push myself up, exhaustion forgotten.

Lyall smiles, holding out the fur cloak. I clasp the fur between my fingers, the pelt dense and coarse. "It's yours."

How could he still have it? A breathless laugh escapes me even as I blink hard against the sting of tears. "You kept it? All this time?"

He swings the cloak over my shoulders, a warm, comforting weight against my back. "Of course. I never gave up, Soren. I believed the gods would bring you back to me. It was only a matter of when."

His words break my heart and make it soar all at once. I take him into my arms, pressing my face into his shoulder. "Thank you for waiting for me."

His hand settles at the nape of my neck, warm as sunlight. "You are worth it, love."

I never thought I'd find someone like him. After so much heartbreak, I'd convinced myself I would be alone forever. Now I know I'll never have to be. I've found the kind of love I thought only existed in my dreams.

"Ready to run?" Lyall asks, his grin full of mischief.

"Hell yeah. So, how do I do this?" How can a pelt of fur change my whole body into a wolf?

Lyall scratches his chin thoughtfully. "I do not know."

"Don't you do this all the time?"

"Aye. It's like asking me how to breathe. I don't know how. I just do it. Mayhap, if you lower yourself to the floor... like this." Lyall gets on all fours. I mimic him, feeling stupid when nothing happens.

"Okay... so what now? Do I have to howl, chase my nonexistent tail—" The colors of the world shift before my eyes. Everything sharpens, like I put on glasses. "Whoa." The fur on my back shivers, making me gasp when it starts to *move*. Fur descends over my arms, crawls down my back.

I close my eyes, terrified of the pain I'm sure will come. Werewolf transformations always look horrible in the movies.

"Soren. Open your eyes for me, love." Lyall's voice is in my head, and there's a burning in my chest. Not like heartburn or anything uncomfortable, more like that pleasant feeling you get when you swallow a warm drink on a cold day. I open my eyes and whimper in delight at the sight of Lyall's beautiful white wolf.

Lyall wags his tail and bumps his nose against my forehead. I realize we're the same height, although he should be bigger than me. It's then that I notice my hands have become paws. Shifting felt so natural, I barely noticed when I'd changed forms.

"This is so cool! I'm a wolf!"

Lyall chuffs, tail swinging side to side. *"Aye, that you are."*

I realize he heard me. *"How can we hear each other like this?"*

Lyall rubs his body against mine. *"It's through our bond. Before, I could feel you, but you couldn't sense me. Now that you've shifted, our bond is no longer one-sided."* He shivers against me. *"Gods, how I missed feeling you."*

The pain in his voice makes me whimper. I grab his tail in my teeth and tug, making him yelp. He spins around and tackles me, and we roll over in the leaves together. I lick one of his ears. *"You're not alone anymore, sweetheart.*

I'm here. I'll always be here, until we're nothing but ash in the earth. Just like you said."

The rush of joy that sweeps through my chest takes me by surprise. It's his joy. I can feel him, as if we share the same heart.

Lyall drops into a play-bow, his eyes bright and focused only on me. *"Then run with me. We'll leave the aches and pains of the past behind, here and now."*

I snap my teeth playfully, blood pumping. *"Let's see who the faster wolf is!"*

The world blurs around me as my paws kick up dirt. Wind roars in my ears, carrying our yips and howls. Side by side, we run, chasing our future.

This is it; I know it. I can *feel* it stretching out before us.

This is the beginning of our forever, together.

Epilogue
Lyall

The wind blows cold off the sea, but with Soren's arm around my shoulders, every part of me feels blissfully warm. As we near the village, I put my arm around his waist, gripping his hip.

"You think people will give us trouble?" Soren asks.

"Wulfric assured me he'd spoken to the villagers and made it clear he would be displeased if anyone provoked us."

Still, when we enter the village and I sense people's eyes on us, I can't keep my hackles from rising. Many of our people still remember the devastation Soren's father brought to our shores. It will take time for them to accept that their blame was misplaced.

"Welcome home, Soren!" a woman calls from her window.

"Thank you," Soren says, offering a smile and wave.

A farmer shouts from his pasture, "Aye, welcome home, lad. I always knew you were a good'un."

To my surprise, we receive quite a few similar greetings on our way to the longhouse. While there are some who cast suspicious or even hostile glares, they heed Wulfric's warning and do not trouble us.

"Well," Soren says, squeezing my shoulder, "that was unexpected!"

"Indeed. It is certainly more than I'd hoped for."

My people can be stubborn, but their hearts are good. It's my hope that someday Soren will be accepted by most of the village.

A new worry makes my stomach churn as we approach the Alpha and Alpha-Mate's' home. I haven't seen Gunnar in the month since Soren's trial. I was surprised when he voted in support of Soren's innocence, but I'm no fool. He may have changed his views, but that does not mean he will see Soren as part of our pack.

Anders has updated me every now and then. Gunnar hasn't gone berserk again. He even implied our brother has been quiet and calm. Arlo's doing, I hope. The witch has been visiting often, but Anders is unsure whether they've accepted their mate bond.

I pray Gunnar will be able to move on and find happiness.

"Nervous?" I ask.

"A little," Soren admits. "I know your brother isn't my biggest fan."

"He will accept you. Just give him time, aye?" I push open the door. The house smells of smoke from the hearth and freshly baked bread.

"Greetings!" Wulfric says, setting a bowl of pickled vegetables on the table. "You're just in time."

The table is loaded with so much food, it's a wonder it doesn't break. My aunt and brothers are already seated. Jamie's beside Anders with Jace, and Kieran sits at Wulfric's side. My heart lurches when I set eyes on Gunnar. When he notices me, the edge of his mouth lifts in a smile that strikes me speechless. When's the last time I saw him smile?

"Lyall. Soren," he says in greeting, tipping his head.

"How are you, darlings?" Arlo asks, bright and cheerful.

Soren and I take our seats across from them. "We're well. You two seem to be quite close." I give Gunnar's foot a kick beneath the table, grinning when spots of color rise in his cheeks.

He coughs. "Aye, well..."

Aunt Helga swoops in on Soren's left. "Here you are, dear." She pours mead into his cup.

"Thank you, Auntie." Soren takes a sip while Helga flushes with delight, eyes sparkling.

"It's so good to have you back at our table."

Soren smiles. "It feels good. Like a part of me remembers what it was like to eat with you all. I missed it."

Helga frowns. "Will you ever remember?"

Soren shakes his head. "Not everything, no. But it's okay. I found my way back, and that's what counts."

There's a touch of bitterness in his scent that tells me he's not entirely truthful. Beneath the table, I take his hand and squeeze, offering whatever comfort I can.

Later, I tell myself.

"Lyall, how is work at the bar?" Kieran asks.

My cheeks warm as I remember dropping a whole bin of dishes the other day. "It is..."

Soren elbows me. "My man is the best barback I have ever had!"

I huff a laugh. "I am not."

Soren shrugs, patting my hand beneath the table. "You just started! It takes time."

Regardless, I am more grateful than words can express. Never did I imagine I would be working with Soren again. *Living* with him. It is as if the gods have finally smiled upon me.

"Pack," Wulfric says, commanding our attention. "Tonight is special indeed. Our family is whole once more." He lifts his flagon in Soren's direction. "Welcome home, Soren."

Soren ducks his head, smiling wide as the others echo the sentiment. If my heart were a mug of mead, it would be overflowing with happiness. After all these years, I have someone beside me at the table. Gone is the envy that ached inside me every time I witnessed my brothers and their mates. I will never feel alone again.

"To Soren!" Kieran lifts his mug.

Soren blushes furiously but lifts his mug too. We tap our mugs together.

"Hey, wait, me too!" Jace says, picking up his cup of water. "To Soren!"

Soren chuckles and toasts the lad. "Thanks, Jace."

Arlo coughs, grabbing my attention. "Sooo, not to steal your thunder, Soren, but Gunnar and I have an announcement to make."

Soren lifts his brows. "Really? What is it?"

I meet Anders's eyes across the table, his expression perplexed.

Arlo looks expectantly at Gunnar, whose cheeks are red as an apple. He clears his throat, then takes Arlo's hand. Helga gasps, hands over her mouth and tears in her eyes.

Arlo smiles big and bright. "We're getting married!"

Wulfric spits his drink across the table. Kieran thumps him on the back.

I look to Gunnar for answers and find his expression carefully guarded. Something's off.

"That is... great news, brother!" I say, plastering a smile on my face.

"What?" Wulfric wheezes, thumping his chest hard. "Why?"

Arlo frowns. "Well, you see, when two people love each other, they may decide to spend the rest of their lives together!"

Wulfric glares at him. "I am aware of what a marriage entails. It's just... surprising, is all." He looks at our brother expectantly.

Gunnar gives him an icy look. "You've been pestering me to take a mate, and now I will. Happy?"

I should be relieved, but I can't help feeling suspicious instead. Gunnar was adamant he would never move on from Leif, and now here he is, announcing marriage to a witch he's recently rejected.

Arlo puts a hand on his chest with a soft sigh. "How could I resist such a handsome brute?" He squeezes Gunnar's hand so hard, Gunnar grimaces.

"Should be interesting," Anders murmurs, not bothering to hide his mischievous grin.

Gunnar clears his throat and reaches for a bowl of beef stew. "Stew, Soren?" He holds the bowl out to my mate. "It always was your favorite."

A surprised smile stumbles across Soren's face. "Thanks. It smells great."

Gunnar remembered Soren's favorite meal. Not only that, he reached out to him. In his own way, Gunnar's making amends with Soren. Mayhap one day, they can be as close as they once were.

"Thank you," I say through our bond.

Gunnar meets my gaze and offers a small smile. *"Hush and eat, snowbrain."*

I tuck in, sharing stories and laughter with my pack, and for the first time in years, I finally remember what it's like to hope.

"So, Arlo and Gunnar. Do you think the Council put them up to this?" Soren plops down on the bed beside me and wastes no time nestling into my side.

I press a kiss to his hair. "It's likely. The Council did ask them to stay behind so they could talk." My stomach flutters, like the time I swallowed a butterfly. "If you could get your memories back, would you?"

Soren hums softly, playing with my fingers. "Yeah, I would. Hearing stories about my life with the pack isn't the same as remembering them. I wish I could remember you most of all. What we were like as kids. The first moment I had feelings for you. Our mating ceremony." He touches his neck where the mating mark should be.

"What if I told you that you could remember everything?"

"That would be nice, but—" Soren goes utterly silent, eyes widening. "Wait... can I?"

I can't help but smile. "Aye. I visited the Council this morning and they told me that if I claim you, your memories should return."

Soren laughs softly. "No way."

I press my lips to his forehead. "Yes way. Our bond will be complete. It will undo the spell that stole your memories."

"All you have to do is bite me?"

I nod and, to my amusement, Soren wrestles his clothes off with such ferocity, it looks like he's fighting a bear. He's naked in seconds and sprawled out before me like a delectable feast. He bobs his eyebrows. "Then put your teeth in me, sweetheart."

I press my lips to the corner of his mouth, drawing in a lungful of his scent. "In time, love. First, let me worship you."

Soren sighs dramatically. "If I have to..."

Laughing, I kiss him again and again. The joy that sweeps through me from head to toe is so intense, it makes my chest ache. He's here. Soren is here with me. I found him again, just as I swore I would. A lump constricts my throat, making it hard to breathe.

"Lyall—"

I kiss him, thumbing away one of my tears when it wets his cheek. "These are happy tears," I assure him, and then he's kissing me on my lips, my damp cheeks, along my jaw. I chart a course down his body with my mouth, finding him hard and eager when I reach his hip bone. I swallow him down, moaning at the earthy taste that fills my mouth.

"Oh god, Lyall," he whispers. My scalp stings when he tugs at my hair. I do just as I promised and worship him, every inch. His breathy sighs and groans fill the room. He's all I can taste, all I can smell. Nothing exists but him, *us*.

"Come here, sweetheart," Soren says, panting.

I give him one last lick and then crawl up his body. He grabs the nape of my neck and hauls me in for a kiss. I could drown in this man, spend hours making love to him again and again, and still my hunger for him would never be sated.

He rolls onto me, blanketing my body with his. Piece by piece, my clothes come off.

My heart races with anticipation when he grabs lube from the end table. I fold an arm behind my head, unable to wipe the smile from my face. "Get me ready for you, love."

Soren bites his lip and slicks his fingers. He sweeps his gaze down my body and shakes his head. "Fuck. You're so beautiful."

Heat blooms in my cheeks. "You're the one who—gods!"

Slick wet heat engulfs me from tip to root. Soren worships me with his mouth, with his fingers as they curl inside me again and again. He brings me to the cusp of completion but always backs off before I can claim my release. It's the sweetest torture, and it feels as if it lasts hours.

"Please, love. Oh gods, please."

The sound Soren makes goes straight to my aching cock. Then my knees are over his shoulders and I'm folded nearly in half. Above me, Soren bites his lip, eyes closing in bliss. He pushes in, and the exquisite pressure reduces me to gasps and whimpers as I surrender to him.

"Okay?" Soren's breath is hot against my damp skin. His forehead rests against mine.

"Aye," I whisper, but it's so much more than okay.

His lips taste like salt when he kisses me, and then he's moving, slow and deep, and gods, he's everywhere. He's all I can feel, taste, and smell as he fills me and fucks me, faster, deeper.

Growls rumble low in my chest. I cover my mouth. "Sorry."

Soren shakes his head, lifting my leg higher. He slides in deep and strikes that spot inside me that has my balls tightening dangerously. "Don't hide from me. Let your wolf out. I want to see him."

Fur prickles over my arms, and my fangs sharpen.

"Fuck, you look so sexy like this, all riled up and wild," Soren says.

"Close," I say in warning as my fangs sharpen. "I... I can't hold it back." I don't want to hurt him, but gods, I need to bite him, to claim him as mine once again.

Soren's eyes darken, and he leans in, peppering kisses along my collarbone. "Bite me. Fuck. Put your teeth in me, sweetheart."

My eyes roll back as his thrusts lose all rhythm and he pounds me into the mattress. My claws bite into the sheets. I can't hold back any longer. A snarl tears from my throat, and my fangs sink into his warm, salty skin. Coppery blood dampens my tongue. Soren's body spasms and with a shout, he's spilling inside me. The bond between us erupts with the pleasure of his release, and I arch up against him as I come messily between us.

We catch our breath. Soren's emotions rush through me, like a ship breaking through the waves. His joy, pleasure, love—it consumes me. Above me, he shudders, pressing his face into my chest. The salty scent of his tears mingles with our sweat.

Oh gods. Did it not work?

"Soren. Love, it's all right." It's strange that I can't feel his grief or sorrow. No, all I feel is... *joy*, warm like sunlight on my skin.

His shoulders heave with laughter, his arms holding me tighter. "I'm fine! So much more than fine." Soren lifts his head, smiling brighter than I've ever seen. "Hey. Hey, Lyall. Ask me something only Past Me would know."

My throat thickens. Could it be...

"Where did I ask you to be my mate?"

Soren bites his lip, eyes bright. "The tree we used to climb when we were kids. We'd race each other to the top. I always won, remember?"

I shove his shoulder. "Aye, but only because I let you! I carved something on the tree. What was it?"

"The rune for journey. You said that's what our lives together would be. A journey."

Tears sting my eyes. "What were your vows when we were handfasted?"

Soren's throat bobs. He takes my hand and holds tight. "I thanked you for giving me a family when I was lost, a friend when I was alone, and a love I would always fight for."

I rub my thumb over his cheek, wiping away a tear. "You remember."

He kisses the palm of my hand, eyes closed tightly. "Everything. All of it. Gods, Lyall. I never thought I'd find someone like you."

I pull him into my arms, showering his lips, his cheeks, his forehead with kisses. "But you did. We found our way back together, my love."

Soren claims my lips in a kiss that takes my breath away. Between kisses he whispers again and again, "I love you. I love you."

Long ago, I promised I would find him. The longer I searched for him, the more I feared it wasn't a vow I could keep. Yet here we are, our hearts and souls made one, Soren's body warm in my arms.

I found him, just as I promised, and this time, nothing but death itself shall ever part us again.

Thank you for reading! I hope you enjoyed Lyall and Soren's story.

There were numerous times I almost gave up on writing it. The past year has been incredibly challenging. Between the horrific genocide in Gaza, the fascistic current administration in America, and my own personal struggles with depression and anxiety, it was truly difficult to care about writing a book of all things.

A huge thank you to Lark's Literary Nest for her feedback on the early versions of the draft, and to my family, friends, editors, and readers who gave me their support through the most difficult year of my life. Even now as I write this on 2/10/2026, I can't say things are better. But they're bearable. So thank you. Writing a book will not fix what is wrong in our world. So why bother, right?

Wrong. Stories about queer joy and happy ever afters are so important right now. If my books can make someone's existence less painful even for a little while, then I have served my purpose. We all deserve love and happy endings and no matter what they try, they will never erase us or silence us.

Hate will never win. Keep resisting, always.
Love,
CJ

About CJ

CJ Ravenna loves to tell stories where the ordinary meets the extraordinary. Her books often feature an explosion or two, possessive and protective werewolves who adore their mates, steamy and swoony romance, and of course a happy ending.

Scan the code to sign up for my newsletter. You'll get access to a library full of bonus content from my books, exclusive sneak peeks, and more!

Also By CJ Ravenna

The Lycanthrope Protection Agency Series

To Hunt A Moonborn Beast (Gabe & Max)

Child Of The Moon (Gabe & Max)

The Moon Aways Rises (Gabe & Max)

The Moon Over The Oak (Zach & Ryan)

Redemption Under The Moon (Ben & Isaac)

Fire and Moonlight (Eddie & Vico)
A Paranormal Yakuza Duet

Secrets & Sake (A Paranormal Yakuza Duet Book 1)

Curses & Kitsune (A Paranormal Yakuza Duet Book 2)
Viking Wolves

Heart of a Wolf (Kieran & Wulfric)

Taming of a Wolf (Anders & Jamie)

Devotion of a Wolf (Lyall & Soren)

www.ingramcontent.com/pod-product-compliance
Lightning Source LLC
LaVergne TN
LVHW091621070526
838199LV00044B/887